Bewitching

MURRAY AND TIDSWELL
PARANORMAL INVESTIGATIONS

BOOK FOUR

J.E. NICE

First published in Great Britain in 2023 by
Write Into The Woods Publishing.

ISBN 978-1-912903-41-2

Cover design and typesetting by Write into the Woods.

www.writeintothewoods.com
www.jenice.co.uk

Other Books
By J.E. Nice

The Last War Series:

Matter Of Time
Despite Our Enemies
In My Bones
With A Scream

*Murray And Tidswell
Paranormal Investigations:*

Beginnings
Becoming
Belonging
Bewitching

No Masters Or Kings:

No Masters Or Kings
In Feverish Haste

Find them all at www.jenice.co.uk

For my mum.

And with thanks to Bucky the dog for putting up with me standing in the patch of bluebells at the back of our local woods, waiting for a fae.

1
Bethany

As weeks went, Bethany had had better ones, although she couldn't quite remember when. There had been an assumption that this round of exams would be different. She was older now, more experienced with this type of thing, and yet somehow there was more pressure. Pressure that was seeping into every aspect of her life.

She found a fallen tree trunk to sit on and took a deep breath of the air. While there was a road close by, it was easy to block out the noise and smell of petrol to focus on the bird song and scent of the trees as they eased their way back to life.

Something inside Bethany lifted.

Springtime had always been her favourite.

She took another deep breath. There wouldn't be much more of the stress, surely. She only had a few exams left and then she'd say goodbye to school. There would be a week or so of celebrating with friends and then a summer job to find. The anxiety of getting her results and then, all being well, she'd go to university in September and start afresh.

Her stomach twisted, but she ignored it.

University would be wonderful, full of new friends, new opportunities, new possibilities. No one would know her, she could be whoever she wanted to be.

Her stomach twisted again, harder this time.

With a shaky breath, Bethany closed her eyes and lifted her face to the shafts of sunlight that filtered through the trees.

Everything was going to be okay.

She inhaled deeply and caught a trace of something floral. Opening her eyes, she looked around and then found her feet, following her nose until she reached a muddy path off the well-used track. There hadn't been rain for a few days and the mud was drying hard so it was easy to walk over as Bethany ventured down the path.

She stopped when she came across a clearing filled with an array of dazzling purple bluebells.

'Wow.'

It came out in an exhale, barely a word. As if in response a breeze ripped through the clearing, rattling the bluebells, and there was that glorious smell again. It wasn't until Bethany was exhaling a lungful of air that she noticed the man sitting on a tree stump a little further down.

Heart jolting, Bethany turned to leave.

'Don't be scared,' said the man.

Bethany hesitated. He must have been in his early twenties and was attractive enough that her throat felt like it was closing, her cheeks immediately turned red and sweat beaded in the small of her back.

'They're pretty, aren't they?' the man said, looking over the bluebells. 'This is my favourite spot to see them. Most people go to the so-called bluebell woods, but what's the point in such a view when the paths are filled with people who don't appreciate the quiet required?' He breathed in and smiled. 'I'm glad I'm not the only one to appreciate these ones, but I do hope you won't tell too many people about this place.'

There was something disarming about the man and Bethany found herself smiling and nodding.

'I won't,' she managed.

There was a pause. It would have been easy to leave but for some reason Bethany remained in place. The man continued to watch the flowers and she took the excuse to study him some more. His skin was white and pale, almost reflective of the flowers he was admiring, while his hair was the darkest she'd ever seen, cut short but with a floppy bit at the front that was somehow endearing. As he turned and met her gaze, her heart squeezed with just how green his eyes were.

'My name's Fen. What's yours?'

What sort of a name was Fen? Was that short for

something?

'Bethany,' she said as the questions fell over one another in her mind.

'I tend to come here when I need quiet,' said Fen. 'When my world gets too busy or loud.'

Bethany nodded.

'Me too. The woods, I mean. I like walking through the woods when it all...gets too much.'

A smile touched Fen's lips and Bethany's stomach somersaulted at the sight.

'Hard to believe that someone so young would find the world too much. But, of course, a lot is piled onto young people these days.' He tilted his head to the side, studying her.

'I'm eighteen,' she told him defensively. Fen didn't seem to react so Bethany wrapped her arms around herself and said, 'And I have exams. To get into university. It's a big deal.'

'Very,' Fen agreed. 'I can understand why you're stressed.'

Bethany relaxed a little, her arms dropping back to her sides.

'And Mum and Dad won't stop arguing.'

'That must be difficult,' said Fen.

'And I don't...' Bethany sighed. 'I just don't want to be here anymore. What if I fail these exams and can never leave?'

Fen looked into her eyes and grinned, showing off pearly white teeth and making the breath catch in Bethany's throat.

'Oh, Bethany,' he purred. 'You'll find freedom. There is always a way.'

2

Erica

Erica Murray walked straight into Alfie's back as he stopped without warning on the narrow path leading into the woods. Peering around him, she listened closely but only heard the birds singing in the trees off to the right.

'What? What is it?' she whispered, goosebumps rising on her arms despite the warmth of the spring day.

'Look,' said Alfie, pointing. 'Someone's cut the ivy.'

Moving to stand beside him as best she could, Erica followed Alfie's pointing finger into the woods and saw what he was talking about. The two trees joined by ivy had been easier to see in the winter as the woodland became sparse. Now that the trees were bursting back to life, these two particular ones were becoming lost and buried again. The ivy winding up each trunk joined the trees at the top, and the gap created between them had become a gateway leading to other worlds. At least, that was how Alfie had described it. Erica knew the gap between those trees had the potential to lead to a world of demons and that was enough as far as she was concerned. Now, the ivy growing up the left tree was going brown and dying.

Erica frowned.

'How do you know someone's cut it and it's not just dying on its own?'

Alfie grinned down at her, his blue eyes flashing as his hand found hers.

'I would like you to think that it has something to do with my magnificent powers of foresight, but in all honesty, the trees told me. Which is why we're here.' He headed into the woods, pulling Erica behind him. She'd been looking up at the nearest ash tree when he'd started moving so was unprepared to be pulled off balance. Still, she regained her composure without letting go of him and followed him into the woods. They walked along the path for a while until Alfie slowed and let go of her hand.

'Right,' he said. 'Close your eyes.'

There had been a time, not so long ago, when Alfie telling Erica to close her eyes would have been met with suspicion and perhaps a hint of excitement that she wouldn't admit to. Now she closed her eyes easily, knowing that this was part of the lesson but secretly hoping that he might take the opportunity to kiss her.

She smiled as his lips touched hers, his arm snaking around her waist. She opened her eyes.

'That's not how you talk to trees,' she murmured, wrapping her arms around his neck.

'No, but I think every lesson should start with a kiss. Don't you?'

Erica nodded.

'And end with one.'

Alfie smiled.

'I thought the lesson could end with something else.'

Erica's body tingled at the thought and she pulled him down for another kiss as a sign of her approval. They could have stayed that way for the next hour, standing in the middle of the woodland path, entangled as they kissed. A breeze moved the branches and new leaves over their heads, and they parted. Perhaps in the summer they would have stayed in those woods for hours, talking and kissing and exploring one another, but it still wasn't quite warm enough. Erica pulled her coat around her and inhaled deeply. The smell of the woods was wonderful whatever the season, but there was something electric about it in spring, as if even the soil was waking up. The air was full of tree sap, wood, fresh leaves, flowers opening and soil turned to mud by late April showers.

Alfie looked around them and then chose a tree to the left, placing his palm on the trunk. He gestured for Erica to do the same. The bark was rough beneath her hand, and also somehow warm.

'Now, listen. Close your eyes if it helps,' Alfie murmured.

Again, Erica did as she was told. At first, nothing changed. The murder of crows that lived in the treetops in the corner of the wood were cawing to one another. Elsewhere some songbirds were arguing over territory. The leaves rustled and branches creaked as another breeze swept over them.

'Remember, listen to your own breathing. Block everything else out.'

Erica closed her eyes to concentrate on the rise and fall of her chest and stomach, listening to the air rushing in and out of her nose until the birdsong fell quiet and the woods became silent.

'Can you hear that?' Alfie's voice was barely audible, only a whisper behind her breath. 'Can you hear someone else breathing?'

Yeah, you, thought Erica, but the more she concentrated on that other sound, the less it sounded like Alfie's breath. She wanted to say it didn't sound human, but Alfie wasn't human so that wasn't a great description.

She listened closely to the other breath.

Witch.

Erica smiled. The voice was earthly, a whisper on the breeze.

'Hello, tree,' she whispered back.

Then there came another voice.

Ric.

In one swift motion, Erica opened her eyes, stepped back and removed her hand. Eyes wide, she turned to Alfie. The voice hadn't been his. He'd also never called her Ric before. It had to have been her imagination. Her subconscious willing the word out of the rustling leaves. It had been ten months since Rick Cavanagh, her supposed future husband, had left to travel through time. He called her Ric. He was the first person that popped into her head, but on consideration, her family called her Ric, her best friend, Jess, called her Ric. Even Jess's five-year-old daughter had taken to sometimes calling her Ric.

Erica shuddered. It hadn't been a voice she'd known.

Alfie drew her close, wrapping his arms tightly around her as she pressed her cheek into his chest.

'It's okay,' he murmured in her ear. 'It was that tree beside you. That's all. It didn't mean to scare you.'

Taking a shuddering breath, Erica pulled herself away from the warmth of Alfie and approached the tree.

'It said my name? I wasn't even touching it.'

Alfie nodded.

'The "E" and "A" may have gotten lost in the wind. You're a quick learner, soon you won't need to touch any of them to hear them.'

Erica smiled and placed her hand on the trunk of the tree that had spoken her name, her fingers brushing over the bark in an apology.

'Hello,' she murmured.

There was no response. She glanced back to Alfie. He made a show of closing his eyes and taking a breath.

Erica inhaled deeply and closed her eyes, feeling the trees around her. She blocked out the birdsong, concentrating on her breathing and then on the tree's breath.

'Hello. I'm sorry for my reaction. You startled me,' she whispered.

Friend, said the strange voice.

When Erica opened her eyes, they were full of unspent tears. She brushed them away and turned to Alfie, grinning.

'I think the tree said it wanted to be friends.' She threw her arms around him in a quick hug before turning back to the tree. 'How long before I can hear them the way you can?'

'That depends. It takes practice,' Alfie told her. 'But you'll get there. Now, let's go see the gateway, shall we?'

Erica whispered goodbye to the tree and followed Alfie further into the woods.

'Second lesson,' he called to her over his shoulder. 'Can you feel anything untoward in the woods? Is there anything evil here?'

'Nope,' said Erica.

Alfie stopped and looked back to her.

'And how do you know that?'

'Because you wouldn't have let me come in here if there was.'

Alfie hesitated and then sighed.

'Right. I may have done these lessons in the wrong order.'

Erica watched him, a smile playing on her lips as she absent-mindedly noted the brown curls around his ears and the way the top buttons on his loose shirt were undone, revealing wisps of brown chest hair. He didn't seem to feel the cold in the same way that Erica did.

'I can't sense anything untoward,' she told him with a self-assured smile. She at least had some confidence in being able to sense spirits and malevolent demonic presences. She'd certainly known when there was a demon in these woods and when Jess's house had been taken over by an angry spirit. Alfie gave a nod and then went off the path, treading through the brambles and ferns, towards the two trees that had once met in the middle. Erica stayed on the path at first, watching as Alfie bent over, running his hand over the base of the tree trunk and around the ivy branches.

'Here,' he called to her, gesturing to the ivy.

With a tut, Erica stepped off the path and into the brambles. The thorns pulled at her jeans and caught on her coat, and twice she felt the prick of them against the skin of her legs. She reached Alfie and crouched as best she could to see what he was pointing at.

The ivy had indeed been cut.

'Who would do this?' Erica asked, brushing her fingertips against the cut. She looked up towards the top of the tree. 'Why cut the ivy on one but not the other?'

Alfie scratched at the light stubble on his cheek thoughtfully.

'The tree's healthy enough. The ivy does tend to strangle them, but it's not doing that badly.'

Erica straightened and put her hands on her hips, surveying the gateway that they now stood on the edge of.

'It's shut, right?'

'It is.'

'Does this change anything?'

Alfie glanced at her.

'It could do.'

Erica had been afraid of that.

'How could it change things?'

Alfie sighed, looking up at the trees.

'There's a possibility that damaging the gateway like this could force it to open and remain open.'

Erica's bowels loosened at the thought.

'Or,' Alfie continued. 'The gateway could be gone. Lost to this world, never to reopen.'

Erica watched him.

'So…how do we know which one it is?'

'We don't. It all depends on how the ivy was cut.'

Alfie moved his hand through the gateway and Erica held her breath. Nothing happened.

'Surely this just means that the demon can never get back through here?' she murmured, stepping closer to him. He moved away from the gateway, taking her with him.

'In theory,' he said. 'Don't worry. I'll keep an eye on it.' He refocused on her. 'Shall we go back to talking to the trees? There's a fallen one back on the main path. We can sit there and chat with them.'

Erica was still staring up at the damaged gateway.

'That's it? The ivy's been cut, we don't know what will happen next, let's go sit on a dead tree and talk to the living ones?'

Alfie shrugged and made his way back to the path, gripping Erica's hand and dragging her with him.

'That's all we can do.' He turned on her once they were back on the narrow, muddy pathway. 'And don't take this as permission to go exploring. I still don't want you going near the gateway, or what was the gateway. Okay? Do you promise?'

'Even if the gateway's shut?'

'Even if you think the gateway's shut.'

Erica searched Alfie's expression, trying to decide if she was going to be angry about the slight patronising tone he'd adopted. His blue eyes were hard, but there was concern there, an urge to keep her safe no matter what. She relented.

'I promise.'

Alfie softened and smiled, squeezing her hand.

'Right. Lesson three,' he said, leading her back to the main path and that fallen tree. The wind picked up, lifting Erica's hair and sending a shiver through her.

'Actually, I think maybe I should go home.'

'Why? It's still fairly early,' said Alfie, stopping and turning back to her.

'I know but I have work to do. A couple of clients to call back and I need to speak to the estate agent. I'm viewing some flats tomorrow.'

Alfie shifted uncomfortably.

'And you still won't give any consideration to moving in with me?' he asked.

Erica's stomach twisted, as it did every time he mentioned her moving in with him.

'Moving in with you in the land of the fae, somewhere through a gateway like that one.' She pointed back to the trees they'd left behind. 'In the secret garden of the cemetery, surrounded by fae and magic and no internet connection?'

Alfie pursed his lips.

'You'd save a lot of money on rent, though.'

Erica laughed.

'Think about it,' she said. 'I'll finally have my own place to do with what I want, and you can come and stay whenever you like. It means that we can walk through these woods and then you can come home with me.'

A slick grin grew on Alfie's face.

'We don't need a flat for that. We can make love in the woods.'

'I'd rather have a bed,' Erica pointed out.

'A bed of leaves.'

Erica gave Alfie a look.

'Or up against a tree.' He winked at her. Erica tried not to smile back, but it was too late, the image was in her head.

'Would the trees appreciate that? Seems a bit rude.'

Alfie shrugged.

'They've seen worse.' He held out a hand to her. 'Come on.'

'What? Right now? It's too cold,' said Erica, wrapping her coat around her again for emphasis.

Alfie sagged for a moment and then approached her, slipping his hands beneath her coat, under her jumper and top, to brush over the bare skin of her back. She could have stayed there, enveloped in his warmth, but that was the moment there were voices and a family of four appeared around the corner.

'See, if we were in a flat, that wouldn't happen,' Erica whispered to Alfie.

He gently kissed her ear lobe, sending a thrill through her.

Erica made it home two hours later, her body chilled and tingling still from Alfie's touch. She checked her reflection in the rear view mirror of her sky blue Mini Cooper and discovered a leaf caught in her hair. Grinning at the memory of how it got there, she pulled it out and dropped it on her parents' driveway. Her family's Labradors barked as she entered the house, the young black Bramley throwing himself at her while old, golden Daisy wagged her tail furiously. Erica greeted both with ear rubs and kisses, and shouted hello to her parents.

'There's post for you on the table,' her mother shouted back from somewhere in the living room.

Erica wandered into the kitchen and found the letter addressed to her on the dining table. Who would that be from? The estate agents had been emailing her. Perhaps it was from the bank, but the envelope was strange. It didn't have the little plastic window at the front and her name and address were handwritten. She studied the handwriting until she finally realised what it reminded her of. Hurriedly, she ripped open the envelope and gently removed the letter from within. She opened the pages and scanned down to the name at the bottom. Her hand went to her mouth as tears pricked her eyes.

It was from Rick.

3

Jess

'Are we there yet?'

That really depended on the destination. Was Jess close to covering her face with her hands and screaming? Yes, she was. Was Jess close to investing all of her savings into a scientist who could invent a mute button for children who continually asked if they were there yet? Yes, she was.

Instead, Ruby was asking if they were close to her grandparents' house and, thankfully, the answer this time was yes. Perhaps that was part of the problem. Five-year-olds would keep asking and asking, and eventually the answer to this particular question would be yes, which hardly deterred them from repeating the question over and over on the next journey. As if they somehow sped the process up.

'Yes, love. We're there.'

'No we're not,' said Ruby, looking out of the

window. 'We're still moving.'

Beside Jess, Marshall tried to cover up a laugh. He failed and it came out as a snort. She gave him a hard sideways look before twisting in her seat to look at her daughter.

'We're just coming up to the town, Rubes. Okay? We'll be five minutes. If that.'

'So we're not there yet.'

'Technically, no, but you asking us all the time isn't going to get us there any faster.'

Ruby raised an eyebrow at her mother. It was a look that both melted Jess's heart and infuriated her. She'd learned the look from Jess who, in turn, had learned it from her mother. Jess turned back to face the road and sighed.

'Nervous?' Marshall asked.

'Yup. Aren't you?'

'Meeting my future in-laws for the first time and trying to explain to them why they've never met me before but here I am, engaged to their daughter? Nah. What's there to be nervous about?'

Jess looked over and caught Marshall smiling to himself. Her eyes drifted down to his thick arms and broad chest. Marshall was a big man and a career in engineering and helping people with their gardens had given him muscle in all the right places. They'd been together almost a year and Jess often wondered if she'd ever get tired of watching him drive. In the beginning, he'd driven her in his van. He'd pick her up on a quiet day and they'd have lunch together. One afternoon, she discovered he'd cleared the tools from the back. Jess smiled. It had been a while since they'd had sex in the back of his van. Sure it had been uncomfortable, but Jess made a mental note to suggest another go when they were back home.

'Stop it,' Marshall murmured, snapping Jess back to the car.

'What?' She turned away, back to the road, as Marshall slowed the car and they passed the big sign that welcomed them to the market town of Chipping Briar.

Marshall glanced over at her with that endearing lopsided smile of his and gave her a wink. Jess grinned and risked placing her hand on his thigh to give it a squeeze.

'See, Ruby. Here we are,' she declared. 'Just got to get to the car park now and then the pub.'

Ruby didn't answer and when Jess looked back to check, the girl was staring out of the window. The sky may have been drab and heavy with cloud but the plant tubs decorating the entrance to the town were overflowing with daffodils. Jess smiled and relaxed. Her parents had moved to this town after Jess had left home but that didn't matter, being with her parents was like going home, and she hadn't seen them for a whole year. She hadn't yet told her parents the full truth about her new business venture working with Erica as paranormal investigators. Jess stiffened, her shoulders rising to her ears. She was turning up with a new fiancé, a new dog and a new career chasing ghosts. Well, it was their own fault for going on such a long cruise to see the world. Jess bit her lip. Somehow she didn't think that argument would go down well.

There was no more time to consider it. She directed Marshall to the end of the town, down a road on the left, another left and into the town's main car park. Marshall exhaled slowly as he squeezed the car into one of the few remaining spaces and turned the engine off.

'Nice place,' he murmured, turning to Jess. 'Ready?'

'As I'll ever be.' Jess glanced back to Ruby. 'Ready to go see Granny and Grampy?'

Ruby nodded eagerly.

'Can I show them Bubbles?' she asked.

'You can tell them all about Bubbles while I hold her,' said Jess, turning to Marshall. 'Ready?'

'Better to just do it rather than think about it anymore.' Marshall gave himself a defiant nod and they both climbed out of the car. Jess went to the back to get Bubbles while Marshall walked around to unstrap Ruby.

'Hello, love.'

Jess turned just as Bubbles jumped out of the car. Her mother, who had been rushing towards her from the footpath that wound into the car park, stopped and stared down at the large Bernese mountain dog. 'My, he's bigger than you said!'

'Granny!' came Ruby's voice, followed by the five-year-old running around the car and throwing herself into her grandmother's waiting open arms. Then Marshall appeared. Jess's mother squeezed Ruby, blinked at Marshall and then glanced at Jess. 'You must be Marshall,' she said, regaining her composure. Marshall nodded.

'Lovely to meet you, Mrs Tidswell.'

'And you. Please, call me Ginny. And this must be Bubbles.' Ginny bent to stroke the dog's head.

Ruby was immediately beside her. Just as she went to open her mouth to begin a monologue lecture on Bubbles, Jess asked, 'Where's Dad?'

'We're meeting him at the pub, I just wanted to pop into one of the independent shops over there and then thought I'd meet you here. Come on, let's go find him.'

Jess and Marshall exchanged a look as Ruby and Ginny led the way back onto the footpath and into the town, Bubbles pulling on the end of her lead and dragging Jess along.

They reached the high street, turned left and wandered along until Ginny ducked to the left and into one of the old buildings. The warmth of the pub hit them immediately along with the smell of stale beer and the sound of the cash register going over the low chatter of people sitting at tables. Towards the back, at a table for six, was Jess's father. He grinned as Ruby ran into his arms.

'You've grown so much,' he told her, planting a

big kiss on her cheek. 'Oh my, that's a big dog.'

'This is Bubbles,' said Ruby, chest full, chin high. She ran over to Bubbles and tried to take the lead from Jess.

'Not yet, sweetheart,' Jess told her. 'Let's all just calm down, yeah?' Jess stroked the dog's ears as Bubbles panted, taking in the strange room, new people and new smells. 'Hi, Dad.' Jess gave her father a hug, and then he turned on Marshall.

'And you must be Marshall.'

'Yes, lovely to meet you.'

The two men shook hands and Jess exhaled slowly. So far, so good.

'I'll get us some drinks,' her father declared. 'Gin and tonic? Wine? Apple juice for those of us under the age of ten?'

'A coffee would be good,' Jess told her father as she took a chair and gestured for Marshall to sit beside her. Opposite, Ginny was making Ruby comfortable.

'A pint, Marshall? Or a coffee?'

'A pint would be good,' Marshall said. 'Do you need a hand?'

'No, no.' Jess's father wandered off with a smile.

'I'm Ginny, he's Eddie,' Jess's mother told Marshall who nodded. 'And is he all right down there? This place is very dog friendly.'

'Her. Bubbles is a her,' said Jess, before telling Bubbles to lie down. Bubbles gave a soft whine until Jess got close and told her to sit. Bubbles sat down and eased to the floor, sniffing the carpet, her eyes lighting up as Jess produced a chew toy from her bag. Bubbles immediately got to work, strange new surroundings forgotten.

'You always did want a dog,' said Ginny, watching her. 'Did you say Paul gave her to you?'

'In a way,' said Jess, sitting back and relaxing a little. 'Paul bought her, changed his mind and decided she should be Ruby's dog and I should take care of her. So here we are.'

Ginny shook her head.

'He always was a strange man.'

'Yes.'

There was a silence until Eddie brought over a tray of drinks and placed one in front of each person.

'What are we talking about?' he asked.

'How strange Paul is.' Ginny flashed Ruby a grin and the girl beamed back. 'Just turning up one day with a dog.'

'Ah. Yes. Well. How is he?' Eddie asked awkwardly.

Jess smiled to herself.

'Getting married.'

Both of her parents looked up at her.

'And, actually, we have some news on that front too. Because, we're also getting married.' Jess flashed them her engagement ring.

Ginny stood up with a whoosh, hand over her mouth, and pulled on Jess's hand for a closer look.

Eddie, however, stared at Marshall.

'Doesn't Ruby have any headphones she can listen to a video with?'

Jess looked past her mother to see her father watching Marshall. Ruby looked up at her mother eagerly.

Reluctantly, Jess fished out a tablet and child size pink headphones and pulled up a video series for Ruby to watch. They all waited until she was engrossed and then Jess opened her mouth, but her father got there first.

'You barely know each other,' he hissed.

Jess sighed.

'I know we haven't been together long. But we know each other, Dad.'

'Are you pregnant?' her mother asked in a whisper.

Jess had expected this, and although the question still made her stomach twist, she did a good job of holding it together.

'No. I'm not pregnant. I'm in love.'

Her parents looked from her to Marshall who attempted a smile.

'I know this must come as a shock,' he told them, clearing his throat. 'But your daughter is the most amazing person I've ever met. And so is Ruby.'

'He makes us happy,' Jess added. 'He keeps us safe.'

Her parents exchanged a glance.

'But it's only been a few months,' said her father.

'It's been nearly a year, Dad. And how long did it take you to know you wanted to marry Mum?' Jess asked.

There was a pause and then a smile bloomed on Eddie's face.

'You always have been hard to argue with,' he told her, taking Ginny's hand. Her mother grinned.

'Well, congratulations. To both of you,' she said. 'We should have bought some champagne. Maybe later. A new dog, a new husband-to-be. And a new job. You haven't told us much about this new business of yours with Erica. Is it a marketing agency? I remember you saying you were planning on setting one up together.'

Jess tried to keep a handle on the spinning conversation. She was in danger of losing control of it, if she ever had control.

'Erm, not exactly. But I guess we're something of an agency.'

'What does that mean?' Ginny sat back and sipped her gin and tonic.

'Sounds a bit like a mid-life crisis,' Eddie interrupted, looking back to Marshall. 'Quitting your job, setting up a business, getting engaged so quickly.'

Jess had trouble arguing against that.

'It is odd how it all worked out, I guess,' she offered.

'And what do you do, Marshall?' Eddie asked.

'I'm a handyman,' said Marshall.

Jess's heart pounded.

'He helps elderly and vulnerable people, Dad. That's how we met. He was gardening for my neighbour and offered to fix our broken fence.'

'The one I offered to fix for you?'

'Yeah, but, remember, I thought the neighbour would fix it because he said he would. Well, he didn't. And then Ruby and Marshall met through the fence, and by the time I'd reached them, she'd convinced him to save all the worms he was digging up from Mr Horton's garden, and then he offered to fix the fence.' Jess shrugged.

Ginny smiled at her, a small knowing look passing between mother and daughter.

'Does it pay well?' Eddie asked. 'Being a handyman.'

'Well...sometimes,' said Marshall. 'I enjoy being my own boss. Some clients pay me well and others...don't pay at all.'

Eddie raised an eyebrow.

'Some clients just want a chat and some company, and I don't feel right taking money out of their small pension just because they had a dripping tap and were lonely.'

Eddie softened.

Under the table, Jess squeezed Marshall's hand.

'And he's wonderful with Ruby, ridiculously supportive of both of us and a whiz with the dog,' Jess added. 'So, how was the cruise?'

'Oh, it was wonderful,' said Ginny, taking the

bait to change subject. 'Of course, like any holiday, the memories will have faded soon, but we have our next adventure planned out.' She grinned at her husband and something inside Jess flipped sickeningly.

'What does that mean? What new adventure?'

The cruise hadn't come as a surprise. Eddie had already been retired for two years when Ginny took early retirement. They took their savings and immediately booked the cruise they'd been talking about for so long. They wanted to see the world. It was something they'd mentioned over and over for as long as Jess could remember, and this was their chance. Their last chance. They reminded her of that often. There had never been any talk of what would happen afterwards.

'Are you going on another cruise?' Jess asked. 'You've just been around the world. Did you miss somewhere?'

Ginny's eyes twinkled.

'No. This one is closer to home.' She giggled. 'We've bought a house.'

Jess frowned.

'You have a house.'

'Yes, well, we're selling that and have bought a new house. A renovation project,' her mother told her.

'It's on the other side of town. We've had our eyes on it for a while and it came up for auction while we were away, so we bid for it online and won,' said her father.

Jess swallowed on the bile rising in her throat.

'You've sold your house?'

'Not yet,' said her mother. 'But it's on the market. We spent most of what we have buying the new house, but we can't live in it yet. By the time the sale has gone through on our old place, the new house will be functional and the sale will fund the rest of the work. That's the plan. You'll love it, Jess.'

'Is it...bigger?' Jess frowned. Why would they want to move from their beautiful finished detached house to take up a full renovation project?

'No. It's a clean slate. Everything at home is done. What else are we going to do now that we've seen the world?'

'I don't know. Relax? Read books? Garden? See friends? Spend time with Ruby?' Jess was aware of her rising pitch.

'I'd quite like to learn some building skills,' said her father.

'And I'll get a completely blank canvas for some interior design and landscaping,' said Ginny.

There was a silence. Marshall looked at Jess, squeezing her hand, and then glanced at Ruby who was giggling, engrossed in her screen.

'I guess we've all come here today with surprises,' he said.

'Yes,' said Ginny, putting down her glass. 'Come see the house. Maybe you'll understand then.'

'Now?' Jess murmured.

'Finish your drink,' said her father.

4

Rick

BRISTOL, 1864

There were certain things that people didn't
consider before deciding to travel through time.
One of those things was currency. Victorian Bristol
didn't use the same money as the modern world,
and without prior planning, Rick Cavanagh would
have landed in the past in some trouble. Poverty
was nothing new. It was a constant, especially in
the cities, and the Bristol he landed in was a little
gloomier, a lot smellier and, arguably, rougher on
the streets than the Bristol he'd grown up in. The
noise was different too. Instead of the roar and *pfft*
of the buses and traffic, there were snorts from
horses and clopping of their hooves on the cobbled
roads. Some things were still the same, however.
After arriving and getting his bearings, Rick had

wandered around the city to see what he recognised.

The Bristol Grand hotel on Broad Street was newly opened and appeared fresh and modern compared to Rick's surroundings. It was also called the White Lion, which threw Rick at first. He couldn't help but smile. One day, in the distant future, he and Erica would visit the Bristol Grand when searching for a reception venue for their wedding. Erica loved the old façade, the historic feel, and now here Rick was, visiting it only months after it had opened. He considered booking a room and staying there, but first he needed to think through his financial situation.

Finding a nearby pub, Rick bought a pint and a pie and sat in a darkened corner to eat and think. While he had money, he didn't have enough to travel endlessly through time until the pocket watch Alfie had given him did something and called him back to Erica. That was relying on the idea that it would ever do that; that Alfie had been telling the truth. If Rick was going to survive and potentially live a life of some luxury wherever he was, then he'd need to earn some money.

He sighed, wishing he was the sporting type. Someone who remembered the results of matches, so he could travel to the right time and place the right bets. But that had never been him. His skills were in people, which was what had led him to join the police as soon as he could. Surely those skills would get him through.

Of course, this was a fantastic opportunity. He had a blank slate, he could try whatever he wanted. On the other hand, he was a man from the future, with no papers or references to help him get hired, or even convince people he was who he said he was.

Back in the police, in his own time, there was a whole department dedicated to producing that paperwork, the passports, working out the currencies and backstories, ensuring everything moved smoothly for each case. Now Rick was on his own.

The other thing that Rick knew was Bristol. This was his home turf. He was Bristolian, born and bred, and he'd never left the city. He'd been born here, grown up here, developed a career, fallen in love, married and started a family here. Right up to the point where he'd stupidly gone after the escaped murderer Rachel Green, travelled back and bumped into Erica before they were supposed to meet. After everything that had happened, here he was, still in Bristol, albeit a completely different time period.

That would have to change.

He'd left Erica to see the world and that was what he planned to do. For all he knew, Erica would be ready for him within a few months. Perhaps she would change her mind about Alfie, or the irritating fae would mess up. Either way, there was a chance that Rick didn't have much time.

Once he'd filled his belly, he strode in the direction of Temple Meads railway station, wondering if it would look any different. The fashion tugged at his gaze as men and women strolled past him, some in a hurry, some not. The women gave him furtive glances. Rick purposefully wore a long brown coat to cover his clothing. It was easier than constantly changing outfits to fit the time he was in. Underneath were jeans and a shirt, which would have to go. He'd buy something on his way back from the railway station, he decided, as a woman in a green dress caught his eye. She smiled at him and he smiled back. He'd need a hat too. All the men were wearing hats.

Temple Meads was different, although when Rick would later stop and think about it, he recognised the building before him as the one hidden beneath layers of new build in his own time. Its simplicity compared to what he was used to was stunning, as was the detail in the design. The smoke, on the other hand, was worse than the pollution of modern Bristol. Puffs of it rose from behind the building as an engine stood idly waiting. The smell of the burning coal gripped something in Rick and he approached, grinning, shoving his hands deep into his pockets and taking in lungfuls of the dirty air.

That night, having dined in the hotel restaurant, Rick sat on the bed and took out the paper and pen he'd brought with him. The pen was noticeably out of place, but easier than carrying ink around. His new clothes were neatly folded at the end of the bed, waiting for the morning and his first day in a new job, as an apprentice learning to drive the steam trains. His stomach churned with the nerves of the day and the excitement of what tomorrow would bring. Before he attempted sleep, however, he crouched over the paper and wrote a letter to Erica.

Beside him, on the covers, was the pocket watch Alfie had given him, glinting gold in the lamp light as Rick described the city to Erica. He made sure to date it and enclosed a piece of that day's newspaper in the envelope when he was done.

Getting the letter to arrive at the right time would be tricky, but nothing Rick couldn't handle. It would take some explaining to the postmaster and perhaps a little extra cash, but Rick had worked everything out.

He fell asleep that night with the pocket watch in his hand, a part of his mind always waiting for it to do something, to tell him to come home.

5
Erica

Erica woke early but not as early as her mother, Esther, who had been awake at dawn and up within minutes to drink tea and tend to her herbs. She made her daughter a coffee while Erica spread margarine and jam on some toast.

'You should have something more filling,' said Esther. 'Toast won't last you long.'

'I'll be okay. I'm meeting Gran at the cemetery in a couple of hours, I'll grab something at the café.'

Esther sighed, placing Erica's coffee on the table beside her toast.

'Or I could make you some porridge.'

Erica's stomach churned and she shook her head. She opened her mouth to thank her mother but decline the offer when Esther sat in the chair beside her and frowned into her eyes.

'What's wrong? Something's wrong. Is it Alfie?'

Erica sat back.

'What? No. Why do you think it's Alfie?'

Esther pulled a face.

'You know why.'

'I thought you liked him now that you know him better.'

Esther sighed.

'I see how he loves you, but I don't trust him and neither should you. You can't trust the fae.'

'What about Gran and Eolande?'

'Yes, well, I don't approve, but you know what your grandmother does if you try to tell her not to do something.'

Erica agreed as she sipped her coffee.

'So it's not Alfie,' Esther continued. 'But something's wrong.'

Erica sighed and reached into her pocket, pulling out the envelope containing the letter from Rick. She handed it to her mother who carefully opened it.

'It's from Rick. From where he is now. In the past,' she told Esther.

Esther's eyes widened as she started to read, and she gave a small wistful sigh.

'How romantic.'

'Is it?'

Esther looked up at her daughter.

'You're not happy about it? The man is travelling through time and writing you love letters. Look at this! He's gotten a job driving steam trains. Don't tell your dad, his head'll explode. And he misses you. And he's thinking about you.'

'And he left me,' said Erica.

Esther stopped and passed the letter back to her daughter. There was a moment of silence as the two women considered the situation, and then Bramley whined from his basket. He got up, stretched, and gave another cry, placing his head in Esther's lap and looking up at her with large brown eyes. She stroked his ears absent-mindedly.

'If he had stayed, would things be different now?' Esther asked, standing and collecting the dogs' bowls. Daisy's ears pricked up, her eyes opening at the sound. She made more of a show of yawning and stretching than Bramley had done, until both dogs were sitting obediently, watching Esther fill their bowls with breakfast.

'I don't know,' said Erica truthfully. 'I know you don't like Alfie, but I do. And the more time I spend with him, the more...' She drifted off and sighed, filling her mouth with jammy toast. 'I love him,' she said around the food.

Esther's shoulders sagged. Erica swallowed.

'What if I'm like Gran?'

'Stubborn, strong-willed and far too adventurous for your own good?' Esther placed the dog bowls on the floor and gave the signal for the dogs to eat. She leaned back against the worktop. 'Ever since you left that marketing job you've become more and more like her.'

'You mean ever since I met Alfie?'

Esther shook her head.

'No. You left that marketing agency without another job. I would never have done that. Neither would your father. But your gran would have. Although she'd have made a scene on the way out and I'm very glad you didn't.' She moved to sit back beside Erica. 'And while I don't necessarily trust Alfie, I do trust you.' Esther gave her daughter a warm smile and took her hand, squeezing it. 'Do you have any way of responding to Rick?'

'Nope. I don't think so.'

'Then forget about it for now. You don't need to think about it yet, do you. Not if there's nothing you can do about it.'

'No.' Erica looked down at her toast, no longer hungry. Esther watched her.

'Here.' She stood and searched through her bottles in a cupboard until she found the one she was after, placing a couple of drops into Erica's coffee. 'For your nerves.'

Erica smiled.

'Thanks, Mum.' She gave Esther a tight hug.

'Now, finish your toast, wash your hands and take the dogs for a walk.'

Erica laughed.

'And here I was thinking I might as well get some work done as I'm up early.'

'Work while walking,' said Esther, smiling and returning to her garden.

Erica took Bramley and Daisy into the woods. They kept to the main path although she furtively glanced at the now broken portal whenever they drew close enough. When they reached the fallen tree trunk, Erica stopped and looked around. The dogs were busy sniffing; they were alone. Closing her eyes, Erica placed a hand on the nearest tree.

'Hello,' she said out loud, focusing on her breathing until the sounds of the woods drifted away.

Hello.

Erica jumped and grinned, but kept her eyes closed and her hand on the tree.

'Lovely to meet you,' she told the tree.

And you, witch.

'Is all well in the woods today?'

All is well.

'Good. I'm glad to hear it. Thank you for talking to me.'

Rain is coming, said the tree.

Erica shifted her weight.

'Oh. Thank you. I best get the dogs home, then.'

He took her.

Erica stopped, fighting to keep her concentration focused and her eyes closed.

'Who took who?'

Fae. She was happy.

A silence followed as Erica waited for more.

'A fae took someone?' she asked quietly.

The tree remained silent.

'Okay,' said Erica. 'Can you tell me when?'

There was no response. Erica waited until a cold, wet nose prodded her free hand.

'Okay. Thank you. Have a nice day.' She opened her eyes and dropped her hand from the tree to find Daisy looking up at her and wagging her tail. 'Hey, girl. Sorry. Shall we carry on?' Erica started walking and the dogs led the way. 'A fae took a girl,' Erica repeated under her breath. From whatever angle you looked at it, it didn't seem good. Except that the tree said she was happy. The girl was happy? Did that mean she went willingly? Or had she been happy and now she wasn't?

They turned a corner and Bramley trotted off down a muddy, narrow pathway, following his nose. Erica went after him.

'Bram! Come back. Where are you going?'

Daisy trotted after her.

Erica stopped when she found Bramley with his nose between bluebells. She clipped on his lead to be on the safe side and then, finally, looked up and around.

'Wow.'

The bluebells were beautiful this year. They spread across the woodland floor, to the right and left of the path, around tree stumps and patches of ferns and brambles, filling the local area with glorious colour. Erica took a moment to appreciate them and then bent to take a photo before leading the dogs back to the main path.

She was still considering the tree's words as she led both dogs on leads from the woods, up the residential roads to where she'd parked her parents' car. The houses on either side were large and detached, much like her parents' house, with gardens out the front, some with double garages and tarmac driveways. Some houses had gravel with weeds sprouting through on their front gardens, some had paved over them for more parking, but some still had lawns although not necessarily well kept. Erica hesitated as they walked past one particular house. On the front lawn was a semi-circle of mushrooms, a curve going out towards the road from the front door, around the garden and back towards the main front window.

Erica smiled. A fairy circle that encompassed the house. Was there any meaning to that? She made a mental note to ask her mother and then jumped as the front door opened. Daisy lifted her head and Bramley wagged his tail in greeting.

'You,' said the woman who appeared. 'You're his girlfriend.'

Erica blinked. The woman was in a soft, blue dressing gown and fluffy slippers, her long brown hair was brushed, and from this distance it looked as though she'd been crying.

'Sorry?' Erica called.

The woman left the house and walked down the driveway. Bramley, sensing Erica's unease, stopped wagging his tail and stepped closer to Daisy and

Erica. Erica automatically reached out and stroked his head.

'You're his girlfriend, aren't you? That fae man. I've seen you walking past before.' The woman glanced down at the dogs and seemed to second guess herself. 'Maybe you're not.'

Erica's heart had twisted at the word 'fae'.

'Man taller than me, curly brown hair, often in a white shirt and jeans?' she asked quietly.

The woman nodded, studying Erica's face.

'He's a fae, or whatever they call themselves.'

'How do you know that?' Erica asked.

The woman's bottom lip quivered but she held herself together.

'I need his help. He's not here with you?'

'No, but I'm seeing him later. How do you know about him?'

'Can you ask him to come here? I need his help. Desperately. No one else can help. He's our only chance. Please? Please, will you ask him to come?'

Erica's stomach turned and beside her, Daisy whined. They all jumped as Bramley gave a short, sharp bark.

'You need help from the fae?'

The woman gave a fast and passionate nod.

'Please. Ask him? I'll pay you. I'll pay him. Whatever he wants. Please.'

'Okay, all right. I'll ask him,' said Erica, reaching into her pocket. 'Here. My name's Erica. Here's my card, it has my email and number on it. I'll ask him later to come round. Okay?'

The woman took the card with trembling fingers, and for a moment looked as if she might give Erica a hug. She glanced down at the dogs and apparently thought better of it.

'Thank you. Thank you so much. Later, yes? Tell him to come as soon as he can. Please. Okay? Thank you.'

The woman stepped away, wiping a hand over her red eyes, and Erica took that as sign that she was free to leave. The dogs were eager to get back to the car so Erica let them drag her along. Once they were safely in the back, Erica sat in the driver's seat and went over the conversations with the tree and then the woman.

A shiver ran through her.

Starting the ignition, she headed for home. She wouldn't see Alfie until that afternoon and dwelling on what had just happened wouldn't help if she didn't have more information. She pushed it from her mind as she drove, but the sickening nausea in her stomach only grew worse.

6

Erica

Minerva handed Erica back the newspaper clipping from 1864 and sighed.

'Bloody typical,' she said, pulling a woolly hat onto her head. 'It's always the man that gets to go have the adventure, isn't it?'

Erica stared at her grandmother in the passenger seat of her Mini Cooper, her fingers brushing over her stomach which still wouldn't settle.

'I don't think that's what's happened here.'

'Isn't it? You tell him you're not ready and he runs off to have fun.'

'Do you really think Victorian England is fun?'

'Of course it is! Unlike all the poor wretches living through it, he can leave whenever he wants.'

Erica looked out the window to the trees of the cemetery in front of them.

'I'm having fun too,' she pointed out.

Minerva grinned, her eyes twinkling. It was an

expression you didn't really want to see on your nearly ninety-year-old grandmother, but it was a common occurrence with Minerva and Erica had long ago gotten used to it.

'Yes. I'm rather glad you're finally having fun with Alfie.'

'And work,' Erica added. 'I ran our ghost tour on Saturday. It was a fun one.'

'In the hotel?'

Erica nodded.

'With a group of ten tourists who were staying there. It was wonderful. We met three spirits.'

'Real spirits?'

Erica gave her grandmother a look.

'Of course real spirits.'

'And you're being careful?'

'Yes. I checked with them all first. I told them no one had to come out and say hello if they didn't want to.'

Minerva laughed to herself.

'I think most people ask the living those questions instead of the dead.'

Erica shrugged.

'The living are paying to be there. The dead live there. It's only polite.'

'Yes, it is.' Minerva patted Erica's knee. 'Good girl. Shall we brave the wind?'

Erica rammed her hat over her head and ears. The wind, an edge of a spring storm passing over the north of the country, caught the door and ripped it from her hands. Muttering gratitude that she hadn't parked close to another car, Erica got out and slammed the door shut.

Minerva joined her as she locked the Mini, wrapping her coat tight around her.

'Should I tell Alfie about the letter?' Erica asked, looking around the cemetery.

'Might as well. You know him. He'll already know. He probably knew before you knew. He might have even known before Rick decided to write the letter.'

Erica smiled. That was the problem with being in a relationship with a fae, it was hard to keep secrets. She corrected herself: it was hard for her to keep secrets from him.

'That's true.' She sighed. A gust of wind caught her breath and disappeared with it towards the city. 'Coffee?'

Minerva nodded and led the way to the small cemetery café, joined to the chapel. At least, it had once been a chapel. Now, it was a community centre situated in the heart of the beautiful Victorian cemetery that had been discarded and left to nature until a group of volunteers had taken it back. Minerva's husband, Erica's grandfather, had been one of those volunteers. His grave was near the back entrance, with the other more recent burials and cremations. Erica glanced up at the chapel as they passed, wondering if Rick would visit it. Perhaps he would stand where she was, looking up at the building and see it as a working chapel. The cemetery would be manicured, without the backdrop of ash trees that had self-sown over the years. The café certainly wouldn't be there.

A shiver ran through her, despite the wind dropping, and from the corner of her eye she saw a shadow. Someone approaching. It would be Alfie, she thought, turning to meet him with a smile ready.

There was no one there.

Erica stared into the empty space as the wind returned, blowing back her hair. When she was small, Minerva had taught her to always believe her gut.

'If your gut tells you something is real, then it's real. It doesn't matter what logic or science or the evidence suggests. If your body tells you that it's real, then trust in yourself,' she'd said.

Erica exhaled slowly, searching for any hint of a person who might have dipped behind a gravestone or vanished behind a shrub. There was no one. She turned back to the chapel and took another slow breath, feeling for anything out of the ordinary. The wind made it difficult, but there it was. A presence. A shape. A sense that she wasn't standing there alone.

It wasn't a spirit. Erica knew a spiritual energy when she was standing next to one. No, this was something else.

'Rick?' she murmured.

'Erica?'

Minerva's voice made her jump and look up the steps leading to the café. Her grandmother, one hand on her hatted head, braced against the wind, squinted at her. 'Are you coming?'

'Yes,' said Erica, giving the chapel one last look. Whoever or whatever her companion had been, they were no longer there. Erica jogged up the steps to catch up with Minerva and fell into the café.

In an instant the wind was gone, replaced with warmth and the smell of strong coffee. Minerva had nabbed a table in the corner, pulling off her hat and coat. A small family were seated at one of the other tables, and the two remaining small tables were occupied by couples reading newspapers. Erica ordered four coffees and two croissants, and then joined her grandmother.

Minerva was watching the small children playing in the corner.

'Any word from Jess? Has she told her parents yet?'

'She messaged to say they got there safe and Marshall's been welcomed into the family. Apparently it was a bit awkward. Her parents assumed she was pregnant again.'

Minerva shrugged.

'Understandable given the speed and what happened last time, I guess.'

'Paul never proposed to her after she got pregnant.'

'No. Thankfully. Just think, there's probably another timeline somewhere, a parallel world, where Jess and Paul did get married. Do they think they got divorced before or after she met Marshall?'

Erica looked at her grandmother as their coffees were placed on the table.

'She wouldn't have met Marshall if she'd married Paul,' Erica pointed out. 'She wouldn't have bought that house.'

'Rubbish. Those two are meant to be. The universe will be pushing them together, no matter what timeline or world they're in.'

Erica smiled, her fingers trailing over the hot ceramic of her coffee cup. She watched as Eolande and Alfie appeared from the trees and made their way to the front door of the café.

'Who do you think the universe is pushing us towards?' she murmured.

Minerva followed her gaze and smiled.

'Well, it screamed at me to marry your grand-father, and I listened. Then, when I needed her the most, it pushed me into Eolande's arms. Do you hear the universe screaming at you?'

Erica laughed.

'Are you kidding? I'm only just learning to listen to the trees, never mind the whole universe.' Her smile faded at the memory of earlier that morning in the woods.

They greeted their fae lovers as Eolande bent to kiss Minerva's cheek and then sat beside her. Alfie wasn't quite so demure in the close, warm public place. He took Erica's hand, sitting beside her and then leaned forward to kiss her lips.

'Steady,' warned Minerva. 'Grandmother here.'

Alfie smiled, searching Erica's eyes and her heart pounded. What did he see when he did that?

'What did we interrupt?' he asked, sitting back and looking to Minerva and Eolande. He raked a hand through his brown hair, managing to somewhat tidy what the wind had messed up.

Minerva glanced at Erica and then sipped at her coffee.

'How the universe tells us what to do. Jess has taken her new man and dog to meet her parents for the first time.'

'How's it going?' he asked.

'He's been accepted, as well he should. They're made for each other,' said Minerva.

Erica dared to glance at Alfie as her grandmother spoke, but he avoided her. Minerva had taken Eolande's hand and squeezed it, making the tall, elegant woman smile.

'Fancy a walk?' Erica asked Alfie quietly.

Finally, he looked at her, tilted his head and then nodded.

Standing, he took both their coffees and went up to the till, asking the woman serving to pour them into takeaway cups.

'You don't mind us going?' Erica asked Minerva.

'And give us some quiet time together? How very

dare you,' Minerva declared, shooing them away with one hand while turning her attention to Eolande. As Erica went to follow Alfie, Minerva called after her, 'But you're still taking me home.'

'Of course. Call me when you're ready.' Erica made a show of putting her phone in her pocket.

The front door of the café was sheltered from the wind and Erica was tempted to grab an outside table for them to sit at and talk, but Alfie had other ideas. He strode down the steps and into the trees, pausing to check she was following. Once she caught up he handed her a coffee and they wandered down the path, the wind pushing them along at times.

'Something weird happened this morning,' she shouted to him. He didn't respond but glanced back to her. 'I took the dogs for a walk in the woods and talked to a tree. It told me something about a fae and a girl. It said he took her.'

Erica studied Alfie's back and, while he did well to hide it, his step faltered, his shoulders flinching.

'Then, on the way out, past this house, a woman came rushing out and asked me to ask you to pay her a visit. That you were the only one who could help?'

Alfie stopped and turned back to her.

'Who?'

Erica shrugged.

'No idea. That big house with the double garage and fairy circle of mushrooms on the front lawn.'

It might have been the chilled wind but Erica could have sworn that Alfie paled.

'What's going on Alfie?' she asked over the wind.

He looked up and met her eyes.

'I don't know. She asked for me in person? How does she know me?'

'She just called you a fae. Called me the fae's girlfriend.'

The corners of Alfie's lips twitched up at that and his gaze travelled over her until he reached her eyes and a raised eyebrow. He sighed.

'You don't know them?' she asked.

'No. But I know what a fairy circle in the garden can mean,' he said. 'I'll go visit them later.'

'I'm going to see a house this afternoon, just after lunch. Do you want to come with me? We can go see this woman and her fairy circle afterwards?'

Alfie smiled, reaching to take her hand as they continued walking.

'If you want to come with me to visit this person, I can't stop you, can I? Nor should I try. Do you want me there? At the viewing?' he asked.

She gave him a strange look.

'Why wouldn't I? You're the main reason I'm moving out.'

'I've told you, you don't have to waste money on rent and bills. We can just stay at mine.'

Erica immediately shook her head. Up ahead was a bench, tucked away in a small alcove, looking out over the cemetery and protected by the trees.

Alfie sat and trailed one arm along the back of the bench for Erica to snuggle into.

'We've talked about this,' she told him. 'I don't want to live in your world.'

'And you think I want to live in yours?'

Erica looked up at Alfie and caught him smiling. He kissed the tip of her nose.

There was a pause as Erica pondered how to broach the new subject.

'I take it you know about the letter?'

'The letter from Detective Rick Cavanagh? Of course.'

Erica relaxed, sipping her coffee.

'Is it weird?' she asked. 'Talking to my current lover about my future husband sending me love letters?'

Alfie shifted position slightly and Erica shifted with him.

'Nothing is ever set in stone,' he murmured in her ear. 'When I first saw you, I knew I'd give you my heart. Then I saw that your heart belonged to another and I let you go. And now? Who does your heart belong to now?'

Erica seemed to melt into Alfie as he spoke, his breath light and warm on her skin, making her toes curl.

'You,' she whispered, although she didn't hear herself speak. The wind caught the word and threw it away. But this was Alfie, she knew he'd heard. At first she regretted the response. She didn't want to hurt him; she didn't want to hurt Rick, either. Yet, in that moment, Alfie did have her heart. He entered her thoughts whenever she took a moment to stop. He gave her comfort when she needed it the most. His very presence was enough to make her feel safe. Despite all that, Rick did something to her that Alfie never had.

Erica slipped her hand into Alfie's and pushed her cheek into his chest, closing her eyes, being careful not to spill her coffee, and listened to his heart beat.

Fen

'Take my hand and step through.'

She'd done so willingly although with some trepidation. Nerves were to be expected. He was nervous too. He'd invited women home before, brought them to his house, given them whatever they wanted and made love to them for two days straight before taking them back. He left them with their friends and families, wondering if the whole thing had been a glorious dream.

This time it would be different.

Bethany wasn't like the others.

He wanted to take it slow this time; no jumping into bed, not even a kiss. He wanted it to be special.

Fen stood back and watched Bethany take in his world. Her eyes were wide, her breath coming hard as she looked around at the bright greens and lush browns, breathing in the pungent smell of the flowers and the woods. She still held his hand and now she gripped it.

'It's okay,' he told her in a soft voice. 'You're safe with me.'

She nodded but didn't smile. Oh, how he wanted to see her smile.

'Come with me.' He led her down the path and into what the humans would call a village. A village of fae. Some looked out their windows as Fen and Bethany passed, most ignored them.

'Brought another one home, have you?' someone called.

Fen gritted his teeth.

'This is different!' he called in a sing-song voice, hoping Bethany wouldn't read too much into it.

They made it to the end of the village and a small house made of timber, built into a large oak tree. Fen opened the door and led Bethany into the cool darkness, pausing to let her eyes adjust.

'Take a seat,' he told her, gesturing to some chairs positioned around the fireplace. 'I'll get a couple of drinks and we'll talk. What would you like?'

Bethany looked up at him with the same wide eyes.

'Tea?' he offered.

She nodded.

'I'll make us some tea. You make yourself at home.' Because this is your new home. He didn't say that last bit out loud, he managed to stop himself in time.

He rushed to make the tea, filling the teapot with leaves and hot water, placing cups on a tray and at the last moment finding a tin of shortbread biscuits he'd brought back from a previous outing to the humans' world.

All of these he placed on a small table in front of Bethany. He poured her tea and offered her a biscuit. She took one and held it, staring at the tea.

Fen sat down and tapped his foot against the wooden floor, trying to find the words.

'Were you ever told fairy tales as a child?' he ventured.

Bethany didn't move. Fen swallowed hard.

'I am a fae,' he announced. 'Not born of your world but born of this world and able to move between the two. We have a long history together, my people and yours. And sometimes it happens that our two people come together. That our souls are destined to be entwined. And you see, Bethany, I hoped you would come across me in the woods today because you are for me. I am for you. We are meant to be together.'

Fen pressed his lips shut to stop any other words falling out and waited for her reaction. His heart dropped, stomach turning, as Bethany frowned. She put the biscuit back in the tin and turned to him.

'You said you'd take me away from it all.'

'And I have!' Fen gestured to the house. 'We will get to know each other and you'll see. We'll fall in love and marry and live here.'

Sheer terror passed over Bethany's eyes.

'But I don't know you.'

'But you will.'

'And when I said I wanted to get away and leave, I meant I wanted to go to London.'

There was a pause as Fen sagged back into his chair.

'Oh.'

He didn't like London. It was too busy with too many people and creatures. He preferred woodland, he preferred home.

'Well, you can go home whenever you like. I promise you.'

Bethany met his eyes and his insides jolted with pleasure and a type of comfort.

'I want to go home. Take me home.'

It was how Fen imagined being stabbed would feel. A sharp pain, a tightness in his chest, and for that moment the shock rendered him unable to breathe.

'But...we're meant for each other.'

Bethany shook her head.

'No, we're not. Take me home.'

Fen placed down his tea cup and steadied himself.

'Okay. I will take you home. But give me thirty minutes. Talk to me for thirty minutes. Give me that chance and then, if you still want to go, I will take you home.'

8

Jess

'Here it is,' said Eddie. 'What do you think?'

Jess wasn't listening. They were standing on the pavement, looking up at the imposing grey brick house. Her parents were to her right and Marshall, Ruby and Bubbles were on her left. The house was double-fronted with a beautiful, although rotting, Victorian porch. The windows, five in all at the front, were dark. Curtains could be seen in some, faded by summer days and coated in a haze of cobweb. Otherwise, there was darkness. The front door and porch gave way to an overgrown path of broken patio slabs that led to the pavement, and a small brown picket fence, partially hidden by tall weeds, marked the boundary.

'There's a big garden at the back,' said her mother.

'And a garage. Come and look.' Eddie led them to the side of the house where a dropped kerb led to an equally dilapidated driveway and small garage that looked like it was waiting for a light wind to come along and knock it down.

'It's…a lot of work,' said Jess.

Her parents nodded eagerly and Jess exchanged a private wide-eyed look with Marshall.

'The garage is coming down but there's asbestos so that'll be a few thousand,' said her father. 'Probably some in the house too. That'll need sorting first thing. Strip all the wallpaper.'

'Oh, yes, the wallpaper looks vintage. But not in a good way,' said Ginny, grinning.

'Strip the floors. The carpets are either vibrant seventies or disgusting. Strip the bathrooms and kitchen. Re-plaster everything, new floors and we're away.'

Jess blinked at her father as he beamed at her.

'Meanwhile, I'll cut back the garden so we can see what's what,' her mother added. 'It's all overgrown. You can't even see the true size.'

'How long has it been empty?' Marshall asked.

'Eight years,' said Eddie. 'The last owner moved into a care home and he hadn't been able to update it at all before he went. Then the family had a big argument about it. It fell more into disrepair. Apparently they couldn't shift it. No one brave enough to take on the work. Then, recently, the owner's son sadly passed away and his children said enough was enough. They lowered the price, put it up for auction and that's when we saw it.'

Marshall nodded, giving the house an appraising look.

'You forgot about rewiring and plumbing,' he murmured.

Eddie looked up at him and his features softened. Jess watched in horror.

'Oh yeah, good thinking,' her father said, giving Marshall a smile. 'Would be great to make this a family project,' he added, glancing to Jess. 'If you want to help.'

'We're both quite busy, Dad. But maybe, I guess. At weekends. Maybe the weekends when Paul has Ruby.'

Eddie was still looking at Marshall.

'And then there's Bubbles to think of,' Jess continued, staring at Marshall, trying to get his attention. He was too busy staring up at the house.

Ginny led them back to the front and opened the little gate. They all stopped as Bubbles gave a whine. Jess snapped round to the dog.

'Is she bored?' Eddie laughed.

'Yeah.' Jess attempted a laugh. 'Yeah, that's probably it.'

Ginny walked up the path, brushing past the weeds, and moved to the window on the right.

'This is the living room. We're contemplating knocking down some walls but need to speak to a builder.' She cupped her hands around her eyes and looked through the window. 'Come here, Jess. What do you think?'

Jess went to follow and stopped as Bubbles gave a sharp, high-pitched bark. The dog sat down and refused to move, leaving Jess at the end of her lead giving her a little tug.

'What's up, Bubs?'

The dog whined again and pulled Jess away from the house. Frowning, Jess handed the lead to Marshall and joined her mother as Bubbles cried and gave another high-pitched bark. What was she scared of?

Jess cupped her hands and looked through the dirty window. The room beyond was dark, as expected, with the seventies carpet of brown and orange swirls that her father had mentioned. There was no furniture although there were some outlines on the walls where furniture had once stood and dips in the carpet that had once housed the legs of a sofa. The walls were a dirty magnolia and cobwebs hung from a couple of the corners, up on the ceiling. Jess smiled. The ceilings were decorated with ornate coving and dirty cornices. She could see what her mother was seeing. A light, beautiful room with the period features brought back to life. The back wall could be knocked through, presumably the kitchen was on the other side. Or it could make a lovely snug, put a TV on the wall and a sofa with a couple of beanbags for Ruby to sink into when she visited. Jess could almost become jealous. She opened her mouth to tell her mother when something in the room moved. Jess's chest tightened, squeezing at her heart, her breath stopping.

She blinked and it was gone.

'What was that?' she asked gently.

'What? Oh, the carpet? I know, terrible, but it'll get pulled up,' said Ginny.

'No. No, the...didn't you see it?'

'Can you see the ceiling? Beautiful, isn't it. Just needs a good clean and a lick of paint.'

Jess blinked again and searched the room. To the back left was the door that led into the hallway and Jess watched as the door moved. It wasn't much, and maybe it was a trick of the eye, but she could have sworn that it had opened a couple of centimetres.

'Is there anyone in the house, Mum? Maybe the old owners are here collecting things?'

Ginny gave her a quizzical look and then turned back to the quiet street. The house was at the edge of the town on a narrow road that would have once been filled with horses and carts taking produce to the market on the high street. The road eventually opened up onto a street of modern houses, but here it hadn't been widened. The town council had left it as it had always been, although the cobbles had been removed at some point, and the small green area opposite with a line of trees had been left to stand. It was probably just that bit too small to build anything worthwhile on. Ginny gestured to the lack of cars nearby.

'It doesn't look like it. And anyway, we've got the

keys. We completed last week. It's our house now. Why?'

Jess blinked and there it was again. A shadow, or something dark, tall enough to be a man, walking past the doorway. Whoever it was, they were in the hall. Jess stood back and desperately tried to work out what she should do next.

'How about some lunch before we go in and give the tour? I don't know about everyone else, but I'm hungry,' Eddie called, breaking the spell.

'Me too!' shouted Ruby.

'Oh, yes, we'll have that pub lunch.' Ginny pulled on Jess's sleeve, dragging her away from the window. Marshall raised an eyebrow as Jess returned to her family.

'You all right?' he murmured as Jess's parents led the way back to the high street.

'Not really. I saw someone in there,' she whispered so that Ruby wouldn't hear. Her daughter was skipping ahead until she appeared between her grandparents, taking both their hands and swinging their arms a little too hard. Bubbles tried to follow but Marshall held her back.

'Probably shadows of the trees from the back garden,' said Marshall, slipping an arm around Jess's waist. She nodded. That would be it. What was happening to her if she kept jumping to ghosts and demons? She needed this weekend. She needed a break. Jess took a deep breath and followed her parents and daughter into the warmth of a pub.

This pub was also dog friendly and Eddie ruffled Bubbles' ears as she lay down at his feet. Jess caught herself watching the dog as Marshall placed some drinks on the table and handed her parents a menu.

'The chips here are wonderful,' said Ginny. 'Triple cooked.'

Jess's stomach grumbled at that, her eyes scanning the menu as her mind whirred.

'Can I have chips, Mummy?' asked Ruby.

'Sure,' Jess told her. 'And a sandwich. What sandwich do you want?'

'Cheese.'

Jess nodded.

'Okay.'

They put their order in and Jess waited until her father came back with their table number written on a wooden spoon before she broached her next question.

'When are you starting the work?'

'On Monday, unless you want to help us start this weekend,' her mother said.

'It'd be great to get your expert eye on the place, Marshall,' said her father, bringing his pint to his lips.

'Sure, no problem. I'd love to help,' said Marshall, glancing at Jess. 'I've always wondered about property development. I think what you're doing is great. A real adventure, if not a bit daunting.'

'It's definitely scary.' Ginny gave a nervous laugh. 'But I can't wait to get stuck in. What's the point in having all this free time and our pensions if we're not doing what we always wanted to do?'

'I didn't know you always wanted to renovate a house,' said Jess.

Her mother shrugged.

'Some dreams come to you when you're young, some come to you on the day you retire.' Ginny grinned at her husband and the two clinked their glasses. Jess gave a weak smile. 'Like you,' her mother continued. 'Quitting your job to start your own business. That's an adventure. What is it you and Erica are doing again? I know you've told me but I still don't really understand it.'

Jess cleared her throat and fumbled with the thin cardboard coaster under her drink.

'Erm...'

'They help people who are worried or curious about their property,' said Marshall for her. 'Jess mostly does the accounts and contract work, and the research. Looking into the history of properties. Their biggest client to date is a hotel in the city. Isn't it?' He gave Jess a look and she nodded, glancing sideways at Ruby.

'They were worried about their hotel?' asked Eddie.

'A number of staff had said they'd heard voices when there was no one there,' Jess told them.

There was a pause and then Eddie laughed.

'They thought there was a ghost? How does you researching the property help with that?'

Jess cleared her throat again.

'We're paranormal investigators,' she said, not looking up, not making eye contact. 'We went in to find out if there was a ghost. And now we run ghost tours there. It's turned into a regular gig. It's fun and it means we're profitable.' She ventured a look up and found her parents staring at her.

Ginny took a sip from her drink and placed her glass back gently on the table.

'This is because of Erica's grandmother, isn't it.'

Jess opened her mouth, but no words came so she closed it again.

'Actually it's because of me,' she said finally. 'A man I used to work with called me up and said he thought he was going mad. His wife had died just after they'd had a baby and he could hear her voice on the baby monitor.'

'And was she a ghost?' asked her father. Jess studied him for a moment, trying to work out if he was taking her seriously.

'No.'

'Of course she wasn't,' said Ginny. 'Ghosts aren't real. It was his grief, making him hear her.'

Jess nodded.

'That's what I thought too. And Ric. Turns out we were all wrong.' She sighed. 'His wife had faked her own death. She was wanted by the police and they'd caught up with her.' Jess took a deep gulp of her drink so that the rest of the story didn't spill out. It was enough that her parents were learning the true nature of her new job, there was no need to bring time travel into it.

'That's...' Ginny shook her head, unable to find the words. She looked at Ruby. 'Dangerous.'

Jess laughed, startling them all.

'It's okay, Mum. We're safe. We have things in place.'

'Oh? Like what?'

'Processes. Procedures. We're being professional about it. Don't worry.' She wouldn't mention the fae, the way they'd beaten back a demon in a woods, or how Minerva's coven of witches had banished a vengeful spirit in Jess's own home. She looked up at Marshall. 'And Marshall keeps us safe. Marshall and Erica's family.'

'Erica's grandmother,' Ginny repeated. 'I always knew there was something about her.'

Jess smiled and nodded.

'Yeah. There's something all right.'

9
Jess

The rest of lunch passed smoothly after Ruby interrupted to tell her grandmother about the latest cartoon she'd been watching. Ginny patiently listened and asked Ruby questions while Eddie and Marshall disappeared into a conversation about pipes and different types of flooring. Soon, with stomachs full, they were leaving the pub and returning to the Victorian house.

Jess began to regret finishing Ruby's chips as they approached. A cloud must have passed over the sun and a chill breeze found its way under her coat. She huddled into herself, wishing Ruby was holding her hand instead of her mother's. Marshall had Bubbles' lead and nearly tripped over the Bernese mountain dog as she hesitated. Jess watched her closely, noting her drooped, pinned back ears. Bubbles glanced up at Jess, catching her eye and giving a small whine.

'What's wrong?' Marshall asked, trying to pull Bubbles along with him.

Jess kept her mouth shut and her eyes on the front door as her father produced a key and stepped inside. Ginny followed, leading Ruby who stopped without warning and was accidentally pulled through the door. Ginny turned back.

'Are you okay?'

Ruby didn't answer. She was looking up at the walls and ceiling.

'It smells funny,' she said after a moment's consideration.

'Yes, it does. There's a bit of damp. No one's lived here for a long time,' Ginny explained.

Ruby glanced back at Jess who meant to give a comforting smile but couldn't quite do it in time. Ruby followed her grandmother through the house and into the kitchen, pulling a face as she went. Jess stepped inside carefully. The chill from the spring breeze turned colder inside the unheated house, sending a wave of goosebumps over her skin. She shivered and stopped on the threshold.

'What's wrong?' Marshall whispered behind her.

'I don't know,' said Jess quietly. 'I saw something through the window, Marsh. I know I did.'

'Want me to go first?' he asked.

Jess shook her head. She took a couple more steps forward and entered the house, glancing up at the walls and ceiling as Ruby had done, wondering what her little girl had sensed. The walls were covered in a thick textured wallpaper, the ceiling with textured paint. The floor had a threadbare carpet that was potentially covering the original Victorian tiles, and Jess was distracted for a moment by the urge to pull up the carpet and find out. She walked forward through the hallway, past the stairs and stopped at the door to the living room. The door that she'd seen move, the door where she'd seen...something.

Now there was a light square reception room. The sunshine of the spring afternoon shone through the large bay windows and any notion of there being a dark presence suddenly seemed ridiculous. Jess almost laughed. She turned back to Marshall and her smile fell.

Bubbles was refusing to enter the house.

Marshall sighed and stared at the dog.

'Come on, Bubs. Nothing to be scared of. See?' He held out his arms and did a silly little dance, but Bubbles only sat down and turned her brown-eyed stare onto Jess. 'What's wrong with her?'

Jess stepped over to Bubbles, crouching and rubbing the dog's ears as Bubbles thrust her head into Jess's lap.

'What can you sense?' she quietly asked the dog. Bubbles licked her cheek. Jess kissed the top of her head and took the lead from Marshall. 'Come on, baby Bubbles. In you come. Let's go see if there's a ball to play with or a chew inside, huh?'

At the mention of balls and chews, Bubbles' ears

pricked up and she delicately stepped inside the house. Keeping her tail between her legs, she followed Jess inside, glancing over her shoulder every now and then to see if Marshall was still behind them.

The kitchen was also filled with light from a large window at the back.

'I didn't think Victorian houses had big kitchens,' said Marshall, giving the room a quick inspection from the doorway.

'No, this is a later extension. Nice, though, isn't it?' said Ginny. She'd seated Ruby at a small table that looked new and had put the kettle on. 'We don't have everything in yet but we have the essentials. The kitchen is up and running, and we've bought a kitchen table we might have to take turns at. Oh, does Bubbles want to see the garden?' Ginny did a double take at the dog. 'Is she all right?'

'Oh, yeah, she just…gets a bit anxious in new places,' said Jess, studying Bubbles. 'Shall we go see the garden?'

Bubbles looked up at Jess expectantly.

The garden was potentially large. At the front, nearest the house, the ground was almost bare, with patches of dying grass and mud. Around the sides and at the back, weeds and grass grew so tall there was no guessing what might be lurking beneath it all. A frail tree stood in the back corner as if it hadn't noticed that spring had arrived. Bubbles brightened as they stepped out of the house and pulled Jess into the mud.

'Great. Thanks,' Jess muttered, studying the tree.

Marshall appeared beside her, taking a deep breath.

'The house seems nice. And I reckon I can get your dad to like me if I help out,' he murmured in her ear. The sensation of him standing so close sent a thrill through Jess and she had to stop herself from grabbing onto him.

'Yeah. Might be original tiles under the hall carpet,' she said. 'Do you think that tree's dead?'

Marshall looked over at the tree and grunted.

'Probably. But your mum said she wanted a project. I can remove it for her, if she wants.'

Jess looked up into Marshall's eyes and smiled.

'You're too good for me,' she told him.

He grinned, leaning down and kissing her with warm lips.

'Never,' he whispered, his hand lingering on her waist. 'Think they'll let us sleep in the same bed?'

Jess laughed, pushing Marshall away.

'We're engaged! Ruby's sleeping with us too, though.'

'Oh.' Marshall frowned. 'Your dad said she had her own room.'

Jess shrugged.

'I don't care. She's staying with us.'

Marshall gave her an appraising look which Jess tried not to notice from the corner of her eye.

'But we'll be back at the old house. What's going on?' he asked gently. 'This is because you think you saw something?'

'I did see something,' said Jess before the doubt could creep in. 'I think.' Her brow creased and she moved as Bubbles tugged on the lead, following a scent. Marshall stepped with her.

'Maybe it's like the nightmares you have?' Marshall suggested. 'Your mind playing tricks. It's like now you expect something to go wrong.'

'Maybe.' Jess pursed her lips. 'But shouldn't I be trusting my gut?'

'Yeah. And what does your gut say?'

Jess sighed.

'Something's not right.'

'But not necessarily with the house?' Marshall asked. 'So maybe the something that isn't right is that your parents accepted me when you didn't think they would? Or the fact that they bought a house without telling you?'

'Or that Bubbles didn't want to go inside,' said Jess.

'She does get anxious sometimes,' Marshall reminded her.

'And Ruby? Ruby stopped at the door.'

'She's seen stuff too, Jess. She had bad dreams after that whole ghost in her room experience. Maybe she's a little nervous the same way you are. And Bubbles is probably picking up on that.'

Jess's shoulders sagged.

'Yeah. You're right. That makes sense. That's probably all it is.'

Bubbles relieved herself and they ventured back into the kitchen. Eddie found an old towel to wipe the dirt from the dog's paws.

'I mean, it doesn't matter at the moment, I guess,' he said as he bent to wipe the last paw. 'But still, it would be nice to keep the mess to a minimum.'

'So,' Ginny started, placing cups of tea on the kitchen table for people to help themselves. 'What are the plans for the weekend? Would you like to help with the house?'

Jess noticed that an alternative wasn't offered.

'Sure,' said Marshall before Jess could open her mouth. 'I'd be happy to help. Where are you thinking of starting?'

Jess glanced up at the large man beside her, her heart aching with love. He was so desperate to impress them.

'Mum, Dad,' she warned, 'Marshall's been working hard all week and he's got a lot on next week. It might be nice if he could relax a little this weekend.'

Marshall gave her a quick look and then shook his head.

'Nah, I love doing this stuff. Especially in a house like this. It's part of the adventure.'

'See?' Ginny turned to Jess. 'He gets it. That would be wonderful, Marshall. Thank you. Where would you recommend starting?'

'It would be good to look at the pipes,' said Eddie. 'And wiring. But we need a plumber and electrician for that.' He gave Marshall a sideways look that made Jess stiffen and clench her teeth.

'I can take a look,' said Marshall. 'I do some electrics and plumbing. Let's see how bad it is.'

'He fixed my washing machine,' Jess told her father. She didn't mention that the incident had led to Marshall babysitting Ruby, which had led to him kissing Jess for the first time, lifting her up onto the kitchen worktop while she wrapped her legs around him. The memory was there now, though, and Jess leaned into Marshall to feel his warmth against her.

'Speaking of adventures,' said Ginny, looking at Ruby. 'You could have a camping trip here. What do you think? Spend a night here? We've got a little pop up tent and some sleeping bags. Might be fun for you and your mum and…Marshall. Right?'

Ruby looked up at her mother with wide eyes and Jess instinctively shook her head.

'Not if there's damp in the house, Mum.'

'Oh, right. Yes, I guess that's right.'

'How about a tour?' Jess asked before her mother could have any other ideas.

Ginny brightened.

'Yes! A tour. Come on, girls. I'll show you upstairs while the boys talk electrics.'

Jess looked up at Marshall and he gave her an encouraging smile. Ruby, on the other hand, gave her a dirty look. She silently took Jess's hand and they followed Ginny back into the hallway and up the stairs.

The steps creaked at they climbed and Ruby's hold on Jess's hand tightened. When they reached the landing, Ginny continued into a bedroom, but Jess and Ruby stopped.

'Mummy?' came Ruby's small voice.

Below them, the hallway was still light from the sun filtering in through the living room window. On the landing, however, the light dimmed more than it should have. The doors were all open and yet it was as if a shadow hung over the space. A chill ran through Jess that logically made no sense. Unless there was a window open. There had to be a window open.

What Jess couldn't quite explain was the feeling on the back of her neck that they were being watched. Taking a shaky breath, Jess turned and opened the door to the bathroom with a creak.

'Oh, that's the bathroom,' said Ginny, re-appearing. 'Obviously needs a lot of work. Although the toilet and taps function properly. Just everything needs replacing.'

Jess stepped inside and tentatively opened a cupboard.

It was empty.

'Handy, isn't it? We can put our towels in there,' came her mother's voice.

'Mummy?' Ruby asked in a quiet voice as Jess

stepped back onto the landing and Ginny disappeared back into a bedroom.

'Yes, sweetheart?'

'Who's that?'

Jess's heart jumped into her throat and she looked where Ruby was pointing, into the bedroom at the back. Keeping Ruby behind her, Jess ventured over to the bedroom and peered in.

'Who's who, sweetheart? What did you see?'

'He's not there anymore,' said Ruby.

Jess stared back at her daughter, exhaling slowly as her options ran through her mind.

'Mum?' she called.

Ginny reappeared.

'Ruby thinks she saw someone. Can we do a check of the house? Maybe someone's snuck in.'

Ginny paled and then laughed, but Jess's expression must have done the trick. She called the men upstairs and every cupboard and hatch was checked, including the loft.

'There's no one here, Rubes,' said Marshall, scooping the little girl up in his big arms.

'No,' said Ruby, holding onto him tightly. 'He's gone now.'

10

Rick

BRISTOL, 1864

Breathing in the heavy city air as he walked, Rick wondered if he'd ever been this happy as a single man. The years he'd spent with Erica and their baby certainly beat working on steam trains in terms of happiness, but without them, alone in the world, this happiness almost matched it. Rick had always wanted to travel, so the idea of travelling through time appealed. Not only would he see the world but he'd see it through the different periods. He'd witness the changes and great moments. He'd be there to see Apollo 11 launch, stand in the crowd as JFK drove by moments before he was killed, he'd be at the back as the Berlin Wall was pulled down and maybe he'd even help to build Stonehenge. There were no limits, and yet the joy that filled his chest from being in the city he grew up in and working on steam engines, returning to the room he'd rented covered in dirt and dust, was indescribable.

Maybe he didn't have to see anything else. Maybe he could just stay here until Erica was ready for him.

Smiling, Rick rounded a corner, moved over so as not to bump into a couple walking towards him, and was yanked off the pavement. Something gripped the fabric of his jacket and pulled so hard he lost his footing. Sprawled on the ground, the light of the street lamps dimmed and Rick looked up, trying to work out what was happening. Finding his feet, Rick stood and picked up his hat that had rolled across the ground. When he turned, he found himself staring at two large men. Rick stopped, his chest twisting, bowels loosening. Either side and behind him were dirty brick walls. He'd been pulled into a tight alleyway and these men were blocking the only exit.

Rick didn't move, he didn't speak. He waited for them to do something.

One of the men held out his hand.

'We'll be taking what's in your pockets,' he said.

Rick looked down at the man's hand and then back up into his eyes. As a police officer, he'd faced scarier moments than this. Drunk or high men, twice the size of him with who knew what in their pockets, just waiting to stab him or to spit in his face. One teenager had tried to run him over once, in a desperate attempt to escape with a stolen car. Rick had certainly been through worse than this, but back then he'd had a panic button, he'd known that other officers were on their way. He'd had a team.

Now, it was just him. Alone in a dark alleyway with two bulky men, over a hundred years from his friends and family and colleagues.

Just how much of the men's bulk was muscle? Rick studied them both.

'Hand over what's in your pockets or we'll take it from you,' said the man again.

Rick didn't move.

The man gave a tut and they advanced on him. Before Rick could open his mouth to question them, retort or scream, the silent man punched him hard in the gut. The air rushed from Rick's body as he bent over double, struggling to inhale. He was pushed over, back to the ground. Something hard hit his head and in the blinding pain, everything went black.

Rick woke with a shiver. Opening his eyes, the night sky was above him. Sounds of the city sleeping reached him and he attempted to sit up. He was still where he had fallen, lying in the tight alleyway, the cold, wet walls around him. His head pounded as he moved, vomit finding its way up his throat. He spat it out, groaning, holding his head in his hand and checking his fingers for blood.

He sat there for a moment, waiting for the world to stop spinning and his stomach to settle. What had happened?

Those two men had attacked him, beaten him, left him for dead.

Panic rose in Rick and he began patting down his pockets. His wallet was gone along with his money. That wasn't a problem. He had a stash back in his hotel room. Lifting his sleeve, he found his time travel device still attached to his wrist. Maybe they hadn't worked out how to get it off. Holding his breath, hot tears pricking his aching eyes, he reached for the inside pocket of his coat.

Rick let out a loud wail that came from deep within his gut.

'Shut up!' someone shouted back in response.

Rick sat in the alleyway and cried, his shoulders heaving in sobs. How stupid he'd been, how reckless, to go back into a different time thinking that anything good would come of it. He'd broken the law of his own time, he'd broken the laws of time travel, he'd left the woman he loved in the arms of another man, and now he'd lost the pocket watch that would tell him when it was time to go home to her.

11

Erica

'It's a bit pokey,' said Alfie, looking around the bedroom of the small flat.

'Well, it's a one bedroom flat. What were you expecting?' Erica muttered, asking herself as much as him. The flat was on the small side, but then she was just one person with one other person staying over when it suited him. How much space did she really need? It even came with a garden, if you could call a tiny square expanse of concrete a garden.

'I don't like it.'

'No, me neither, but I can afford it.' Erica sighed and looked up into Alfie's frustrated blue eyes. 'I need to move out of my parents' house and if I get somewhere like this, then I'll make it nice. I'll make it a home. And then you can come visit and stay as much as you like. Just think of the freedom.'

Alfie   looked   around   the   bedroom   again,

wrinkling his nose.

'You can do better.'

Erica crossed her arms.

'Can I? Tell you what, you have a look at all the lettings around here and you find me something better in my budget.'

Alfie sighed.

'This is it, huh?'

'This is what I can afford.'

'You know where's bigger than this?' Alfie asked.

'Don't say your place.'

'My place,' said Alfie.

Erica pursed her lips. Alfie had what constituted a two-storey house, and while this flat was made of brick and concrete, Alfie's home was tree and wood and leaves. It was green and earthy and always smelled amazing, especially after the rain. Not to mention it was rent-free. However, it lacked an internet connection, and was situated in a different world.

'I just need the business to grow a bit more,' she murmured to herself. 'A few more clients a month and I can afford something a little bigger. A little nicer.'

'With a proper garden.'

'I don't need a proper garden, Alfie.'

He raised an eyebrow at her.

'Of course you do. You need to practise talking to the trees and we can't have sex in that.' He gestured towards the concrete outside.

Erica flinched, her neck burning as the estate agent chose that moment to come in search of them.

Alfie flashed him a smile and put an arm around Erica, whispering in her ear, 'Whoever heard of a witch with a concrete garden?'

Erica sighed.

'It's nice,' she told the estate agent.

'It is, isn't it,' he said, looking from her to Alfie and back again. 'Seen everything?'

'What, the bathroom and the bedroom? Yes, we've seen them both.' Alfie rolled his eyes. 'And I think we can do better.'

'A shame, then, that it's me renting the place and not you,' Erica told him.

'Does that mean you want to take it?'

Erica paused as the estate agent waited eagerly for an answer. They all jumped as the phone in her pocket began singing.

'Oh, sorry.' She pulled out the phone. It wasn't a number she recognised. 'Sorry, I have to take this.' She pushed past Alfie and the estate agent, making her way through the front door. The men followed.

Erica answered before she was out of the flat.

'Hello?'

'Hello. Is this Murray and Tidswell Paranormal Investigations?' came a woman's voice.

Erica exhaled quietly in relief. She really needed to get a business phone instead of using her personal one. With every potential client call, there was a fear that something bad had happened.

'It is. This is Erica Murray speaking, how can I help?'

'Oh, thank god. We met this morning. Outside my house. You were walking with your two dogs and I asked you about your...boyfriend. Do you remember?'

A chill ran through Erica.

'I do remember.'

'Have you spoken to him?'

'I have, yeah. I told him.'

'He hasn't been to see us yet. We really need to talk to him. Please. He's the only one who can help. Unless you can? I didn't realise you ran a paranormal investigation agency. Can you help?'

'Maybe,' said Erica. 'What's the problem?'

'Our daughter has gone missing. A fae has taken her.'

Erica went cold and turned on her heel to find Alfie watching her curiously.

'We'll come now. Both me and Alfie,' Erica told the woman. 'We're about twenty minutes away and leaving now.'

'Oh, thank you. Thank you so much.'

'I'm coming too?' Alfie asked as Erica hung up.

'Yes. That was the woman who asked me to ask you to talk to her.'

Alfie's smile was gone in a second.

'We're going to talk to her. Right now.'

Alfie's jaw tensed, but he agreed.

'Is everything all right?' asked the estate agent.

'Oh, yes, something work related has come up,' said Erica, brushing away the worry in her tone with a hand gesture.

'This is the business that you run?' asked the estate agent. 'What is it that you do? Some sort of building or surveying work?'

'Surveying. Yeah, something like that,' said Erica.

'She's a paranormal investigator,' Alfie told him.

The estate agent looked between them again and then laughed.

'You talk to ghosts, huh?'

Erica had learned recently that there were two types of people. When told what her business was, one type would think it all a joke, while the other type would proclaim how they often watched paranormal television shows before peppering her with questions. She preferred the latter.

'I try,' she told the estate agent. 'But it's less about talking to ghosts and more about putting people's minds at rest. There's usually a logical explanation for the things they've experienced.'

'Well, there would be,' said the estate agent. 'And you charge them money to tell them they're idiots?'

Erica glared at the man. He didn't seem to notice.

'The world must seem very small to you,' Alfie told him in a quiet voice.

Erica took Alfie's hand and squeezed it.

'I'll be in touch,' she told the estate agent before unlocking her car with a beep and climbing into the driver's seat. Alfie plonked into the passenger seat and watched the estate agent getting into his car.

'You're not taking this flat, are you?' he asked, still staring out of the window.

'Probably not. I mean, I would have done if he hadn't just pissed me off.'

Alfie laughed as Erica started the ignition.

They pulled up outside the detached house in the leafy, residential road near the woods.

'Now, this house is nice,' Alfie proclaimed.

'Yup, well, when I win the lottery, I can get a house like this,' Erica mumbled. 'Do you want to tell me what this is all about before we go in?' she asked.

Alfie's features darkened.

'Not yet,' he told her. 'I'm not sure yet, but I have an idea.'

Erica gave a short nod and climbed out of the car, walking up the driveway and ringing the doorbell.

Alfie stayed behind her, his hands dug deep into his jean pockets. He was looking up at the windows above them so Erica took the opportunity to breathe deep and close her eyes, steadying herself.

The door opened and the woman who had stopped her when she was walking her parents' dogs appeared. Her eyes were still red and more tired than before.

The woman gave Erica a small smile which vanished when she laid eyes on Alfie.

'Come in, please.'

She glanced back at Alfie as they entered the house and followed her into the living room.

'Take a seat.' She didn't offer them drinks, sitting down in an armchair and fretting at her own fingers, pulling at her fingernails.

'Do you want to tell us what happened?' Erica asked after a moment of silence. 'What's your name?'

'Clare,' said the woman, her eyes still on Alfie. 'One of your kind has taken my daughter. You need to bring her back.'

Erica turned to look at Alfie. He glanced at her and then sighed, sitting forward, elbows on his knees.

'Why do you think a fae has taken your daughter?' he asked.

'How do you even know the word "fae"?' said Erica, her stomach twisting. She wasn't sure she wanted to know the answer. At the back of her mind she was acutely aware that Alfie was a lot older than her, that he had a history and that it wasn't necessarily one she would approve of. She'd read the fairy tales, the folklore, and while she wasn't sure just how much of it was true, she knew enough.

'There's no other explanation,' Clare told Alfie before turning to Erica. 'He came visiting when my daughter was little. We didn't think anything of it. He was friendly and kind, he did some work around the house for us. He told us he was a neighbour so we thought he lived around the corner, certainly not in the woods. Then, on my daughter's sixteenth birthday he sat down with me and my husband and explained that our little girl was meant for him and that one day she would fall in love with him and he would take her away to make her happy. It was horrible! He wasn't allowed in the house after that. She didn't really know him all that well, so we just kept telling her to avoid strangers. We did our best.' Clare's chin creased and the tears spilled from her eyes. She got up to fetch a box of tissues and sat back down, wiping her face.

Erica swallowed to keep the bile from rising.

'And she's gone missing?'

Clare nodded.

'When? How long has she been gone for?' Erica asked.

'She disappeared this morning. She didn't come home from her walk.'

'Have you called the police?'

'Why? Why bother? They can't help. You.' Clare pointed at Alfie who didn't move. 'You can help. You're a fae. Just like him. He told us all about your kind. How you often have soulmates in humans. How you fall in love with them and take them away. You can go and get her back. I've been all through the woods, shouting her name and his. They've gone. Where have they gone? You have to know. You have to.'

'Hang on. Hang on,' said Erica, determined to find a reasonable explanation, wishing that Alfie would say something. 'How do you know this guy is a fae?'

Clare met her eyes.

'He told me.'

'Yeah, but...' Erica started.

'What's his name?' Alfie asked.

Clare and Erica both turned to him.

'Fen,' said Clare. 'He said his name is Fen.'

Alfie pursed his lips and then stood up.

'We're leaving,' he said, taking Erica's hand. She stayed sitting on the sofa.

'What? No. No, you can't. You have to help me. You have to get my daughter back. Please.' Clare was on her feet, tears streaming down her cheeks, moving to block the door.

'Alfie,' Erica said gently, looking up at him. 'Do you know Fen?'

His eyes had hardened and as he looked down at Erica, her heart began to pound.

'I know of Fen,' he said. 'And what he says is true. If he has seen that your daughter is meant for him and now she's gone with him, there isn't anything I can do. There's nothing I should do.'

'Wait a minute.' Erica stood up, pulling her hand out of Alfie's grasp. 'How old is she now? What's her name?' she asked Clare.

'Bethany,' came Clare's small voice. 'She's just turned eighteen.'

'Then she's an adult and old enough to make her own decisions,' said Alfie.

'But she knew nothing of the fae?' Erica asked.

Clare shook her head.

'She might have met Fen once when she was little, but she wouldn't remember and he didn't age. He didn't age,' she repeated, eyes pleading with Erica.

Erica clenched her teeth, setting her jaw with determination.

'He took her into your world,' she said quietly to Alfie. He watched her with a hard expression. 'We have to help her.' Erica stepped closer to him, staring up into his eyes. 'Alfie, she needs our help.'

He shook his head.

'It's not our place to interfere.'

Erica stepped back as if she'd been punched. Alfie flinched at the horror in her expression, but she turned away before he could respond any further.

'I'll find your daughter,' she told Clare. 'I promise.' Erica shot Alfie a look over her shoulder. 'Do you have a photo of her?'

Clare nodded and took a photograph from the top of a nearby cabinet, pushing it into Erica's hands.

'Thank you. Thank you so much.'

Erica shot Alfie another look and, with a simple

gesture, ordered him out of the house.

They drove to Erica's parents' home in silence. Out of the corner of her eye, Erica saw Alfie watching her, opening his mouth to speak but then closing it again.

What possible excuse could he have? What could he possibly say to justify these actions?

12

Erica

'What are you doing?'

Erica kept her lips pressed together as she pulled into her parents' driveway, the gravel crunching beneath the Mini's tyres.

'I'm going to ask my mum for help and get some things, and then I'm driving you to the cemetery. You're going to open the door, point me in the right direction and then you're going to leave me alone.'

'Erica.'

'No.' Erica turned on Alfie. 'Why don't you want to help her?'

Alfie remained silent long enough for Erica to give a small growl and get out of the car, slamming the door behind her.

'Stay there!' she ordered, not trusting herself and not wanting her mother's wrath involved.

Much to her surprise, Alfie did as he was told.

The Labradors welcomed Erica home and she took a moment to cuddle them.

'Hello, love. How was the flat?' her mother asked from the kitchen.

Flat? Erica had completely forgotten about the viewing.

'Oh, horrible. Pokey little place with a concrete garden and an arrogant, horrible estate agent,' said Erica, walking into the kitchen, trailing the dogs, to find her mother sitting at the table sipping a coffee.

'Not the right place, then?'

'No. Where's Dad?'

'He's popped out. What's wrong?'

Erica searched her mother's eyes for a moment.

'A girl's gone missing and her mother says a fae's taken her. I need to go into the fae world and bring her back.'

Erica's mother stared at her and Erica waited. Carefully, Esther placed her cup back on the table and considered her next words carefully.

'How old is she?'

'Eighteen.'

'Did she go consensually?'

'I don't know.'

Esther exhaled slowly and then stood.

'It's spring. Fae are known to take young people this time of year. They use bluebells to do it.'

'What?' Erica followed her mother across the kitchen.

'All the bluebells in the woods. They release a

wonderful scent that is known to make the young people more...placated. It makes it easier for the fae to convince them to leave this world.'

'Bluebells?' said Erica as Esther rifled through her bottles and jars.

'Yes. Here.' Esther handed her daughter a bottle. 'This will remove the charm the fae has placed on her. She'll hopefully only need a sip, not too much. She'll be thinking clearly in no time and then you can find out if she wants to go home or not.'

Erica took the bottle and gave her mother a quizzical look.

'You don't think she'll want to go home?'

Esther shrugged.

'I told you to stay away from Alfie, but you love him so you stay with him. This girl is eighteen. I couldn't tell you what to do when you were eighteen, and your grandmother couldn't tell me what to do when I was eighteen. Maybe she'll see in this fae whatever it is that you see in Alfie.'

Erica swallowed against her dry throat.

'He is helping you, isn't he?' Esther asked, watching her daughter.

'He's in the car,' Erica said weakly.

'And he's helping you?' Esther repeated, more pointedly this time.

Erica ran a hand over her face.

'I don't know,' she said. 'He seems to think it's none of our business and we should let them get on with it. The girl's an adult now. This fae seemed to wait until she'd turned eighteen.'

Esther leaned back against the kitchen worktop and sighed.

'That's what Alfie was going to do,' she murmured. 'He saw you in my belly, announced to us all that you were meant for him and then tried to befriend us.'

Erica shuddered. Esther's eyes softened as she watched her daughter.

'And look what happened. I kept him away from you for as long as I could. You met him in your thirties and now you're together. Sometimes I wonder if he'd have taken you away at eighteen, given the chance.'

Erica shifted her weight.

'Are you seeing him with new eyes?' Esther wondered.

'Maybe with the eyes you see him with,' Erica told her.

Mother and daughter looked at one another in silence.

'Well,' said Esther, breaking eye contact. 'Go find this girl and see what's what. And take Alfie with you.' She herded Erica to the front door, opened it and both women stopped as Alfie stared wide-eyed at them, hand raised ready to knock. He lowered his hand, looking from Erica to Esther and back again. Finally, he cleared his throat and appeared sheepish.

'Erica,' he started. 'I'm sorry.'

Behind Erica, her mother made a small noise.

'I want to help,' he finished.

Erica shrugged.

'Good. Thank you. We're leaving now.'

Alfie turned back for the car while Esther held Erica back.

'Never thought I'd hear the day a fae apologised,' she whispered to her daughter. 'Be careful and come back to us. Okay?'

Erica promised and hugged her mother, saying goodbye to the dogs and jogging back to her car.

She pulled out of her parents' driveway and waited a while before she broke the silence between her and Alfie.

'Would you have come for me when I was eighteen?' she asked quietly.

Alfie turned to study her and then he nodded.

'I nearly did,' he told her. 'But I knew your mother wouldn't allow it. Your grandmother wouldn't allow it. They'd be angry and I know better than to anger your grandmother, and didn't want to annoy your mother any more than I already had. I needed them on my side if I was going to get a chance to meet you, to be with you.'

'You wanted to meet me that badly?'

Alfie gave a small smile.

'More than anything.'

Something inside Erica shifted and melted.

'Why, then? Why didn't you want to help me?'

'Because,' said Alfie. 'I know how Fen feels. If

this woman is for him then he's been waiting a long time for her. We all wait a long time for the person who is meant for us. Do you know how long Eolande waited for your grandmother? The agony of waiting until the person grows into an adult is bad enough without having to wait until they're in their eighties.'

Erica started. She'd never considered Eolande and her grandmother's relationship from that angle.

'But she did wait,' Erica said. 'And so did you. So why couldn't this Fen wait a little longer?'

'Why should he? She's an adult, capable of making her own decisions. Our worlds are very different,' said Alfie, reaching out and brushing the tip of his finger against Erica's hand. 'We try to live partly by your rules. Waiting until you turn of age is one of those rules and not one that all of my kind follow.'

'No,' said Erica. 'Have you taken girls into your world before?' The question came out so quietly that she wondered if Alfie had heard her.

'Yes,' he said after a heartbeat. 'Every now and then, for a weekend. For a night.'

'For sex,' Erica clarified.

'They consent,' said Alfie.

Erica didn't doubt that.

'Did you ever use bluebells on me?' she asked, and then jumped when Alfie laughed.

'No! I didn't need to. I didn't think to,' he added

to himself. 'I'd waited so long to meet you, going over every possible scenario, but then when it came to it, I wasn't ready. I didn't know quite what to say.' He looked back to her. 'You were so beautiful, more than I could possibly have imagined, and I saw you and that your heart belonged to another, and it was...it was like I couldn't breathe. I may have attempted to use some charm magic but it certainly wasn't thought through.'

Erica reached out and took Alfie's hand, squeezing it.

'I really need your help to find this girl,' she murmured.

'You have my help.'

Erica smiled and glanced at him.

'Why did you change your mind? I thought this was none of our business?'

'It isn't, but these are your world's customs,' said Alfie. 'And I will help because I love you. Because I am meant for you. Because my heart is yours.' He lifted her hand and kissed it, pressing his soft lips against her skin.

Erica's body tingled, suddenly alive.

She pulled in through the cemetery gates and parked the car. They bypassed the café, where they would usually stop for a quick drink, and headed straight for the Secret Garden. A small patch of the cemetery enclosed by walls and closed to the public by a wooden gate. Beyond the gate were ash trees, self-sown close together, and a bench sitting in the grass. Through those ash trees was the hidden doorway to the fae's world.

Alfie took Erica's hand. They had to stay connected otherwise Alfie would walk through into a different world while Erica stayed behind among the trees.

'Are you sure?' Alfie asked.

Erica studied the man she loved.

'When was the last time you took someone through here, just for sex?'

Alfie frowned, looking down at her.

'Why does that matter?'

Erica shrugged.

'It doesn't, I guess. Morbid curiosity. I don't really want to know but...you've done this before. Just because you didn't do it with me...because you couldn't do it with me...if you could have, you would have charmed me and seduced me and convinced me to follow you through these trees. And then what? What would have happened next?'

Alfie blinked.

'I would have done my best to make you happy and waited for you to fall in love with me,' he said quietly.

'Because that's what your kind does?'

'Sometimes.'

'Sometimes?'

'Sometimes a fae and a human will go through, fall into bed together, spend a glorious forty-eight hours making love, and then the human will decide they want to stay. It's been known to happen.'

Erica's stomach churned.

'Has it happened with you?'

Alfie smiled then, his eyes lighting up, and he wrapped an arm around Erica's waist.

'No,' he said. 'I waited for you, Erica. There were others while I waited, but they weren't you. I only wanted you.' He leaned down and kissed her lips. 'And there are bad fae. Just as there are bad humans. We try our best to keep everything...good. And I know of this Fen. I have no reason to believe he's bad or that he'll hurt this girl.'

Despite the feeling in her stomach, Erica couldn't help but wrap her arms around Alfie for a hug.

'Still, we need to know,' she said quietly, stepping away from him, taking his hand and letting him lead her into his world.

13
Bethany

Bethany woke to the heavy scent of flowers. She knew she wasn't home before she even opened her eyes. Groaning, she blocked out the morning sunlight with a hand over her face and peered around the room. She was lying in a double bed and with a jolt she raised the covers to her chin and checked the space beside her. The other side of the bed was not only empty but still perfectly made. No one had been over on that side. Checking beneath the covers, Bethany found she was still wearing the same clothes as the day before and she exhaled in relief.

That was when she noticed the ache in her head. Groaning, louder this time, she sat up properly, pushing the covers away, and took stock of her surroundings. The bedroom was small with wooden walls and a soft looking rug on the floor. The bed was just big enough for two, the sheets clean and fresh smelling. There was a large window where the morning shafts of sunlight made their way in. Either side of the bed were small tables. The one nearest her held a small vase filled with bluebells and the other table held a jug full of water and a glass. Bethany was about to reach for it when she stopped herself.

She'd asked Fen to take her home. She'd given him thirty minutes on the promise that he would take her home. Why wasn't she home?

Those thirty minutes came back to her slowly. He'd talked more about being a fae – whatever that meant – and he'd asked her questions about herself. She'd been guarded at first, but eventually she'd sipped her tea and eaten the biscuit. Fen had lit a small fire in the hearth and then, as it grew dark, he'd prepared her a meal. They'd eaten and talked and by the end of the evening she was even laughing at his stories and poor jokes.

Frowning, Bethany climbed out of the bed and stretched.

It had been a nice evening, and now it was time to go home. Head throbbing, Bethany found her shoes by the bed and wandered over to the door. Opening it a little with a creak, she peered through but didn't see any sign of life other than the great oak the house was twisted around.

It was a lovely house. She couldn't deny that. As she wandered through, trying to remember where the front door was and the way back home, she heard a soft singing. She stopped and listened. The words weren't English and she couldn't catch their meaning. The tune was soft and gentle, somehow easing the ache in her head.

Following the sound, she found Fen in the galley kitchen, singing to himself. She watched him for a moment. He was dressed in dark linen trousers and a shirt with the top buttons undone. His feet were bare and clean, and his dark hair tussled from where he'd slept. Where had he slept?

Bethany cleared her throat and then coughed. She hadn't realised quite how dry her mouth was. Fen turned to her, the singing ceasing and the ache in her head returning with a harsh throb. Hand on her forehead, eyes narrowed against the pain, Bethany leaned against the oak doorframe.

'Can I go home now, please?' she croaked.

Fen rushed to bring her a drink of water which she declined.

'I'll drink when I'm home.'

'But you sound dehydrated,' he said.

Bethany frowned.

'How? I drank tea last night with you.'

Fen shrugged.

'I don't know. Here. Just a sip and then I'll take you home.'

Relenting, Bethany took the glass and sipped the water. There was a sweetness to it and a freshness that soothed her head immediately. Before she knew it, she'd drunk the whole glass.

'There,' said Fen, grinning. He did have a lovely smile. It lit up his green eyes, making them twinkle. In the light of day, having slept well, and now that the pain in her head was easing, she could accept that Fen was handsome. 'Isn't that better?' He took the glass from her.

'Now can I go home?' she asked.

'Absolutely. Come on.'

Fen led her out of the house and through the village. Unlike before, there was no one around. Fae must sleep in, Bethany decided, staying close to Fen and trying to hurry him up. They reached the edge of the village and the treeline where bluebells were growing as a carpet across the woodland floor.

'I don't remember these,' Bethany murmured.

'You don't? They were here, I promise you,' Fen said. 'Are you sure you want to go? You could stay. We can get to know each other.'

Bethany shook her head.

'I want to go home.'

Fen pressed his lips together and sighed, but still, he led the way through the door. The light dimmed, the colours weren't so lush and vibrant, the peaceful sound of the ancient sleeping woodland was replaced with the road of nearby traffic, and the smell of trees and bluebells now had a tinge of pollution.

Bethany pulled a face.

'I want to go to London,' she murmured, mostly to herself, as she looked around the woods near her home. 'I have to go home, finish my exams and then I can go.'

'Can we still see each other? You know, I had a good time yesterday. I hope you did too?'

Bethany looked up into Fen's intense eyes and something inside her gave way. After all, London would be just as dim as these woods. It would be louder and smellier. Now that she was back, her body yearned for the bright colours and sweet smell of Fen's world.

'You can come back any time,' Fen was saying. 'You're welcome any time.' He reached out and took her hand. The sensation of his warm skin against hers sent a spark through her body, leaving a tingling in its wake.

Fen's eyes lit up as he watched her.

'You feel it too,' he murmured.

Bethany tried to disperse the feeling by shaking her head.

'I have to go home,' she repeated.

'We're meant to be together,' Fen whispered, still holding her hand. 'I've seen it. I know it. And I know that you feel it too.'

'I'm going home.' Bethany took her hand from Fen's and turned away.

'I'll come to London with you.'

Bethany stopped and turned back to the fae.

'What?'

'I'll come to London with you.'

'But you don't like London.' They'd discussed it

at length the previous night.

Fen shrugged.

'I like you. And I want you to be happy.'

Bethany's heart skipped, her stomach jolting with pleasure.

'Okay,' she said before she could think.

Fen brightened further.

'We can go now, if you like?'

Bethany blinked.

'I need to finish my exams.'

'I'll bring you back then. Just...spend the day with me? Or a couple of days. In London.'

Bethany could see no harm in that. She pulled out her phone and sent a quick message to her mother so she wouldn't worry, then she took Fen's hand and stepped with him back into the fae world.

14

Jess

Naturally, Ruby was awake before any of the adults in the house, even before Bubbles. She waited until her stomach grumbled and then pushed against her mother's shoulder. The bed was cosy with three of them in it, but now that she was awake, the warmth was becoming stifling. It was Marshall. How could one person give off so much heat?

Jess murmured but didn't wake.

'Mummy?' Ruby hissed. '*Mummy?*'

Marshall groaned and rolled over. Ruby pulled a face and then held her nose so close to her mother's that they nearly touched. 'Mummy!'

Jess woke and stared into her daughter's eyes.

৪০০৪

It took a moment for Jess to breathe, her heart racing at opening her eyes to find her five-year-old so close. Gently pushing her daughter back, Jess glanced to Marshall's sleeping form and then down to Bubbles on the floor. The room was too closed in and now she was wide awake. Not that she was annoyed about that. Her dreams had been uncomfortable, full of moving shadows and whispers from unknown voices until, at one point in the night, glowing demon eyes had woken her with a start. It had taken her a while to get back to sleep after that.

Rolling over, Jess checked the time on her phone. It was six, which wasn't bad for Ruby when she wasn't in her own bed.

'I'm hungry,' Ruby whispered.

Jess nodded and pulled the covers off. Ruby climbed out of bed first, followed by Jess who moved considerably slower. Bubbles opened her eyes as their feet touched the carpet, and stretched, yawning wide, her tongue lolling out of her mouth.

Silently, in their pyjamas, the three of them padded downstairs into the kitchen. Jess quietly poured Ruby the cereal her mother had bought specially, and then found a tin of dog food they'd brought with them for Bubbles. With both of her girls eating, Jess took a moment to rub the sleep from her eyes. It was too early to take a cup of tea to Marshall and too early for her parents to wake, but this was now the start of Jess's day. With that decided, she turned to make herself a cup of coffee. While the coffee machine whirred, she found some cartoons on Ruby's tablet, and then opened the back door for Bubbles to go out into the garden.

Her parents' house was lovely, especially with the spring morning light finding its way in. Why on earth did they want to leave this? The kitchen was modern and tidy, the flooring was relevantly new, and the windows were big. The whole house was light and modern with no sign of malevolent shadows. Sighing, Jess took her coffee and stepped out onto the patio with the dog. While Bubbles sniffed at the pristine flower beds, considering which one to relieve herself on, Jess lifted her face to the sky.

'What do I do?' she asked the Universe.

It was a question she would normally ask the tarot cards that Minerva had given her for her birthday, but she didn't like to attempt reading the cards in front of anyone, especially Ruby. Ruby would ask questions and Jess still didn't have the answers. Or at least, not answers she could give to her daughter yet.

For a moment, the light around Jess brightened. A wisp of cloud must have moved across the sun, but still, it felt like a sign. Jess pulled out her phone, checked over her shoulder to see that Ruby was still engrossed in her cereal and cartoons, and messaged Erica.

Hey. Are you awake? I need to talk.

She stood on the patio, pursing her lips, biting her tongue and watching Bubbles finally choose a spot to relieve herself. Sitting on one of the patio chairs, Jess placed her cup on the glass table with a clink and carefully put her phone next to it.

After ten minutes, there was no reply. Jess chewed on her lip and picked up her phone, staring at the screen. Erica would be with Alfie, she realised, in his world, cut off from modern technology. She searched her contacts and sent a new message.

Hi. It's Jess. I'm so sorry to disturb you, especially so early, but Erica isn't replying and I need to talk.

Placing the phone back on the table, Jess looked up at the morning sky and took a breath. There came a horrible noise as her phone vibrated against the glass. Jess scooped it up and answered it.

'Hi. Sorry, I know it's early. Thank you for calling. I hope I didn't wake you?'

'I've been up a while,' said Erica's mother. 'I'm an early bird. Up with the sun. What's troubling you? Is everything okay? I'm afraid Erica is with Alfie.' Esther sighed hard.

Jess opened her mouth and stopped.

'Is everything okay? With Erica?'

'Well...' Esther hesitated. 'She's disappeared off into the fae world. A teenage girl has gone missing

113

and her mother has asked Erica to find her. Actually, she wanted Alfie to find her. But Alfie said no. Don't get me started on that. And Erica wasn't happy about it either. Alfie came good in the end and has gone with her. I just hope he's looking after her. I hate it when they go off into his world. I always worry she won't come back. But it's the same with my mother and Erica is so like Mum.'

There was a silence as Jess tried to process all those words.

'That's...scary. How old is the girl?' A cold dread gripped Jess's insides.

'Eighteen.'

The air inside Jess escaped in a rush through her lips.

'Devil's advocate, technically she's an adult. Why does Erica have to go running after her?' Jess said slowly.

'She's just going to check on her, not drag her out. Although I'd rather she dragged the girl out,' Esther told her.

Jess nodded.

'I wish she'd told me. I could have come back to help.'

'No, no. Alfie's going with her. And she knows how important this weekend is for you. Have your parents met Marshall yet? How's it going? Do they like him?'

Now it was Jess's turn. She took a deep breath and allowed the words to come out in a rush, just as

Esther had done.

'They seem to like him, which is great, but they've bought a new house. It's an old Victorian house and a complete mess, a renovation project, and they're really excited about it. And, I mean, it's fine, of course. It's their money, their retirement. But they're going to sell their lovely, finished house for this mess of a thing and who knows how dangerous it is, but that isn't the worst bit. There's something…in there. Ruby didn't want to go into the house and then Bubbles didn't want to, but Marshall just said we're all still a bit tender from last year's…stuff. And he's right. We probably are and they're probably picking up on my nerves, but I saw *something*. A someone. Through the window, in the house. Someone *moving*. And then Ruby saw someone upstairs, but there was no one there, and then she said he'd gone. *He*. My parents don't believe in ghosts and what if this isn't a ghost? What if it's something worse? What do I do?' Jess had buried her head in her free hand, curling herself up on the chair.

There was a pause before Esther replied.

'What would Erica tell you to do, I wonder.'

'To work the job,' came Jess's muffled voice. 'But…that's what she does. She goes in and senses spirits and talks to them. I talk to the clients and deal with the paperwork. I don't think my parents will be up for me writing them a contract and sending them an invoice.'

Esther chuckled.

'You're capable of more than you think, Jess. You did wonderfully when the spirit was in your own home. Remember?'

'No, Erica and Minerva did great. I just protected my family.'

'And that's what you're going to do now,' Esther told her. 'If it's a spirit then you can talk to it. You don't even have to ask for a sign or anything, just explain the situation to it and ask for it to go away, or to be quiet, or to not interfere. It can be that simple, especially in this case.'

'And if it doesn't? If it's like the spirit we had in our house? Or not a spirit?'

There was another pause.

'I can come and help,' Esther said gently. Jess closed her eyes tight and shook her head.

'I don't want to trouble anyone.'

'And I'm not sure what use I would be,' Esther admitted. 'Spirits aren't really my thing. But I can talk to Mum? See if she can help. I can drive her down.' Esther sighed softly into the phone. 'Try talking to it,' she repeated. 'And if that doesn't work then call me back and we'll get it sorted. Give it time. It'll be fine. Just because horrible things have happened in the past doesn't mean they will again. You've had six months of easy jobs, things have been going great. Keep hold of that. This will be fine too. Okay?'

Jess nodded.

'Yeah. Okay. Thanks. I hope things go okay with Erica.'

'I'm sure they will. I might come to you just to take my mind off the whole thing.'

They said their goodbyes and hung up. Jess remained staring at her phone as her mind whirred. She wasn't sure how long she sat there. Bubbles shoved her wet nose into Jess's arm, became bored and disappeared back into the house to find Ruby. Just as Jess was stirring, preparing to move and discovered her coffee had gone cold, her phone began to ring. She stared at the name that popped up.

'Hi again,' she answered.

'Hello, love. I realise I told you to take your time but I didn't take my own advice and Mum never sleeps,' said Esther. In the background came the muffled voice of Erica's grandmother, Minerva. 'Hang on, I'm putting you on speakerphone. You'd think she still lived here, given the hour,' she added in a mutter.

'Hello, Jess, love!' came Minerva's voice. 'I got a taxi! Marvellous things. Never too old for a taxi. How are your folks? Do they love Marshall?'

Jess laughed.

'They're warming to him,' she told them. 'Especially as he's offered to basically work all weekend on their new house.'

'Yes, Esther told me about their new venture,' said Minerva. 'And what you and Ruby may have seen. Esther's right, you know. Just talk to whoever might be there. First and foremost, always be polite. Explain the situation. If there's a spirit, they may just be wondering what's going on. Treat them like a friend.'

'What if it's not a spirit? What if it's not friendly?' Jess asked, keeping her voice low.

'Then you keep out of there until one of us can get there,' said Esther. 'It's bad enough that Ric is going into a whole other dimension without you having to deal with anything unfriendly on your own. This is all your fault, you know.' That last bit was aimed at Minerva.

Jess opened her mouth to protest but Minerva got there first, because Minerva always got there first.

'Oh, pish! Nonsense. They're living, Esther. Let them get on with it. Erica will be fine because she's our girl. And Jess can absolutely do this, because she's our girl too.'

Warmth spread through Jess's chest. 'You can do this, Jess,' Minerva continued. 'Remember everything you've learned. Consult the cards if you need to. You are not alone. And I mean that. We're just on the end of the line, but right there with you is a lovely man who will protect you and your baby at all costs. Make use of him, Jess. Ask for his help. You may need to step into Erica's shoes, so ask Marshall to step into yours. Metaphorically, of course. You are more than capable.

'Be polite, explain the situation to the spirit and then see what happens. If the spirit turns on you or you suspect it isn't a spirit, then you call us. Let's do this one step at a time and not jump to conclusions. All right?'

Jess was grinning into the phone. She gave a defiant nod.

'Right. Thank you. Thank you so much. I really mean that.'

'Of course, love. We're always here for you.'

Jess wanted to hug them both. Still smiling, they made some more small talk before hanging up. Jess plonked her coffee cup on the kitchen worktop and scooped up Bubbles and Ruby, ushering them back upstairs to wake Marshall.

They needed to talk.

15

Jess

By the time Jess's parents had ventured down-stairs, Ruby was sitting at the table surrounded by paper and colouring pencils. She directed Marshall what to draw while he drank a coffee. Jess had just finished clearing their breakfast things and offered to make something for her parents.

'You know you're our guests. We should be making you breakfast,' said her mother.

Jess shrugged.

'But you don't want to get up at the same time as Ruby and Bubbles. Trust me.' Jess gave her parents a smile and then watched as her father rubbed his hands together.

'Poached egg on toast,' he declared.

Jess's smile fell.

'No,' she said. 'It has to be something I can make.'

'Pancakes!' screeched Ruby, making the adults

flinch.

'You've had breakfast, Rubes.' Marshall regained her attention and tapped the paper in front of him. 'Come on. I have no idea what I'm doing, what should I draw next?'

There was a pause as Jess's parents considered what they had in the cupboards. Eventually, Eddie sighed.

'Well, now I want pancakes,' he grumbled, ruffling Ruby's hair. 'Is that okay?' he asked Jess, pulling an apologetic face from behind Ruby.

'I can help!' shouted Ruby.

'Okay. Pancakes for the grandparents,' said Jess. 'Assistant Chef Ruby, can you please tell me where we keep the eggs?'

From her seat at the table, Ruby giggled and pointed to the fridge.

'Wonderful,' said Jess, fetching the eggs. 'And where do we keep the flour?'

Ruby gave this some thought and then pointed at a random cupboard. Eddie crept up behind her and whispered in her ear. She moved her pointing finger to a different cupboard. Jess opened it and found the packet of flour.

Once the pancakes were made, Jess delivered them and two coffees on a tray to the patio table in the garden where she'd ordered her parents to sit. Marshall kept Ruby at the kitchen table, furiously colouring in a hastily drawn unicorn.

'That was impressive,' said Ginny as Jess emptied the tray. 'You didn't even make any mess but Ruby was involved the whole time.'

'Well, I'd just cleaned up our mess. I didn't want to make more.'

'Clever,' said Ginny, giving her daughter a smile. 'And thank you for the breakfast outside on such a lovely spring morning.'

'Yes, you should come visit more often,' said Eddie, taking a bite of his pancakes. 'Good hearty breakfast before we start work on the house. Is Marshall ready?'

'Whenever you are,' said Jess. 'And I'll come too. There's something I want to try, but I'm going to need you to look after Ruby while we do it.'

Eddie and Ginny looked up at their daughter.

'What do you want to try?' asked Ginny, placing down her fork and turning her full attention to Jess.

Jess opened and closed her mouth under the scrutiny of her mother.

'I just... Okay, I spoke to Erica's mother this morning about yesterday. About what Ruby might have seen.'

'Sometimes kids think they've seen things when they haven't,' said Eddie. 'It was probably a shadow.'

Something inside Jess twitched.

'And sometimes shadows aren't just a trick of the light,' she told her father. 'Sometimes they're something else.'

'This is about ghosts again?' said Ginny, sipping her coffee.

'Yes,' Jess replied slowly. 'And I want to try telling whatever might be there what's going on. Honestly, even if you don't believe in that stuff, where's the harm?'

'Then why can't you do it with Ruby?'

Jess stared at her mother.

'Because I don't want to have to explain these things to her.'

'Why not? Ghosts aren't real. It's just a bit of fun, isn't it? Why are you doing this, Jess?' Ginny asked, not giving her daughter time to answer. 'Can't you just be happy that we're keeping busy? That we're excited by this project? Your fiancé, who you chose to spring on us, understands. Why don't you?'

Jess frowned, her mouth still opening and closing in a form of protest.

'Okay, I think things are getting out of hand,' said Eddie, shoving the last of his pancakes into his mouth. 'Let Jess do whatever she needs to in order to feel comfortable. I, for one, would love to look after Ruby.'

'Thank you, Dad.'

'Why don't you feel comfortable? This isn't your childhood home. What is it that makes you feel so uncomfortable?' Ginny stared up at her daughter and raised an eyebrow, the same way that Ruby did.

'I...' The memories of the previous summer rushed through Jess's mind. She couldn't possibly

123

explain them to her mother, how would she start? Well, Mum, nearly a year ago now... Maybe Marshall and Erica were right and this was all in her head. She was dwelling too much on what had been instead of all the positive experiences she'd had since. All the spirits Erica had talked to, all the moments of connection and contact. The hellos, the flickering lights to answer questions, the joy in clients' eyes as they realised their loved one might still be there and they had another chance at goodbye. That all meant something, and it meant more than a demon in the woods and a supposed poltergeist in her daughter's bedroom.

'Never mind, Mum. Maybe you're right,' Jess relented, her shoulders sagging.

Ginny sipped her coffee.

'But we'll still look after Ruby. How long will it take?' asked Eddie. 'We could play catch in the garden. On the muddy bit, anyway.' He grinned.

'Not long. Thanks, Dad. She'll love that. Bubbles too.'

'Someone'll have to look after Ruby and the dog while we're working, anyway,' Eddie told his wife. 'And I want to spend some time with my grand-daughter.'

'If I can keep helping, I don't mind driving up here on weekends,' came Marshall's voice. He'd stepped out onto the patio, Ruby in front of him, holding his hand as she led him out. 'And Ruby's an excellent handyman assistant. Aren't you, Rubes?'

Ruby nodded.

'I'm in charge of making sure he has the right things,' she told her grandparents.

Eddie clapped his hands.

'Wonderful. Can we get over there now and take a look around?' he asked Marshall. 'Unless you and Ruby have plans?' He looked down at his grand-daughter.

'No. No, we should go now. Get it all over with,' said Ginny, standing and taking her unfinished pancakes and coffee into the kitchen. Eddie sagged back, shrugging at his daughter.

Jess gave Marshall a look.

'You guys go on ahead, if you like. I'll follow with Mum and Bubbles,' she said gently, following her mother inside.

Twenty minutes later, Marshall had managed to get Ruby's car seat into Eddie's car. Jess helped and said goodbye to Ruby, promising to follow, then watched them pull away before going back into the house. Her mother was going through a kitchen cupboard.

'There's so much to sort out,' came her muffled voice. 'We should have started when we first won the house auction, but everything moved so fast. Still—' Her head reappeared along with a selection of pans, '—we still have time, even if we put this place on the market tomorrow.' She turned to Jess. 'Do you want to help me?'

'Mum, what's so bad about me trying to talk to whatever's there? If you don't believe in ghosts then can't you just humour me?'

Ginny sighed and gestured for Jess to sit at the table. She did so and her mother sat opposite her.

'The cruise was all about us,' Ginny started after a moment's contemplation. 'Just me and your father, travelling around the world. It was like we were twenty again. It was glorious. This new house is also about us, but suddenly it can be more than that. Especially as this new fiancé of yours is good at DIY, a fiancé who, as I mentioned, you surprised us with. One moment you're seeing a man and the next you're marrying him. I wondered if you might want to help with the house although I'd understand if you didn't. But then suddenly you're telling me that the house I want to turn into the home of my dreams is haunted.'

Jess squeezed her eyes shut.

'I made it all about me,' she murmured, opening her eyes and looking at her mother. Ginny gave a subtle nod. 'I didn't mean to ruin anything,' Jess told her. 'I still don't want to ruin anything. I just...I want you and Dad to be safe. That's all.'

'And instead of focusing on the damp or the structure, you decided that the house must be haunted?'

Jess blinked.

'Does the house have structural problems?'

'Of course not. We had a survey done.'

Jess pulled a face.

'Okay.' She sat back, considering her next words. 'Okay. I didn't tell you about how serious things were with Marshall because you and Dad were reliving your twenties and travelling around the world.'

'We were still talking, you could have told me. All this time he's just been a name you mention every now and then.'

'We talked once a month and most of that was you telling me about the places you'd seen and then talking to Ruby. I didn't really get a chance, but I see your point. I could have said more. I don't know why I didn't.' Jess shrugged. 'It was a busy year. Moving house, settling Ruby, getting Bubbles, trying to work out a new business alongside meeting Marshall. The thing with Marshall has been this huge whirlwind. If I'd have known we'd get engaged so quickly, I definitely would have introduced you to him, gotten him on a video call, let you have a chat with him.'

'And you're happy with him?'

Jess smiled.

'I am. I've never been so happy as I am right now. I really love him, Mum.'

Ginny nodded, smiling back.

'And it's obvious how much he loves you and Ruby. And the dog.'

Bubbles took that opportunity to make a noise from where she was lying under the table. Ginny laughed.

'She's knows when we're talking about her,' Jess explained.

'And Marshall seems lovely. And handy. How wonderful to be marrying a man who's good with his hands.'

Jess grinned and then tried to force her lips back down. Ginny gave her a knowing look. Jess's expression fell away as she considered her next step.

'Mum, other things have happened in the last twelve months. Big, scary things. To do with work, I guess. But they're the reason why I'm nervous about the house. I need to do this. Please?'

Ginny sighed.

'I'm not going to stop you,' she told her daughter. 'I wish you'd tell me what these big, scary things were, though.'

Jess ran her hands over her face. Was she going to do this? Slowly, attempting to carefully choose her words and omit certain details, Jess told her mother about the demon in the woods and the shadowy spirit in Ruby's bedroom.

As Jess spoke, Ginny's eyes widened, her chest rising as she held her breath in places and falling as she exhaled in rushes.

'Oh, Jess.' Ginny stood and wrapped her arms around her daughter. Jess held her tightly, burying her face into her mother's neck. As they parted, Jess quickly wiped the beginning of tears away. 'You know what I'm going to say about this business.' Ginny sat back down. 'I think you should find a job. A normal job.'

Jess shook her head.

'Those were two incidences last year. We've had six months or whatever now of nice, interesting jobs with lovely clients. I'm really enjoying it. But I need you to understand why I'm worried that Ruby and Bubbles were hesitant to go into the house. And that both Ruby and I saw...something.'

Ginny nodded.

'And if there is something, you can get rid of it?' Jess nodded.

'I might need help but yes, I'm confident we can.'

Ginny pursed her lips.

'Tell me about the happy stories,' she said, standing again. 'I'll make some tea.'

Jess smiled.

'Okay. Which story would you like? There was the grieving woman who had just lost her father. Strange things were happening in the house and it turned out to be her father trying to say goodbye. I cried all day at that one, but it was wonderful and peaceful. Or maybe a story about the hotel we work with. The one we hold ghost tours at, or any of the interesting, old buildings we've visited in Bristol. Erica will sometimes find an echo of something. Maybe a memory tied into the brick and stone, or an actual spirit contentedly living out its afterlife there. It's interesting to watch her work.'

'And it's all real?' Ginny murmured, her back to Jess as she made the tea.

'I've seen it, Mum. It's real.'

'Tell me about the hotel,' said Ginny as the kettle finished boiling.

16

Rick

BRISTOL, PRESENT DAY

The Murray family home was quiet. Erica's car wasn't on the driveway, neither was her father's but her mother's car was in the corner. Someone could be home. Rick remained in his rental car on the road, trying to see into the windows from this distance. It was impossible. Erica wasn't home, that was all he needed to know.

Slowly, he climbed out of the car and made his way up the gravel driveway. There was no movement at the windows, no sign of life. Not until he pushed his letter to Erica through the letterbox and the panicked patter of dog paws on the wooden floors inside could be heard, followed by growls and barks. Rick smiled.

'Hey, Daisy. Hey, Bramley. Only me,' he

murmured, trailing his fingers down the door.

There was no point in staying. He walked quickly back to his car, sniffing.

He drove to the cemetery on autopilot, hardly noticing the motorway or heavy traffic as he began to weave through the city. Driving wasn't as difficult as he'd imagined it to be, having spent time in Victorian Bristol. Driving a steam engine was a completely different thing and yet his body remembered how to drive a modern car with ease. He pulled into the cemetery with care, remembering the last time he'd been in a rush and Erica had chastised him for racing around the gravel path. Once parked, he stayed in the car, staring out of the windscreen, up at the chapel and the trees beyond. He didn't know exactly where the fae lived in the cemetery, but he knew Alfie was a frequent visitor of the café. After a moment of only seeing older couples and one young family go up and down the steps leading to the café, Rick got out of the car and made his way over.

A few people were sitting outside, a few more were seated inside. None of them were Alfie. Rick bought a coffee to go, trying not to think what he would do if Alfie didn't turn up. So it was slowly that he took the coffee and slowly that he left the café, wandering through the cemetery, looking for signs of the fae. He ended up at the back of the cemetery, looking down at Erica's grandfather's gravestone.

'Don't suppose you've seen Alfie about?' Rick asked it.

There was no response, although a chill swept over him. Rick closed his eyes to it, hoping to hear a voice. There was only birdsong and the chatter of two dog walkers passing by.

'He's with Erica, isn't he,' Rick murmured, his heart twisting painfully. With a deep sigh, Rick returned to his car and drained the last of his coffee. He would take the rental car back and by the time he got there, he'd have a new plan, he was sure.

The more he thought about it, the more he went in circles. He couldn't go on without that pocket watch, not without speaking to Alfie or Erica, and to get the pocket watch back from the muggers would be dangerous. Was it worth the danger if it was just a trinket Alfie had gifted him to convince him to leave Erica alone? Maybe the pocket watch didn't work. Maybe Alfie had manipulated him. Rick stood outside the car rental garage and, without thinking more on it, twisted the device on his wrist, sending out a circle of bright white light. The flash lasted only a few seconds for him, although there was a scream as someone jumped out of his way. He should have put more thought into where he time travelled. The middle of a pavement wasn't the ideal place. He didn't stay there long, breaking into a run and heading across the Victorian city, in the direction of the cemetery. It took longer than it should have done. The roads were different in this time, the air thick with steam and burning coal, and the stench of horse dung and unwashed humans. There were too many people walking, too many carriages on the uneven roads, too much noise. Eventually, Rick admitted defeat and waved down a cab. By the time they reached the cemetery, Rick had caught his breath and he'd spent the last of what little cash he'd had left after the mugging.

The cemetery wasn't new, even at this time, but it looked remarkably different to the cemetery he'd just visited. The woodland was gone, the ivy growing over the gravestones didn't exist yet. Many of the gravestones didn't exist yet. There were some ornamental trees and a large oak that stood impressively off to the side, a tree that had once stood in an open field and had watched the city grow towards and then around it, as the dead were buried close by, the chapel built to the side and the manicured gardens grew in its shadow. The gardens were beautiful. Rick took a moment to fully appreciate them as he stepped past the threshold and headed towards the chapel. The café wouldn't be there, just as the gift shop wasn't at the entrance gates, but would the fae be there?

Was Alfie even alive in this time? Rick wasn't quite sure how old Alfie was, but he had a feeling the fae was around, somewhere.

'Alfie?' he called gently as he walked around the cemetery. Gardeners stopped, lifting their eyes to him as he passed. He nodded a greeting and moved on quickly. 'Alfie?'

What now? What else was there?

'Excuse me.'

The nearest gardener, an older man with silver hair and dirty fingers, straightened his back as Rick approached.

'I don't suppose there's anyone here called Alfie, is there?'

'Alfred? Of course. Alfred!' the man shouted, making Rick jump. A few paces beyond them, another man straightened and Rick's shoulders fell.

'No. No, that's not the Alfie I'm looking for. Thanks anyway.'

Rick made his way out of the cemetery and sat on the roadside, fiddling with the device on his wrist. He couldn't ask the fae for help. Why hadn't he listened more closely when Erica had spoken about them? Why hadn't he asked more questions? It didn't matter. He was on his own. His mind played out every eventuality, every possibility of how he could get that pocket watch back. Could he simply step in during his own mugging and stop them? No, it was too dangerous, to end up face-to-face with himself. They'd been warned about such things during his training. No, he had to do this in such a way that past him wouldn't see present him. Rick looked up at the sky. He could just leave. Forget about the pocket watch, get on with his life, travel to a new time, start again, forget Erica and his future son ever existed. He could give up on them and what his life could be.

Jaw clenched, Rick twisted the device on his wrist and disappeared in a flash of bright light.

17

Erica

Erica breathed in as she stepped into the world of the fae, just as she did every time Alfie led her through the doorway. The air in his world was sweet and fresh, without a hint of pollution, without a hint that something was wrong. There was the scent of tree leaves and bark, of lush grass and flowers. The sky, from what could be seen through the tree canopy, was blue, and a carpet of bluebells swayed in the breeze at their feet. No matter the season, the weather in this world was always glorious. When it was autumn, the trees were red and gold against a blue sky, or shrouded in a fine mist that curled around the tree trunks. During winter, the outline of the tree branches were stark against either a light blue sky or heavy grey snow clouds. For a month or so, the ground would be frozen and the land would be white until the spring sunshine melted it and things began to grow again. Even when it rained here, the water was fresh and left everything clean, with a smell that felt like home. Erica had never had any doubt that if Alfie had managed to find her and bring her here as a naïve teenager, she would have had trouble leaving. Even as an adult, she had to force herself to leave this world. Each and every time. If it wasn't for her family and Jess, and their business, she would have stayed in there with Alfie from the moment he first took her to his home.

How on earth was she going to potentially convince a teenage girl to return to a life of exams and work after she'd experienced this?

But not everyone was like Erica. She often had to remind herself of that. Not everyone wanted the fresh air and lush grass and beautiful weather. Some people wanted adventure, money, grime and noise. While the fae could offer adventure – depending on the sort one was looking for – the rest generally went against their nature.

Alfie didn't hesitate once they were through into his world. Keeping hold of Erica's hand, he strode towards the fae village. Trotting to keep up, aware of not wanting to crush the bluebells at her feet, Erica breathed in again and stumbled a little as Alfie pulled her onward.

'Stop taking deep breaths,' he muttered.

'What? Why?' Erica drew level with him, but still he wouldn't let her hand go. He rarely let go of her in this world, always keeping her close.

Alfie glanced at her sideways.

'What you call our fae charm,' he told her. 'This time of year, the bluebells are our friends. There's a reason we plant them around the doorways and there's a reason many young humans cross through when they're in bloom.'

Erica gave the bluebells another look as they left the carpet of purple flowers behind. They took on a rather sinister appearance as she considered Alfie's words and remembered her mother's bottle in her bag.

'The smell of them?' she whispered, moving closer to him.

He nodded.

She smiled a little.

'And you don't want me falling under their spell?'

He shook his head, the curls around his ears swaying with the motion. Gently, Erica traced a finger around them, lightly touching his ear. Alfie visibly shivered and stopped, looking down into her eyes.

'Might be a bit late,' she murmured softly, staring up at him. His eyes matched the sky above, and in this world he seemed a little taller, more relaxed. She expected him to snake an arm around her waist, to lean down and kiss her lips, but instead his eyes softened a little, his hand squeezing hers, and then he was leading her through the village again.

Erica stayed close, her stomach somersaulting in disappointment that he hadn't kissed her, that he hadn't given her some sort of permission to jump on him.

Frowning, Erica glanced back to the bluebells left behind. That was quite enough of smelling the flowers.

They walked with purpose down the main thoroughfare of the fae village, houses built into the thick trees on either side, until Alfie led her down a side path to the left. Right down to the end of the path, past more fae homes, until the path narrowed and threatened to disappear into the forest. There weren't many fae around although Erica spotted some peering out of windows. There was some washing hanging out and in one garden, a couple lay naked on the grass, curled up into one another, both breathing deep and fast asleep.

At the narrowest point of the path, between an old oak tree and beech tree, was a large, beautiful home of different shades of timber. Wooden steps led up to the blue front door, curtains shifted in the warm breeze at the open windows, and everything about the place was clean and tidy. A burst of colourful flowers lined each window sill and either side of the path leading up to the door. Alfie strode up the steps and knocked loudly.

'Who lives here?' Erica whispered as loud as she dared, staying at the bottom of the steps. Now that Alfie had dropped her hand, she was aware of how small and alone she was without him by her side. Hugging herself, she stood close to the steps and exhaled in a rush when the door opened and revealed the home's owner.

Eolande was a similar height to Alfie and the very definition of the word elegance. She first looked down the steps to Erica with expressionless eyes before turning to Alfie and slowly raising one quizzical eyebrow.

'I'm looking for Fen,' he told her, his shoulders sagging a little.

Eolande sighed and looked back to Erica.

'You best come in,' she said shortly, turning and leading the way inside. Alfie looked down to Erica and held out a hand. Carefully, Erica climbed the steps and took his hand, not saying a word, hardly daring to breathe, as he led her into Eolande's home.

'*We're* looking for Fen,' she corrected under her breath as she looked around. Eolande's home was much like Alfie's in structure, a bit bigger perhaps, but the atmosphere was different. Compared to Eolande's, Alfie's home was barren and a little cold. Eolande's was full of colour. There were flowers in vases on the tables and window sills, the wooden floors shone as if freshly cleaned and, inexplicably, there was the smell of freshly baked bread. Erica frowned. This wasn't what she'd been expecting at all.

Eolande led them into a living room where there

were two armchairs and a large sofa covered in a colourful throw. There, on one of the armchairs, was a cushion that caught Erica's eye.

'That's Gran's,' she said, nodding to the yellow cushion.

Eolande smiled.

'Yes, it is.'

Erica looked around the room again, seeing the colour with new eyes.

'Gran's home used to look a little like this before she moved into the retirement home.'

Eolande nodded.

'Much of this is Minerva's input. I wouldn't have known where to start.'

A warmth spread through Erica and she took a seat when Eolande beckoned her to. Alfie wandered across the room, gazing out of the window.

'Have you seen Fen?' he asked.

'No,' said Eolande. 'Would you like a drink?' she asked Erica.

Erica glanced at Alfie who met her eyes calmly.

'No, thank you,' she said, giving her grand-mother's fae partner a smile.

Eolande sat on the armchair with Minerva's cushion and gave a short sigh.

'I haven't seen Fen,' she said. 'But he has been seen.'

'Did he have a girl with him?' Erica asked. She froze as Eolande met her eyes and gave a slight nod.

'It is not uncommon,' the fae said.

Erica looked to Alfie.

'How often does Fen bring a human girl back here?'

Alfie's shoulders lifted in a shrug, although his back was now turned to them as he stared out of the window.

'As often as anyone else,' Eolande responded. 'This is our way. Alfie has brought home human girls before. I have brought home human girls, and boys, before. Sex is important to us, Erica, as is love. And before we find the person who has our heart, we must learn and often there is experimentation to be done.'

Erica pulled a face.

'Experimentation?'

Eolande gave a slight shrug.

'Where is the fun, otherwise?'

Erica thought back to the naked couple in the garden they'd passed.

'It is all consensual. If something is non-consensual then there are repercussions. It is our way,' claimed Eolande, stiffening a little as she watched Erica's expression.

'Is it consensual if you're using bluebells?' Erica asked quietly. She was watching Alfie with a keen eye, otherwise she wouldn't have seen him flinch at her words.

Eolande smiled.

'How are bluebells any different to the copious amounts of alcohol your kind drink before falling into bed with a stranger? Is that not consensual?'

Erica turned to Eolande.

'Not always.'

The elegant fae stood and began rearranging the cushions.

'As with everything,' she said with a bored tone. 'You're running after Fen? Do you believe the girl he's with is here against her will?'

'No,' started Erica. 'Her mother is worried, though. I just want to check she's okay.'

Alfie turned back to the room to find Eolande staring at him. She gave him a questioning look.

'And why do you want to find him, Aelfraed?'

'Because it is important to Erica,' Alfie told her. 'You would do the same for Minerva.'

Eolande sighed through her nose but agreed.

'Sometimes it's easy to miss the simple times of bringing someone back into this world for a weekend of pleasure,' she muttered.

Erica's eyes widened and she glanced at Alfie who gave a tentative smile.

'But, of course, love makes that pleasure all the more,' Eolande continued. She turned back to them. 'Fen was here with the girl, but they left this morning.'

'Where did they go?' asked Erica.

Eolande turned her piercing gaze on her and Erica wilted a little, looking away. Alfie stepped closer then, taking Erica's hand and giving a subtle gesture for her to stand.

'I do not know,' said Eolande. 'But the wind whispers that the girl was speaking of London.'

Alfie paled.

'Fen wouldn't go to London,' he murmured. 'We're not London fae.'

Erica smirked.

'You're not city fae? You live in Bristol.'

'London is different,' Alfie told her. 'Bigger. Bolder. More dangerous.'

Erica's smirk faded.

'Would you go to London if Erica asked it of you?' Eolande asked Alfie.

His shoulders sagged.

'The girl's mother said Fen had been visiting since she was a child, that she is the one for him,' he told her.

Eolande gave them both a look.

'You may follow them and check on her wellbeing, but you cannot mess with matters of the heart.'

Erica frowned. Who was Eolande to be giving her orders?

'Bethany is eighteen,' she countered. 'If she chooses to stay with Fen then we can't argue, but I have to check she's okay.'

Eolande turned on Alfie.

'It is what it is,' he told her, squeezing Erica's hand. 'And if they're going to London, then I suppose we should too.' He frowned. 'Even if his heart tells him to go to London, I can't see him complying. I wonder where he's really taking her.'

'What? You think he's taking her somewhere else? Like...kidnapping?'

Alfie searched Erica's eyes.

'No,' he said eventually, after too much time had passed. 'Not like kidnapping.' He gave a small smile. 'He'll take her the long way.' Alfie looked to Eolande for confirmation. 'To talk her out of it.'

Eolande smiled.

'Fen was never the bravest,' she agreed.

Erica opened her mouth to speak but Alfie led her from the room before the words would come.

'Where are we going?' she asked, following Alfie and wondering if she should be dragging her feet and pulling back.

'What we came here to do,' he told her. 'Thank you, Eolande.'

'Yes,' Erica called over her shoulder. 'Thank you, Eolande. You have a lovely home.'

Eolande didn't respond, but when Erica looked back the elegant fae was standing at her front door, watching them leave, her lips and eyes expression-less.

'She doesn't seem happy,' Erica murmured, catching up with Alfie.

'I told you this isn't our way,' he whispered back.

The naked couple had woken and one of them moaned as the other slipped between their legs. Erica looked away hurriedly.

'Well, it's our way and if you don't like our way

then you should stop coming into our world and sweeping us off our feet,' Erica snapped. She glanced sideways at Alfie just in time to catch the smile turning up the corners of his lips. Erica stopped, pulling Alfie to a stop beside her. Smile fading, he looked down at her, searching her eyes.

'What's wrong?'

Erica went up on tiptoe, pushing her fingers through Alfie's hair, one hand slipping around the back of his neck to pull him down until their lips met.

'You're doing this for me. I wouldn't have a clue what to do if you weren't with me,' she told him, the tips of their noses touching. 'Thank you.'

Alfie grinned and wrapped his arms around her waist. Somewhere behind them the naked fae's moans turned into cries of pleasure, and Erica did her best to ignore them despite her body reacting to it.

'You have my heart,' Alfie murmured, evidently reacting to the sounds of sex as well as he pushed up against her. 'And I will follow you anywhere. It is our way,' he whispered before kissing her deeply.

18

Erica

Those four little words stayed with Erica as Alfie led her by the hand through the fae village. *This was their way.*

Her grandmother had told her before she'd been introduced to Alfie that fae loved hard. That had certainly been her experience, both with Alfie and of watching her grandmother with Eolande. While there was something to be said for being loved so hard, there was also something a little...scary. Was that the right word?

'Aelfraed! A bit early in the day to be bringing her home!'

Erica snapped out of her thoughts to find a tall, handsome fae man standing beside his garden gate, leering at her. She moved closer to Alfie as he waved to the man.

'Have you seen Fen?' Alfie called.

The leer and associated grin fell from Alfie's

neighbour's face and he shrugged.

'Maybe I have. Maybe I haven't.'

Alfie stopped walking and turned back. Erica reluctantly followed.

'We know where they're going,' she whispered to him. 'Can't we just go?' Every fibre of her being was pulling her away from Alfie's neighbour but she was tethered, by Alfie's hand clutching hers and by the need to stay close to him. Glancing around, faces were appearing at windows, fae were standing by doors. All eyes appeared to be on them and some were steadily on her, a mixture of disapproving eyebrows and straight lips, curious searching gazes, a knowing smile. Erica could have stood there for hours trying to make sense of it all although her pounding heart and loosening bowels would never have allowed it.

'Alfie,' she hissed.

'You have, then,' said Alfie, ignoring her but tightening his grip. He knew what she was seeing, but this was his home, these were his kind. She had to trust him, no matter what her body was telling her. What other choice did she have at this point? Erica remained close to him and tried to focus on his conversation with his neighbour.

The fae man was busy shrugging again.

'He was with a girl,' Alfie continued. 'Do you know where they are?'

The neighbour glanced at Erica.

'You have yours. Let Fen have his. We don't go

running after one another. The girl went willingly.'

'I'm not going to take her from him,' said Alfie. 'I promised her mother I would check on her. That is all.'

'Her mother?' The neighbour scoffed.

Now that Erica was forcing her attention on him, she realised that his eyes were the colour of those belonging to a dashing hero in a romance novel. Yet, when she shifted her weight from one foot to another, they appeared to change. To her right, they were turquoise, to her left, they were more purple. Were those even eye colours?

'It appears Fen has been working his way into the family since he realised their daughter was for him. He's been waiting for his time. She's only just eighteen.'

'She's long been an adult,' said the neighbour as if agreeing to something.

Alfie shook his head.

'She's just an adult,' he corrected. 'And still a child in her parents' eyes.'

The neighbour screwed his face up while still managing to look devilishly handsome. Erica glanced to his home behind him. How many humans had been seduced to spend a night or a weekend in there?

'She went willingly,' the neighbour repeated, glancing back to Erica. She snapped her gaze from his house to his eyes and tried to hold the stare, squaring her shoulders despite her trembling knees. Alfie must have felt it through their held hands. He placed a foot between them, drawing back his neighbour's attention. 'Just because you wasted your time and waited too long, Aelfraed, does not mean that Fen is in the wrong.'

'I never said that,' said Alfie through gritted teeth.

Erica frowned as the fae's handsomeness ebbed a little.

'Wasted his time?' she murmured. 'Waited too long? Alfie found me at just the right time, thank you very much. He waited just the right amount of time. He did things perfectly.' Erica snapped her mouth shut as she realised both men were staring at her, Alfie with a hint of a smile on his lips.

The neighbour turned back to Alfie, but Erica wasn't done.

'And he didn't need to use charm or tricks or *bluebells* on me,' she told him, her voice a little louder. 'You want to know what consent is? You're looking at it.' She stopped herself before she started shouting, breath coming hard, fingers gripping Alfie.

The neighbour's eyes widened a fraction and he opened his mouth to retort, but Alfie got there first.

'Fen and his lady love have gone, yes?'

The neighbour kept his eyes on Erica.

'As far as I'm aware.'

'Well,' said Alfie. 'We'd best check, don't you think?' He turned to Erica. 'Don't want to go on a wild goose chase, especially not to London. Let's go knock on his door.'

Without waiting for an answer, Alfie led Erica away. She glanced back to the neighbour over her shoulder, saw him glowering after them.

'What's his problem?' she asked.

'Oh, that's a long list,' said Alfie. 'Sometimes I think he's envious. Envy is a bad shade on a fae. It's been a long time since he found love, despite bringing someone new home every week or so.'

'How does a fae find love?' Erica asked after a moment's thought. 'You just keep going between worlds and searching?'

Alfie gave a little murmur as they reached a home at the end of the road. He tapped on the door and turned back to Erica.

'It's generally easier for the fae who fall in love with fae. It's more complicated for the rest of us. Sometimes we come across you when we're least expecting. Sometimes we dream of you. Sometimes we recognise you before you're born.' He gave her a sweet smile at that. 'Sometimes we miss you. Sometimes we find you late. Sometimes we have to wait. Eolande waited decades for Minerva, she found her when she was least expecting, in the cemetery one evening. I waited decades – although thankfully not as many – for you after being intro-duced to your mother when you were growing in her belly.' Alfie knocked again on the door. 'I dreamed of you,' he added quietly.

Erica perked up. She knew the story of how Eolande and Minerva had become a couple, she knew the rift that Alfie had caused when he'd gotten over excited at foreseeing Erica when he'd met her mother, but that was all she knew.

'I didn't know you dreamt of me,' she told him. 'What was the dream?'

Alfie flashed her a smile and then opened the front door. Erica watched, alarmed.

'It isn't locked?' she whispered.

Alfie gave her a look.

'We don't lock our doors here. We've no need to.'

He dropped her hand and walked into Fen's home. Erica paused a moment and then followed.

'Check the rooms, check the cupboards,' Alfie instructed as he walked through the small living room to what appeared to be the kitchen. Erica looked down at the chairs with indents where two people had been sitting. 'I dreamed of your eyes,' came Alfie's voice. 'And of your hair. Of your voice. Then, in another dream, I was shown your smile and your laugh. We kissed, we undressed, we made love.'

Erica's body tingled at his voice as she looked behind the furniture in the living room for clues.

'Is this before you knew about me?'

There was a clatter of Alfie opening and closing cupboards. Erica noted the small vase of bluebells on the coffee table in front of the chairs and then joined him in the kitchen. There, on the window sill, were another two vases of bluebells. She narrowed her eyes as Alfie straightened and put his hands on his hips.

'There's not a lot of food. I'd say he packed supplies before they left, which does suggest they're on their way somewhere.' He met Erica's eyes. 'The first two dreams were before I met your mother. It's probably why I acted like such an idiot when I saw she was carrying you. The last dream was afterwards. A sort of confirmation.'

'And that's how you knew we were supposed to be together?'

Alfie chuckled.

'No. It was just a nice dream, but there was a hint of foresight in there. My own foresight happens a little differently. I knew the moment I saw you growing inside your mother. Don't ask me how.'

Erica wasn't going to. She'd already tried that once, but Alfie hadn't been able to find the right words to convey the experience in a way she understood.

'Which is probably how Fen knows about Bethany?' she said as Alfie made his way to the only bedroom. Erica followed, looking over his shoulder. The bed sheets were crumpled and unmade, and on the bedside table was a vase of bluebells.

'They had sex?' Erica asked, moving past Alfie to inspect the vase.

'No.' Alfie looked back to the living room. 'I don't think so. That chair looks slept in. He probably gave her the bed.'

'How chivalrous of him,' Erica muttered. 'So many bluebells. They're in every room.'

Alfie pulled a face.

'The whole thing reeks a little of desperation, but then, that's Fen. He'll consider his wait for her to have been a long one full of hard work trying to bring her family round to the idea. He loves to be honest, that one.'

'If he's so honest, why all the bluebells?'

Alfie's eyes softened and he gestured for Erica to leave with him.

'Bluebells don't drug a person,' he told her as he closed the front door behind them. 'They help with seduction, yes, but they only nudge.' He glanced at her as she followed him. 'You've just been in a fae home filled with bluebells, do you feel anything?'

Erica took a moment and then said, 'No.'

Alfie grinned.

'Are you sure? By my reckoning, your heart is fluttering.'

Erica bit her lower lip. He was right, her heart was having a light flutter, sending the odd thrill through her.

'Your stomach is flipping.'

Erica placed a hand over her gut to try and keep it still.

'You're wet.'

Erica's eyes shot up to meet Alfie's.

'That's not because of the bluebells,' she

murmured as a throbbing started up between her legs. She stopped when she realised where they were. 'I thought we were going after Fen and Bethany?'

Alfie opened his own front door and ushered Erica inside.

'We need supplies first. And I need you first,' he whispered in her ear as he closed the door, shutting out the rest of the world.

Erica melted a little.

'That's not the bluebells,' she told him breathlessly as his hands wrapped around her from behind, finding their way beneath her top. 'That's just you. Us. That's just us.' It was becoming harder to find words, becoming harder not to turn around and jump on him, or to take his hand and pull him to the bedroom. No, the chairs in the living room were closer. The stairs were closer. Hell, the floor they were standing on seemed clean enough.

'You weren't wet before I suggested you were,' Alfie murmured, his hands finding her breasts beneath her clothes.

Erica blinked, trying to think.

'My heart was fluttering before you said,' she told him.

'That's just because I'm so handsome you can't keep your hands off me,' came Alfie's voice. Erica laughed.

'So you're saying that the bluebells helped nudge me into wanting sex with you right now?' Erica turned to face Alfie, pausing to pull her top over her head. His eyes drifted down as she undid her bra and her hands reached for his trousers.

'Did you want sex with me before?'

Erica nodded and Alfie grinned, taking her hands from his crotch and kissing her wrists in turn.

'The bluebells give a nudge,' he confirmed. 'They would have helped ease some of the doubts Bethany had about coming here with Fen. They would have helped ease her nerves about staying here for the night. But I don't think they were enough to convince her to have sex with him. Does that help matters?'

Erica nodded and then Alfie's lips were on hers.

'Chair or bed?' he asked before lowering his head to kiss along her collarbone.

Erica was about to suggest the floor, or up against the wall, or door. Why move when she could have him right here, right now? But a small voice in her head suggested that somewhere comfortable would be nice and the chairs were closest.

'Chair.' She pulled him into the living room and pushed him into the nearest armchair. Slipping off the rest of her clothes, she climbed on top of him, unbuttoning his shirt as she kissed his lips and Alfie's hand moved between her legs.

Erica had expected the sex to be over quickly, considering how much she'd needed him, but somehow Alfie had made it last. They ended up curled on the chair together, breathing each other in, and for that blissful hour or so, Erica had forgotten about Fen and Bethany. It was just another day in Alfie's home.

Snuggled against his chest, she peered around the room and imagined living there. It would be easy enough, to move in, to forget about the rest of her world. The first week would be consumed with sex, but then what?

What was life with a fae really like?

'If I moved in, if a human moved here,' Erica began, not moving her cheek from Alfie's chest. 'What would life be like? How would they spend their day?'

Alfie gave her a small squeeze of a hug.

'If you moved here, you could leave whenever you wanted,' he told her. 'I'd show you all the doors, you could come and go as you please. You could go to work in your world and come back here afterwards. We'd cook and eat, we'd drink, we'd lay on the grass and look at the stars. Make love in every room, in every position, out in the garden.'

Erica gave a muffled laugh.

'That wouldn't last.'

'It would,' said Alfie, kissing the top of her head as his hand ventured down over her bare hip. 'Of course, we'd have to marry so you could use the doors.'

Erica sat up and stared at him. He watched her,

expressionless, waiting for her full reaction.

'You have to be married to a fae to use the doors when you want to?'

'Security measures,' Alfie explained with a charming smile. He pulled Erica back into him, breathing in her hair. 'Would you want to marry me?'

Erica swallowed, her fingers playing with his chest hair.

'Do other humans live here? Married to fae?'

'They do. Would you like to meet them?'

Erica didn't reply but her immediate thought was yes, she wanted to meet them right then and ask them all the questions. The feeling was so overwhelming that it shocked her into silence. Alfie seemed to know, because Alfie always knew. He kissed her head again, gave her bottom a playful squeeze and then started to move. Erica slid off him and back to her feet, finding her clothes and redressing.

As Erica ran fingers through her tangled hair, she watched Alfie pull up his jeans but leave off his shirt, moving into the kitchen.

Damn those bluebells.

19

Fen

There was absolutely no way that Fen was going to London. It wasn't that he wasn't brave, not exactly. He would certainly do anything for Bethany. His love for her was palpable; he was hers, she was his. He had seen it. He had dreamed it. He had known it the moment he laid eyes on her and had been gifted the visions of her fully grown, smiling at him, laughing at his jokes, naked in his bed. He would move to the human world for her, he would give up his magic for her, he would die for her. But would he go to London? Not if he could help it.

After Bethany had agreed to spend the day with him, he had walked her through his home village and to the forest along the edge. He'd shown her the trees and let her listen to the birds singing. They'd watched the fox cubs playing and Bethany had smiled and laughed, and Fen had caught himself repeating that he would go to London for her.

Why did he keep saying that?

She'd nodded and asked if they could go that moment. She didn't need her exams, she didn't need school. She'd taken his hand and blood had rushed through Fen's ears. Something about the fun they could have together.

It was only afterwards, once they'd returned to his home and packed bags of food before setting out on the forest path towards the doorway to London, that he realised he may have overdone it with the bluebells.

'This is going to be so much fun,' said Bethany as she looked up at the trees on either side of the path. 'You showed me your home, and then we'll spend a day in London, which will become my home. That's only fair, right?'

'Right,' said Fen.

'And then you'll take me home to my parents. Yes?'

'Of course.'

Fen didn't know much about exams or school, but he knew enough about the big city.

'What do you want to do in London?' he asked her. He'd asked her why she wanted to live in London the night before, but she'd only told him in short sentences that she found the city magical. The very mention of the magical city of London had sent a shiver through Fen. She'd been cautious the night before. Now she was opening up, practically skipping beside him. Was it London that made her this excited? This happy?

Fen's heart sank.

'I'm going to be a fashion designer,' Bethany told him. 'I'm going to launch my own line of clothes. Start my own business. I can't wait,' she squealed.

Fen swallowed hard.

'You can make clothes here,' he murmured.

'What?'

'We have dressmakers here,' he told her, a little more firmly. 'You can live here, with me, and make clothes.'

Bethany frowned.

'I don't think it's the same thing.'

Fen grinned as his mind plotted and planned.

'No, it's better. Imagine how different your clothing will be to the others. Sewn with threads imbued with magic. Your clothes will shine and sparkle and everyone will love them all the more because they were made by the clever fingers of a fae's wife.' Fen closed his mouth. He hadn't meant to say that. Watching Bethany closely out of the corner of his eye as they walked, he held his breath.

'Imbued with magic,' she breathed.

Fen exhaled. Maybe she hadn't heard. He realised she had stopped walking, so he turned back for her. She was watching him with soft eyes, a smile touching her lips. Every time he looked at her, he was struck by her beauty. As the afternoon light shone through the tree canopy, as the smile on her lips grew and her soft eyes searched his, she was radiant. He approached her cautiously, not wanting to change anything.

'We don't know each other,' she murmured when he was a couple of steps away.

'We will,' he told her.

Bethany laughed and closed the gap between them, searching his eyes in such a way that his heart began to pound.

'And we will go to London and have adventures together,' she said gently.

Fen's stomach heaved a little. As he hunted his mind for the words to put her off the idea of London, she leaned forward and kissed his cheek.

All words were forgotten.

Fen stared at her with wide eyes as she pulled away. She laughed again and leaned forward to kiss him quickly on the lips.

Fen didn't move. Maybe if he didn't move, she would kiss him again.

'Come on,' she told him, taking his hand and pulling him along the path. 'The sooner we walk, the sooner we're there. Right?'

Right, thought Fen, following her, holding her hand tightly. Except that he wasn't going to London. He couldn't go to London.

20

Jess

When Jess and her mother arrived at the house Marshall was on his back on the kitchen floor, his head underneath the sink. Ruby was holding a cloth and passing it to Marshall when he asked for it. Eddie was bent over double, trying to watch what he was doing.

'Mummy!' Ruby grinned at Jess as they walked in and Jess gave her fiancé and daughter an adoring look.

'Are you being Marshall's assistant?' she asked Ruby, dropping Bubbles' lead and then regretting it as the dog padded over to Marshall and stood on him to investigate what he was doing.

Marshall *oomphed* and attempted to push Bubbles off.

'Get off! You big lumbering fool.' He managed to sit up without banging his head and Bubbles licked his cheek.

Laughing, Ruby pulled on Bubbles' collar and she stepped off Marshall, releasing him.

'Sorry,' said Jess, taking over from Ruby and leading Bubbles out of the way. 'Everything okay?'

'Marshall was just checking the pipework. I thought we might have a leak.'

'No leak,' said Marshall, wiping his hands on his jeans. 'But the pipes are old. They're okay now, but you might want to consider replacing them before you fit a new kitchen.'

Eddie nodded.

'New pipework and new wiring throughout, I think. Can you do any of that?'

'Definitely not the rewiring. You need a qualified electrician for that,' Marshall told him.

'He's not touching electricity,' Jess stated, placing a bag full of food and toys for Bubbles on the table. She pulled her phone from her pocket and checked the time.

'I'm going to...erm...go upstairs,' she said.

Ginny bit her lip.

'To talk to things that aren't there?'

Jess glanced quickly at her daughter who had definitely heard and was looking up at her mother.

'Are you going to talk to the man upstairs?' she whispered.

Jess's insides seemed to liquify and she put a hand on the table to steady herself.

Ginny blinked down at her granddaughter and then turned to Jess who gave her mother a look.

'I'm going upstairs. Could you please look after Ruby and Bubbles? Keep them both down here.'

Jess turned her back on her family and headed for the staircase as Ginny placed her hands on Ruby's shoulders to keep her in place. Eddie had hold of Bubbles' lead.

'I'll go with her, if that's okay?' Marshall said, although it wasn't really a question, his gazed fixed on the back of Jess. 'Stay here. Be good,' he told both Ruby and Bubbles as he followed Jess up the stairs.

Jess jumped as Marshall appeared on the landing behind her, despite having heard that he was following her.

'You're not doing this alone,' he murmured, kissing her cheek. 'What can I do?'

Jess smiled, her heart giving a small flutter. Having the bulk of Marshall behind her didn't make her relax, but she felt sturdier. She took a breath and blew out her cheeks.

'Just stay with me,' she told him.

'Always.' Marshall squared his shoulders and Jess had to rip her gaze from him.

Taking another slow breath, Jess walked into the bedroom where Ruby had seen the figure. There was nothing there other than some original floorboards and a fireplace. She tried to feel the air, the way Erica did. She'd been in the same room as spirits many times now, when helping Erica to communicate with them. Jess usually held the equipment and recorded anything, but she'd felt the cool air, she'd sensed something *other*.

Eyes closed, she reached out for that *other* now, but there was nothing.

That didn't mean that whatever was in this house wasn't here. Although she could hope. Jess cleared her throat and centred herself.

'Erm.' Not the best of starts, how did one start something like this? 'Hello,' she continued, swallowing on her dry mouth. She'd need a cup of tea after this. 'I don't know if you're here. My name is Jess and this is my family. My parents have bought this house and they would like to renovate it. They're going to be careful, do it sympathetically. They don't want to hurt anyone, they just want to make this house into a home again. And we would really appreciate it if you could please let that happen and not scare any of us. Because my daughter saw you and it scared her. We don't mind you staying here and watching, but please don't scare us.' Jess looked around the room. 'Thank you. We really appreciate it.' She went to turn back to Marshall and hesitated. 'My, erm, my friend is a witch,' she added. 'Maybe when she's free, she can come talk to you. If you like.'

She turned to Marshall to find him giving her that lopsided smile of his. Her stomach flipped at the sight. Marshall gave a single nod and held out his hand to her. She took it and he led her down the stairs where Ginny and Bubbles were waiting in the hallway.

'Where's Ruby?' asked Jess.

'Out in the garden with your dad. How did it go?' Ginny looked from Jess to Marshall and back again.

'I don't know,' admitted Jess. 'I've explained what's going on and asked whoever is here to not scare us. Now we wait and see what happens, if anything. Hopefully nothing. Shall I put the kettle on? I'm going to put the kettle on.' Jess dropped Marshall's hand and walked back into the kitchen, spotting her father and Ruby wandering around the garden, hand in hand. Smiling, Jess filled the kettle and switched it on.

Ginny and Marshall followed her in, Bubbles trotting out into the garden to join Ruby.

'And do you feel better now?' Ginny asked, finding four cups and placing a tea bag in each.

'Yes, I do,' said Jess, although her stomach turned and her fingers trembled.

Behind the women, Marshall watched, ringing his hands.

'Good,' said Ginny. 'Then maybe you can help us with the house today?'

Jess sighed.

'Okay. Sure. What about Ruby? A house renovation is no place for a five-year-old.'

Ginny glanced back at Marshall.

'I thought she was Marshall's assistant?'

Jess caught herself smiling and looked back to Marshall who shrugged.

'I reckon she'd be happy to be either of our assistants, depending on what we're each doing. But things might get...dusty.'

'And what about Bubbles,' Jess murmured. 'What are you planning on doing this weekend?' she asked her mother. 'If it's all dirty work, maybe Marshall could help Dad, and you and me can take Ruby and Bubbles out somewhere? We can fetch fancy coffees and cake or go buy supplies,' she offered.

Ginny gave this some thought.

'A shopping trip,' she murmured as Jess poured the water into each cup.

'Great,' said Marshall. 'In that case, I'll go check in the bathroom, see what we're dealing with. If your dad asks where I am...' he added to Jess who nodded. He gave her a wink, sending a flush of pleasure through her, and she blew him a kiss as he turned to go back up the stairs.

Jess turned back to find her mother smiling at her.

'You're very cute together,' she said.

Jess grinned.

'You really do like him, then? You approve?'

'He seems very nice,' said Ginny, before calling her husband in for his tea. 'Thoughtful. Most importantly, he cares about Ruby.'

'He loves Ruby. He's been like a father the moment he came into our lives,' murmured Jess. 'It's like he's always been here with us.'

Ginny beamed.

'Then yes, I approve. Your father does too, don't you, Eddie.'

'Hmm? What?' Eddie ushered both Ruby and Bubbles into the kitchen and gratefully took his tea. 'All went well?' he asked his daughter.

Jess nodded.

'I did what was suggested, now we wait and see.'

Eddie gave a firm nod and sipped his tea.

'And we approve of Marshall, don't we, Eddie,' added Ginny.

'I approve of Marshall,' said Ruby, looking from adult to adult, each with their own drink. Her gaze landed on her mother who gave her a funny smile and then went about getting her a drink of orange juice.

'Well, that's important,' said Eddie. 'And not that you need our approval,' he said to Jess, 'but I think he's great. He knows a plumber who can help out and he's going to sort out the flooring for us. Maybe the walls too, although he said something about knowing a plasterer. Yeah, I think you chose well.'

Jess laughed, gesturing for Ruby to sit at the table for her drink.

'And he loves me and Ruby, too.'

'And that. Of course that,' agreed Eddie. 'When's the wedding, then?'

Ginny's eyed widened.

'We have a wedding to plan!'

Jess rolled her eyes at Ruby and Ruby rolled her

eyes back.

'You do seem a lot happier,' Eddie murmured quietly, watching Ruby kick her legs under the table and sip her drink.

Jess retreated to lean back against a worktop as Bubbles lay down with a groan under the table, Ruby's feet just above her back.

'I'm incredibly happy,' she told her parents. 'I love my job, I love my Ruby and Bubbles. Marshall is like the cherry on the cake. He makes everything amazing. And he wanted you both to like him so badly. So, you know, be gentle with him.' She glanced at her father who gave a playful smile.

'He offered to help with the house, we're not making him.'

Jess sipped her tea, her insides relaxing a little from the warmth.

'Pipework in the bathroom is the same as down here, which is to be expected,' said Marshall, walking into the kitchen and glancing at their cups of tea. Jess turned to make him one. 'I'll send my plumber mate a message, shall I? See what quote he can give you.'

Eddie nodded.

'Great, thanks, Marshall.'

Marshall dug out his phone and started tapping away.

'How much of all that did you hear?' Jess murmured, passing him his tea.

'Of you all talking about how great I am? Not a

word,' said Marshall, grinning and taking the cup from her. He leaned down and kissed her cheek.

'Yuck!' said Ruby before giving her widest grin possible to Marshall. He stuck his tongue out at her.

'Right, what's next?' asked Eddie, putting his empty cup down. 'We should start on something. I want to start on something. Where should we start?' he asked Marshall.

Marshall gave a soft sigh as he thought.

'Well, we can start removing everything that needs to go. Flooring, wallpaper, all that. We can't put anything back though until the wiring and plumbing's been done.'

Eddie nodded in agreement.

'The women folk can help with the wallpaper.'

'Err, excuse me? I did both the flooring and the walls when I bought my house. By myself,' Jess argued. 'The women folk, as you put it, can do all of that.'

'Well, crack on then,' said her father, grinning.

Ruby laughed as Jess gave Eddie a look.

'I've got a steamer for getting the wallpaper off,' he continued to Marshall. 'And I guess we can just rip the carpets up.'

'And put them where? The skip isn't arriving until Monday,' Ginny complained, finishing her drink.

Eddie waved her away.

'It can just go out front or on the drive until then. It's only a couple of days. Come on then, Marshall.

Big strong man like you, you can pull up the carpet, can't you?'

Marshall looked down at his half-finished tea.

'Sure. Where do you want to start?'

'Living room. I think there are original floor-boards under there. Come on.'

Eddie pushed past everyone, and Marshall took a final swig of his tea before passing the cup to Jess.

'While the men are at work, let's talk weddings,' said Ginny, taking a seat next to Ruby and patting the empty space for Jess to sit.

Jess considered offering to help the men but she'd have to talk weddings at some point, it might as well be now with her mother and daughter.

'Want another drink?' she asked her mother, wondering if they had anything stronger than tea.

21

Jess

Even with her head down, tongue slightly sticking out between her teeth as she coloured, Ruby knew there were two pairs of eyes watching her. One pair belonged to her mother, sitting beside her. When Ruby glanced up to check that the other pair belonged to her grandmother, she found Granny with her head down over a list she was writing and a man standing in the corner of the room. She met his eyes and he slowly blinked at her, raising a finger to his lips to silence her.

As if that would work.

Ruby hadn't been brought up to stay silent just because a stranger had told her to not to tell anyone. In fact, her mother said these were the best secrets to share with her and that part of the game of 'not telling anyone' was that her mother always had to be told.

Still, she didn't mention the man's presence. Her

mother and grandmother didn't seem to notice him, or if they did, then they didn't react. He was definitely new to the room; they should have reacted to his presence. Beneath her dangling feet, under the table, Bubbles shifted and emitted a soft growl. Still, Ruby's mother didn't move.

The little girl studied the man in quick glances as she coloured, pretending to be focused on the drawing in front of her. She really should tell her mother about the ghost in the corner of the room.

಼ಃ

Jess watched her daughter colouring, playing keep-the-pencils-on-the-table. Her second cup of tea was finished long ago and her mother was busy chatting about the wedding guest list of people Jess had vaguely heard of.

From the other room, the sound of carpets being ripped up eased to silence, followed by low male mumbles and then, 'Girls! Get in here.'

At the sound of her husband's voice, Ginny jumped to her feet and bolted for the living room, followed swiftly by Bubbles. Wondering how her mother had gone so fast, Jess helped Ruby off the chair and held her hand as they joined the others.

They found their family crowded in a circle in the middle of the room, all staring down. Eddie had been right, there were floorboards under the carpet. Proper wooden, original floorboards, coated in dust and patches of underlay. They would come up beautifully, Jess thought, with a little elbow grease and varnish. That wasn't why Eddie had called them in.

Marshall beckoned her over and they made space for Jess and her daughter.

There, on the floor at their feet, was a definite hatch. A door. An opening into the floor. Jess snapped up to look at Marshall.

'Is there a cellar?' she asked quietly, her mind whirring.

'Nope,' said her father. 'Not that we know of, anyway. A hidden door!' He rubbed his hands together gleefully. 'There might be treasure down there,' he said, his eyes lifting to Ruby. 'Gold and jewels. Or something antique worth thousands. Or a pirate map showing the way to his buried treasure,' he continued, putting on a pirate voice and closing one eye as Ruby laughed.

'Or, more likely, a load of dust and dirt,' said Ginny, taking a small step back. 'Are you going to open it?'

Marshall and Eddie exchanged a look, and then Marshall carefully got down onto his knees and investigated the door. He blew at the dust on the wood, swiped it away with the flat of his hand and found a handle buried neatly in the door. Prodding it, he managed to lift it and then he gave it an experimental tug.

Nothing happened.

Leaning back, Marshall put his significant weight into it and the door opened with a *pop!*

Pulling out her phone, Jess turned on the torch and crouched to get a good look.

'Huh.'

'Huh? What's huh? Is there treasure?' asked her father, moving some old carpet to cushion his knees as he joined her on the floor. Marshall recovered and went onto all fours to look into the opening. Bubbles' head appeared beside him, tail wagging.

Tentatively, Marshall reached in and removed a box coated in thick grime.

A shadow passed over the house. A cloud, perhaps, moving across the sun, blocking out the light for only a moment.

Eddie's eyes widened as he watched Marshall attempt to open the box.

'Maybe we shouldn't,' Jess murmured, aware of a shiver running through her. Had the air turned colder or was it her imagination? She looked up to find her mother holding Ruby protectively by the shoulders. Checking on Bubbles, the dog was just as excited by the box as Eddie.

It had to be her imagination.

They watched as Marshall found the catch and lifted the box's lid.

'Huh.'

'Huh *what*?' Eddie almost screamed.

Marshall lifted a saucer and a small bottle from the box. Jess's eyes froze on the bottle. It was the length of Marshall's hand and made of thick glass. Inside there was a soft amber liquid.

'Please tell me that might be wine.' Eddie's eyes widened.

Marshall held the bottle up and then glanced to Jess.

'There's stuff in there.'

Jess's bowels loosened. She held out a hand and Marshall passed the bottle to her. Something clinked as the bottle moved.

'That doesn't sound like wine,' said her father, his shoulders sagging.

Jess shone her torch into the bottle.

'They look like long nails,' she murmured, peering through the glass. 'Two of them.' She turned the bottle, moving the light a little. 'There's other stuff too.'

'Definitely not wine.' Eddie grimaced.

'Why would someone have a bottle of water with nails in underneath the floorboards?' asked Ginny.

Jess swallowed against her dry mouth.

'It might not be water. Or wine,' she murmured before glancing up at Ruby. She kept her mouth shut, lowering the bottle but keeping a grip on it. 'What else was there?' she asked.

Marshall pulled out the saucer and showed it to her. A small, white, delicate plate with a shallow crack running from the edge to the centre.

Jess frowned.

'A saucer and a bottle,' she murmured thoughtfully.

'Someone's secret stash,' said Eddie, looking down into the hole beneath the floorboards to check for anything else. 'Maybe so they could have a tipple after the missus had gone to bed.'

Jess lifted the bottle again, staring at the liquid. There was a line going through the length of it. At first she thought it to be a defect in the glass, but as she shone her torch on it, she could see it was coloured.

'Wool?' she pondered aloud. 'Or thread. Pink or red, or stained by the liquid.'

When she looked up around the room, she found Marshall and Ginny both watching her. Holding the bottle up to the light, she snapped a photo of it on her phone before placing the bottle and saucer back into the box in Marshall's hands. He closed it, locking the clasp.

'You have an idea about it?' he asked quietly.

She gave a subtle nod as they both stood, and she stepped away to message the photo to Esther along with a question.

'I wonder how Ric is getting on,' she murmured. She wrote the message into the Murray family's group chat so that Erica might see it, just in case. Just before she hit send, Jess chewed her lip and added a bit about the saucer.

'Well, that was exciting,' said Ginny when Eddie couldn't find anything else. 'Nothing like finding some old rubbish under your house. Maybe we should take them to a museum to be looked at?'

'Probably not worth anything,' Eddie agreed, lowering the hatch door and brushing his hand over the catch as it sank back into the wood. 'Good to know this is here, though. Should we make a feature of it?' he asked his wife.

'Definitely. Look at these floorboards! They're gorgeous. We'll get them sanded and varnished and put a glass coffee table over this so we can see it.'

Eddie grinned, giving his wife a kiss on the cheek before surveying the mounds of carpet.

'Best get rid of all this, then.' He clapped his hands.

Marshall handed the box to Jess and helped Eddie drag the rolls of old carpet out the front, ready for the skip on Monday. Bubbles attempted to help, sniffing everything before they lifted it and following them back and forth.

'Shall we do the carpets upstairs while we're on a roll? Or is it time for a cuppa?' Eddie asked as he surveyed the empty living room and its newly revealed floorboards.

'I'll go put the kettle on,' Ginny said, ushering Ruby out of the room.

'Let's go decide where we're starting upstairs.' Eddie gave Marshall a grin and the two men wandered up the stairs chatting as they went.

Jess watched them go before looking down at the box in her grasp. There was an overwhelming urge to put the box back, to the extent that she turned to look at the closed hatch.

'Jess? Do you want anything to drink?' came her mother's voice.

'No, thank you,' she called back, still staring at the hatch. She glanced around the room. 'Did you put this there?' she whispered.

There came no response.

Slowly, Jess wandered back to the kitchen, placing the box on the table as she took a seat. She kept one hand on the box, not able to let it go.

'It's exciting, isn't it?' Ginny asked after Ruby took her seat. Jess sat beside her daughter and rearranged her colouring pencils. Bubbles followed them in and looked between the humans, tail wagging slowly. 'I wonder what other treasures this house is hiding.'

'Hmm.' Jess looked down at the box beneath her fingers.

Ginny looked to her over her shoulder.

'Oh, come on. Lighten up a little. This is meant to be fun! You've done your little talking thing and I'm sure it worked.' Jess's mother glanced at Ruby who was looking up at her with big eyes, kicking her legs under the table.

'Come on, Rubes,' said Jess. 'Draw us something.'

'Okay.' Ruby picked up her pencils and found a clean piece of paper. 'What should I draw?'

'Draw Granny and Grampy,' said Jess. 'Draw the family. You know, like the nice one you did of us when we first met Marshall?'

Ruby nodded and, sticking the tip of her tongue out between her teeth, got to work. Ginny caught Jess's eye.

'She drew a family picture of you all?'

'Marshall included. Right after we first met him,' said Jess with a smile. 'It's still on our fridge.' She hesitated as an idea occurred to her. 'Oh, could we use it for wedding invites or something? It would be lovely to use it in the wedding. It's my favourite.' She winked at Ruby.

'What a wonderful idea,' agreed Ginny, pouring the tea. 'Is Ruby going to be a flower girl?'

Ruby pulled a face.

'I don't know,' said Jess. 'A bridesmaid, maybe.'

Ruby pulled more of a face.

'Or a groomsgirl,' Jess suggested, unable to stop a grin as she watched her daughter. 'So she can help Marshall instead of me.'

Ruby met her mother's eyes.

'Would I have to wear a dress?'

'You could wear a little tuxedo. A special suit,' Jess told her.

Ruby gave this some thought as Ginny frowned and shook her head.

'But she'd look so pretty in a little dress. And it's not like you're planning on getting married again, are you?' she asked Jess, somehow covering the pointedness of the question by sipping her tea.

Jess stared at her mother and opened her mouth

to answer when Bubbles jumped up from where she was lying under the table. She gave a huff, and then ran out of the kitchen and up the stairs. They listened to the thumping of her paws as she reached the landing.

'Maybe the men are coming back down,' Ginny wondered.

Jess tightened her grip on the box.

There was a bark from Bubbles and then a shout that made everything and everyone stop. Jess jumped to her feet and then wobbled, looking down at Ruby who was staring up at the doorway, eyes wide, bottom lip quivering.

There came another yell that was unmistakably Marshall, and then a crash.

'Eddie?' Ginny called, her eyes on Ruby. 'Go check on them,' she told Jess.

Released, Jess grabbed the box and ran up the stairs, leaving Ruby with her mother.

'Marshall? Dad? Everything all right?'

22

Rick

BRISTOL, 1864

He'd thought it through over and over, gone over every possible eventuality, but there was just no way around it. Rick needed to get that pocket watch back. When he flashed to Victorian Bristol, he made sure to go back a little further than he should have done. Finding the road was easy, hiding was a little harder.

There he was, walking down the street, happy, humming if memory served him right. Rick hung back on the opposite side of the road, his hat pulled down over his eyes, a gloved hand brushing something imaginary from his face to conceal his identity. He watched his slightly younger self get accosted and forced into the alleyway. Once they were out of sight, Rick crossed the road, got into position and waited. He closed his eyes against the memories. The fear, his pounding heart, his heavy breathing and the pain from being hit. He remembered the adrenaline though, he let that feed him, along with the anger. Was he out cold yet? Were they fumbling through his coat, searching for things to take? Had they found the pocket watch?

His two attackers appeared beside him, turning into him as they left the alleyway. They stopped as they realised their path was blocked, and Rick enjoyed the moment as their eyes widened in recognition. One of the men turned back to the alleyway.

'How...?'

'Give me the pocket watch,' said Rick, holding out his hand.

The other man snarled.

'It's a trick. A lookalike. It's nothing,' he growled to his colleague, and then his arm was back, his fist curled.

Rick acted on instinct, and before the man could do much else, Rick had punched him, his knuckles smashing into the man's nose. He staggered back as Rick grunted with pain. The other man caught his friend and looked up at Rick.

'Pocket watch. Now.' Rick's growl wasn't intentional but the pain in his hand made it hard to breathe.

It did the trick. The man muttered what sounded like a prayer under his breath and threw the gold pocket watch to Rick. Rick caught it, dug his hand into his pocket, gripping the watch with everything he had. Then he turned on his heel and walked away. No one said anything, no one followed him, until...

'Oi! You there. Stop!'

Rick glanced back over his shoulder and spotted a uniformed police officer next to the man he'd punched. Now he had a choice. He could turn and go to the police officer, explain the situation and try to convince him that he'd done nothing wrong. His identical, unconscious body in the alleyway would probably complicate things. Why hadn't the police officer noticed his body lying there, beaten and bruised?

That made the choice easier. Rick ran.

He ran as fast as he could through the city, jumping out of the way of cabs and the horses who pulled them, pushing past women and men, much to their loud annoyance. There were shouts from behind as the police officer pursued him. Rick swung onto the road that led to the train station and, finally out of sight and with enough distance between him and the police officer to pause, he turned the device on his wrist. There came a cry as the blinding light surrounded him and then he walked calmly towards the train station. He'd returned to the time he'd left, where there was no other Rick lying in the alleyway or wandering the streets wondering what to do next. The police officer would have rounded the corner to find him missing and had probably quickly given up finding him. Rick walked leisurely into the station and straight into another man. Lifting his eyes so he could apologise, Rick came face-to-face with DCI Burns, Rick's boss from the future, and froze.

'Hello, Cavanagh.'

Rick ran. Pumping his legs as fast as he could, he ran until he found the platform he wanted. There was a train waiting there, filling the area with steam and the delicious smell of smoke. Rick leapt onto the train, breathing hard, and innocently asked a nearby member of staff if the train was heading to London.

'It is, sir.'

'Thank you. I was worried I was going to miss it,' said Rick, turning to find a seat.

'Almost, sir. We leave any second now.'

Something untwisted in Rick and he sat, leaning his head back, eyes closed. The train journey would give him a chance to figure out what he should do next. He pulled the watch from his pocket and ran his thumb over it, admiring it gleaming in the dim light.

'That was too close. Nearly lost you,' he told it, an image of Erica's smiling face in his mind. 'That won't happen again.' He tucked the watch into the breast pocket of his shirt so that it was close to his heart, and settled back in his seat. The whistle was blown, the doors slammed shut and Rick turned his head to gaze out of the window as the train began to move.

A familiar face appeared on the platform.

Rick held his breath, heart pounding anew as the train picked up speed as he watched the lanky frame of DCI Burns. His eyes scanned the train, landing on Rick staring out of the window. Burns turned his body to face Rick just as the train left the station and Burns disappeared from view.

23

Erica

'Got everything?' Erica asked as Alfie closed his front door behind him.

'Yes.'

In any other circumstances, Erica would have turned then and continued down the path to the road, leading the way. But this wasn't her world.

She waited for Alfie as he shouldered their bag of provisions and joined her on the path. Taking her hand, Alfie led her back to the road where he stopped.

'Why are we stopping?'

Alfie looked up and down the road.

'Hang on, this shouldn't take long.' He pulled her left when she was sure they should have gone right. 'Cecilia?' he called as they reached a house built into a beech tree. Alfie wandered up the garden path and knocked on the door. 'Cecilia?' he called again.

Erica found herself hiding behind Alfie as the door opened and a woman appeared. There was a beat as Erica realised this woman wasn't a fae and she crept out of Alfie's shadow a little.

'Alfie! It feels like such a long time since we talked,' said Cecilia. Her hazel hair hung down to her hips, straight and heavy. Her eyes were dark green and her lips full. There was a natural beauty about her that made Erica grip Alfie's hand harder.

'A long time. I hope you and Berwyn are well?' Alfie enquired.

'Very,' said Cecilia, looking to Erica as if noticing her for the first time. 'And yourself?'

'Very,' echoed Alfie. 'This is Erica Murray. Erica, this is Cecilia. She married a fae ten years ago.' There should have been more to that introduction but Alfie left it there so that the words hung over their heads.

Cecilia gave Erica an appraising look.

'Erica Murray, granddaughter of Minerva Warner,' she breathed.

'The same,' said Alfie, squeezing Erica's hand.

'Would you like to come in for a drink? I've just made some pastries.'

Alfie turned to Erica who stared back at him.

'Erm, that sounds lovely,' she said slowly. 'But... what about London?'

'You're going to London? Why?' Cecilia looked between them.

'Fen has taken a girl that way,' Alfie explained,

190

his gaze fixed on Erica. 'We promised her mother we would check on her.'

Cecilia gave a nod.

'One pastry and a drink, for the road?'

Alfie raised a questioning eyebrow at Erica, and while everything screamed at Erica to say no, how could she?

'If you think we have time,' she murmured to Alfie. He gave her a sly smile and led the way into Cecilia's home.

The house was much the same as Alfie's. Wooden floors, wooden walls, but it was lighter. There were flowers at the windows and in vases on every available surface but, Erica noticed, no bluebells. A sweet, earthy smell filled the rooms as Cecilia led them through to a small kitchen with large doors opening out onto a lush, green and private garden. Bare-footed, Cecilia padded into the kitchen and began preparing their drinks.

It wasn't coffee, as Erica had been expecting.

'Water with my own special cordial,' Cecilia explained, handing her a glass and a plate with a pastry on it. 'It helps to wake you up without all the stimulants we're used to back in our world.'

'Thank you.' Erica waited until Alfie had his own glass and plate, and then followed them into the garden where they sat on wooden chairs.

'Berwyn made these,' said Cecilia with great pride.

'He's not here?' Alfie asked, taking a bite from

his pastry.

'Asleep,' said Cecilia. 'He wakes early but sleeps in.' Her cheeks flushed a little and Erica didn't need to know any more. Cecilia turned to her. 'We've heard about you, of course. Alfie talks of you. It's lovely to finally meet you.'

Erica smiled, placing her glass down by her feet for lack of a table. Her stomach gave a soft grumble at the pastry.

'How long have you lived here?' she asked. While she was here, she may as well ask the questions.

'Permanently, nine years,' Cecilia told her. 'I wanted to keep in touch with friends and family but a year into our marriage, I just found myself wanting to stay here. This world is much...' She breathed in deep, closing her eyes. 'It's fresher, isn't it. More colourful. More wholesome.'

Erica bit her lip and nodded, taking a small bite from her pastry.

'Are you thinking of marrying?' Cecilia asked.

Alfie, annoyingly, turned to Erica.

'No,' she said, avoiding Alfie's gaze. 'I'm looking for somewhere to live and Alfie keeps suggesting here. But I need an internet connection for work.'

Cecilia frowned.

'You can give up your work if you live here.'

'I don't want to,' Erica told her. 'My friend and I run our own business, I enjoy it. I don't want to give it up and I don't want to lose her. But Alfie says you can only come and go as you please here if you're married to a fae.'

'Yes, that's true. And once you've had a taste of living here, you'll prefer to stay. Trust me,' Cecilia told her. 'Is the drink all right?' she added gently.

Erica glanced at Alfie who was sipping his water, smacking his lips and giving the glass a look.

'It's nice,' he told her.

Erica picked up her glass and took a sip. The water was ice cold and came with a gentle elderflower sweetness. There was something else, although Erica couldn't place it, leaving a delicious aftertaste on her tongue. She drank some more before returning to the pastry.

'Don't you miss your family?' Erica asked.

'No,' said Cecilia. 'But then, my life back there wasn't up to much. Isn't that why we fall into this world? It's certainly why Berwyn managed to coax me through that door twelve years ago. I'd never met a man like him.' Cecilia's eyes glazed, her lips lifting in a soft smile. 'He was so big and strong, but gentle and kind at the same time. He said all the right things, he made me feel safe. Waking up in his bed with his arms around me is still my absolute favourite thing. Plus, of course, they're much more open about sex here.' Cecilia seemed to rejoin them, her eyes focusing. 'The sex is fantastic. Don't you agree that sex with a fae is better than anything else?'

Erica blinked, feeling Alfie's smirk as he turned to her and tried to appear innocent.

'Ah, Berwyn.' Cecilia stood before Erica could answer and a heavily muscled man stepped out of the house and into the garden. He wore linen trousers but nothing else, and Erica fought to keep her eyes on his face, which was chiselled and topped with a mop of dark hair. His eyes, however, were large and almost twinkled. He patted Alfie on the shoulder.

'Aelfraed,' he said in a voice that matched his stature. His eyes found Erica. 'You brought your woman to meet my wife?'

'Good to see you again, Berwyn. This is Erica Murray.'

'Minerva's granddaughter?'

'Yes, so behave yourself.'

Berwyn grinned, flashing white teeth. He slid an arm around his wife's waist and pulled her in for a deep kiss. Her hands trailed on his chest as she said she would fetch him some breakfast.

Berwyn sat at the last remaining vacant chair and studied Erica. She remained still, not wanting to make any sudden moves under his keen gaze. She couldn't even reach out for Alfie, although she wanted to.

'She's a little old,' he said eventually, leaning back and turning to Alfie. Once his gaze was away from her, Erica felt a weight lift. She exhaled slowly, trying to regain control.

'She is not,' said Alfie. 'And what does it matter to you?'

'You should have taken her when she came of age,' said Berwyn matter-of-factly.

Erica bristled.

'Is that what you did with Cecilia?' she asked.

Berwyn's intense gaze found her again and Erica fought to keep her composure.

'Erica isn't like the others,' Alfie said gently, placing his glass and plate down. 'She's Minerva's granddaughter, she's the granddaughter and daughter of witches. One does not simply take her when she comes of age.'

Berwyn grinned and then laughed. Erica flinched.

'You would have if you hadn't messed it up.' He turned his eyes back to Erica and raked his gaze over her.

That was enough.

Erica jumped to her feet and collected Alfie's plate and glass.

'I'll take these back in,' she told the men, giving Alfie a meaningful look.

Hurrying into the kitchen, she found Cecilia pouring coffee into a mug. Erica stopped.

'You have coffee?' she asked.

'Yes, Berwyn prefers coffee,' said Cecilia. 'Oh, thank you. Put those in the sink, can you?'

Erica carefully placed the plates and glasses in the sink, turning back to Cecilia.

'Are you happy?' she asked quietly.

'Incredibly,' Cecilia told her, before slowly

looking up and meeting her eyes. 'Are you?'

'Well, yes.'

'Then why won't you marry him?'

The question hung in the air.

'Did Berwyn... How old were you when you met him?'

Cecilia gave this some thought.

'Nineteen,' she said eventually, having done the maths.

'Were there bluebells?' Erica asked.

Cecilia laughed.

'It was April and I was walking home from a night out with my friends,' she told Erica. 'There was a patch of bluebells in a playground near my home. Berwyn was sitting on the swings.'

'But...you're happy?' Erica checked.

Cecilia sighed and approached her.

'I know all about the fae charm,' she told Erica quietly. 'I know about the bluebells and fae magic. I've married into it. And I heartily recommend it. I age slower here so I can enjoy my husband before we decide to bring children into our lives. You're worried he took advantage? He didn't. He seduced me slowly even though I fell in love the moment I laid eyes on him. We're meant to be. He's mine. I am for him. We were born for each other. Don't you feel the same way about Alfie?'

Erica frowned uneasily.

'Well, yes...'

'Don't you want to be with him?'

'Yes.' The word was out before Erica could think. In fact, it was beginning to feel as if her mouth wasn't connected to her mind anymore. Her thoughts were fuzzy, hard to grab hold of, dancing and skipping around her while she tried to pluck them from the air.

'Then you should marry him,' came Cecilia's voice.

Erica grabbed on to the side of the worktop to steady herself.

'Are you all right?' Cecilia asked, but she was smiling.

Erica's stomach dropped.

'What was in the water?' she slurred.

Cecilia laughed.

'There's more to fae magic than bluebells,' she told Erica. 'I love putting flowers in my drinks. It gives you a buzz.'

'Erica, time to go.'

Erica turned at Alfie's voice, but all she could see was Berwyn, looming over her from the doorway.

'Alfie?' she managed.

A hand took hers and she flinched away at first before recognising Alfie's touch. She let him pull her through the house and back out onto the road.

Laughter followed them.

Once out on the road, Erica stopped, hands on her knees, willing her stomach to give up the fight and let her vomit.

'What. The. Hell,' she said between breaths.

Alfie stroked her back.

'Come on,' he said. 'Let's get that out of your system.'

He took her hand again, leading her gently away from Cecilia and Berwyn's home, back towards his own house. Erica groaned. Why couldn't they have just left for London as planned?

24
Erica

Erica sat on the floor of Alfie's bathroom, sipping the clean, fresh water from a glass he'd given her. There was no sweet taste this time, no strange aftertaste. No magic, no flowers. Just water.

Her stomach ached from the convulsions of vomiting up everything Cecilia had given her.

'What was that?' Erica croaked as Alfie sat on the floor beside her. 'That's not how you try to convince someone to join a community. Or marry someone,' she added, sipping the water.

'No. They've always been a strange couple. I honestly thought Berwyn wouldn't come down. Cecilia can be all right on her own. Sometimes.'

Erica gave Alfie a look.

'Sometimes?'

He shrugged.

'She gets worse every year. He's a bad influence on her.'

Erica rested her head back against the wall and closed her eyes as the room did a little experimental spin.

'Remind me to put my own spell on her next time I see her,' she muttered.

She opened her eyes as Alfie laughed.

'I'm so sorry,' he said, kissing her clothed shoulder and then entwining his fingers through hers and lifting her hand to his lips. 'I thought the water would be fine. It didn't occur to me that she would tamper with your drink.'

'And yet you have the gift of foresight,' said Erica bitterly.

'It doesn't always work,' Alfie murmured, kissing her hand again. 'Do you forgive me?'

Erica met his eyes, searching them before softening.

'Of course. You got me out of there quick enough. You're sitting here with me now.' She squeezed his hand. 'If I ever do marry you, we'll need to move. I'm not having them as my neighbours.'

Alfie laughed again, his gaze staying on her.

'So you still want to marry me one day?'

'I never said I want to marry you.'

'No,' said Alfie. 'But you do.'

Erica gave him a look and sipped her water.

'It's not that simple, is it. Evidently. If I marry you, do we have to live here? It sounds like I'll be giving up my whole life for you.' Erica sighed. 'No wonder Mum didn't want me to meet you.' She looked up into Alfie's large, sad eyes. 'I'm not giving up my job,' she told him quietly. 'I love my life. I love my job. And my family. And Jess and Marshall and Ruby. And I couldn't ask you to leave this world and live in mine because Cecilia is right. Home is dark and dismal compared to here.' Erica sighed through her nose, wondering whether to continue. When Alfie didn't speak, the words pushed themselves out. 'And then there's Rick.'

Silence followed, until Erica glanced up and met Alfie's eyes again. They were no longer sad. She twisted her lips to stop herself from saying anything more. He leaned his head against the wall, mirroring her, and gave a deep sigh.

'You still think about him?' he asked quietly.

'Sometimes. Not as often as I thought I would,' Erica admitted. 'We have a future together. A child. He's my future.'

'Do you want that future?' Alfie asked, not looking at her.

Erica didn't reply. She'd given this so much thought, lying in bed at night beside Alfie, staring up the ceiling, or when out driving, stuck at traffic lights. Was she waiting for Rick to come back? Did she want him to come back?

The memory of when they'd first met, as he'd fought to keep his identity from her as he tried to reunite Jess's friend Steve with his baby son, was still vivid. The feelings he'd evoked. How her stomach had flipped at the sight of him, how her

201

heart had pounded. How she'd *known* that they were meant to be, just from simply looking at him.

Those feelings had been utterly absent when she'd met the present day Rick, and they'd ebbed a little when she'd seen future Rick again. By that point, she'd been with Alfie.

Erica gave Alfie a sideways glance.

'Have you ever used fae charm on me? To get me into bed or whatever?'

Alfie sighed through his nose.

'We've been through this. No, I haven't.' He turned to meet her gaze. 'Why?' There was a sparkle in his eyes that suggested he knew why she was asking, so there was no point in hiding it.

'My feelings for Rick became a little less when we got together.'

Alfie smiled to himself.

'I know.'

Erica looked at him.

'What else do you know?' she asked.

Alfie stared at the roll top bath tub opposite them. He appeared to steady himself before he answered.

'I know that I'm in love with you,' he murmured. 'And I know that you're in love with me.' He squeezed her hand and she squeezed back. 'I know that it's still possible for you to build that future with Rick,' he admitted. 'And I know that if you asked it of me, I would live in your world with you.'

Erica's heart jolted and she fought the urge to

vomit again, sipping her water.

'And I know why Rick left,' Alfie added quietly.

Erica considered him.

'What do you mean? Why he left? He told me why he was leaving.'

'He talked to me first,' Alfie explained. 'Before he went.'

'I know.'

Alfie turned to look into her eyes.

'I gave him a pocket watch.'

Erica gave a hint of a smile.

'I know. He showed it to me. It was beautiful.'

Alfie cocked his head to the side, watching her.

'It was made here, a few centuries ago,' he told her.

'So you...just gave it to Rick?' Nausea forgotten, Erica shifted her position to face Alfie, her head still resting on the wall.

'I did. I told him it would tell him when he should come back for you,' said Alfie gently.

'When will that be?' she asked.

'Whenever you decide.'

Erica closed her eyes for a moment.

'Stop trying to please everyone,' came Alfie's voice, soft and gentle as if carried on a breeze. There was a warmth, telling her his face was suddenly close to hers. 'Please yourself. Forget about my feelings, about Rick's feelings. What do you want, Erica?'

Erica opened her eyes to find Alfie millimetres

from her, concern etched into every part of his face. Giving a small smile, Erica leaned forward and pressed her lips against his.

'What if I choose you? What happens to Rick?' she murmured.

'He has a happy ending,' Alfie told her. 'We all do, whatever you choose.'

'Even you?' Erica bumped her nose against his.

After a long pause, the fae whispered, 'Eventually.'

Erica pushed forward again, kissing him hard but not opening her mouth, acutely aware that she'd just vomited.

She pulled away, putting distance between them.

'Going to clean my teeth,' she announced, attempting to stand up. 'And then we should be getting after Fen.'

Alfie remained sitting, watching her, letting go of her hand.

'My father gave me that pocket watch,' he said gently.

Erica hesitated before slowly making her way to the sink and retrieving the toothbrush she kept at Alfie's.

'He said one day I would find someone, likely a human, who would steal my heart, the way he had stolen my mother's. That the pocket watch would help me find that person. It began ticking in my pocket when I met your mother. It chimed the day you were born.'

It was hard to clean your teeth when your face wanted to cry. Erica fought back the chin wobbles and tears.

'I messed everything up,' Alfie continued, still staring at his bath tub. 'I messed everything up when I met your mother. As you grew, I would see you with him in my dreams and knew I'd lost you, but still that damn pocket watch would chime on your birthday and tick when you were close. You were lost to me but it wouldn't let me forget you. I've had your whole life to practise losing you. I'll understand if you choose him. If he's who you truly want, then I want you to choose him. I need you to be happy.' Finally, he looked up at her and, in the mirror's reflection, Erica met his tear-filled eyes. 'Whatever you choose, if you're happy then I'm happy. And, eventually, there'll be someone else. I'll meet someone new. And you can forget about me. If you want to.'

Alfie found his feet and wandered out of the bathroom leaving Erica staring at her own reflection with her toothbrush hanging from her mouth.

There were no flowers in Alfie's bathroom. There were no flowers in his house. His home was unique in that among the world of the fae. She hadn't really noticed it until now, but he had never had flowers in his home, not even on her first visit. There hadn't been bluebells when they'd met, never any sweet drinks with strange aftertastes. There had only been Alfie and his smile.

Erica spat into the sink.

Because his smile was all he needed.

Wiping her mouth, she met her own eyes again in the mirror, wondering just how much of his words were based on truth and where the magic began.

25
Bethany

The idea of going to London with Fen was more comforting than the idea of going alone. At first, going alone had been an adventure, but the older she grew, the closer the day came, the less Bethany wanted to go to London by herself. But here was a handsome man who seemed kind and gentle, and who wanted to go to London with her. That alone had been worth the kiss.

Sure, he had mentioned marriage, but Bethany had often thought of getting married. That had always been part of the plan; to go to London, start her own business, fall in love, get married, start a family. It didn't have to happen in that order. In fact, maybe it was better this way. Maybe falling in love first would give her something to fall back on, someone to curl up with on the bad days, someone to celebrate with her on the good days.

They had walked in silence for a while until

Bethany had started telling him of the places she wanted to visit when in London. She'd done her research, she knew where she wanted to stay and where she wanted to eat and drink.

'I'm going to the London College of Fashion,' she declared. 'They'll accept me, once I get the grades. Although to do that I need to do my exams. We'll be back for my exams, won't we?'

'Of course,' said Fen.

They were holding hands, and while Fen's hand was warm, soft and comforting, he didn't seem keen on letting her go.

'You could get a job and we could rent somewhere nearby. Or you could stay with me in student accommodation. Or...' Bethany paused, glancing sideways at him. 'We could stay here, in your world?'

Fen stumbled a little and Bethany pretended not to notice.

'You would want to stay here while you become a fashion designer in your world?' Fen asked a little too quietly, as if he was almost asking himself.

'Could I?'

'I don't see why not. Yes, of course you can,' said Fen. 'Although I would have to take you through the door each day. Back and forth. You know, it would be easier if we were married. Once we're married, you can go back and forth between our worlds whenever you like, with or without me.'

'Really?'

'Hmm.'

'We just have a ceremony – I'll wear a beautiful dress that I've designed myself – and then I can go back and forth?' Bethany looked up at the tall, ancient trees around them. That didn't sound like such a bad thing.

'And you would be my wife and I would be your husband.'

'Yes.' And there would be no boyfriends at university, Bethany realised. No experimenting, no falling in love and getting her heart broken. She'd leave school and become a wife.

'And I would provide for us,' said Fen.

'But I would be able to run my own business,' Bethany checked.

'Of course,' said Fen. 'Fae have ways of helping.' He squeezed her hand in such a way that something inside Bethany twisted. She wasn't sure if it was good or bad. 'And each night we'll make love under the stars and each morning again before you go to be a fashion designer.'

Flushing, Bethany slowed and looked at Fen.

'You want to have sex?'

Fen's eyes danced.

'With you, yes.' His expression fell as Bethany swallowed against her dry mouth. 'What's wrong?'

'I haven't...I mean, I don't...'

'You haven't had sex before?'

Bethany shook her head.

Fen grinned.

'Oh, my dearest Bethany. Please don't worry. We'll do everything at your pace. You can tell me when you're ready. And it won't hurt, I'll make sure of it. It'll be fun. It'll be filled with pleasure. I only want to make you happy.' Fen lifted Bethany's hand in his and kissed her skin.

Pleasure rippled through her.

'I'm only eighteen,' she murmured. 'I've never been with anyone. I can't settle down with the first man I...' She couldn't finish the sentence, and apparently this thought had never occurred to Fen because his expression fell.

'Oh. Oh. You want there to be other men?'

Bethany shrugged.

'Or women. I don't know.'

'Oh.'

They continued walking.

'But when we are together I will live for your pleasure,' he told her. 'I'll run the house, keep it clean. I'll cook for you. I'll kiss you and hold you. I'll make you orgasm over and over.'

Bethany stiffened and giggled.

'Let's just go to London and see how that goes,' she suggested. 'We need to get to know each other.'

'Of course,' said Fen with a smile. Then he pointed over her shoulder. She glanced back to find a clearing filled with bluebells. 'Let's rest here a while, hmm? Have something to eat.'

'But the sooner we get there, the sooner we can enjoy it,' Bethany murmured, quietly admiring the clearing. She did feel a little sleepy, and her stomach rumbled at the mention of food.

'Ten minutes,' said Fen, leading her to the clearing.

She followed until he stopped, standing among the bluebells. He turned back to her, leaned forward and kissed her lips. This time she placed a hand on his cheek, not wanting him to leave her.

Ten minutes couldn't hurt.

26

Jess

'What happened?' Jess asked as she reached the
landing. Marshall was there, facing the back
bedroom with Jess's father behind him, peering
around Marshall's bulk.

'We heard something,' said Eddie, keeping his
eyes on the room. 'I heard someone behind me, but
there was no one there.'

'And then this was thrown at us.' Marshall
handed a book to Jess.

Jess took it, turning it over in her hands. *DIY for
Dummies*.

'It's mine,' her father explained. 'Your mother
bought it for me as a new house present.'

Jess gave a small smile at the sweetness before
her frown returned.

'Is everything okay?' Ginny called from downstairs.

'Go down to Mum,' Jess told her father. 'Look

after Ruby and Bubbles. Shout if anything happens.'

Paling, Eddie nodded and carefully made his way down the stairs. Marshall studied Jess.

'What are you thinking?' he asked.

'I don't know,' she murmured, slowly stepping past Marshall and into the bedroom. She wracked her brain. What would Erica do? 'Hello?' she called tentatively. 'Can you hear me? Please give us a sign that you can hear me. Knock or tap. Move something.'

They both waited, Marshall tense, ready to grab Jess. He stepped into the room, following her.

Nothing happened.

'I told you earlier, we'll be making some changes to the house,' Jess continued. 'That includes taking up the carpet. We'll replace it with nice flooring, unless the original floorboards are underneath. I promise, we're going to take good care of this house.'

She waited again, and again, nothing happened.

'Was that your box under the floor downstairs?' she whispered.

The door behind Marshall slammed shut and Jess yelped in shock. Marshall wheeled around and stared at it.

'Eddie?' he called, his voice catching.

'We can put the box back,' said Jess. 'I'm sorry we moved it. We didn't know what it was. We'll put it back.'

Silence met them. Slowly, Marshall reached forward and tried the door handle. The door swung open with ease.

Both Marshall and Jess squealed as sound filled the room. Hand on her chest, Jess apologised, her breath coming hard.

'My phone. It's my phone,' she said, pulling it from her pocket and, seeing Esther's name flashing on the screen, answered the call. 'Hi.'

'Jess, We— Is everything okay?'

'Not really,' Jess admitted. 'Marshall and my dad just had a book thrown at them. And the door just slammed. Talking to whatever's here isn't working well.' She looked around the room as she spoke. Again, she wondered what Erica would do. 'Should I try again? Maybe with a voice recorder?' she thought out loud.

'Not yet,' came Minerva's voice.

Jess froze.

'You're on speaker, love,' Esther explained. 'I saw your message and Mum's still here, so I showed her. We called as soon as we could.'

'Okay. Hang on.' Jess put her phone on speaker and held it up so Marshall could hear. 'You're on speaker too. Marshall's here. He's helping me.'

'Good man,' said Minerva. 'That picture you sent us, of the bottle.'

'Yes?' Jess looked up, meeting Marshall's gaze.

'Looks an awful lot like a witch bottle to me.'

Jess closed her eyes. The moment she'd seen the

bottle, she'd had a feeling about it. When it became obvious there were things inside it, she'd been flooded by memories of her research. She'd read about witch bottles and kept meaning to ask Erica if she'd ever made one.

'What's a witch bottle?' Marshall asked.

'Ah.' Minerva cleared her throat, ready to talk.

'—Something that used to be made to protect a house from witches, which of course never worked, or made by a witch to protect the home or someone living inside it, which of course did work,' came Esther's voice, before her mother could reply. 'It used to be a small clay pot, and then glass bottles became fashionable. They'd be filled with urine and items to aid in protection; nails, thread, hair and the like.'

Marshall pulled a face.

'That bottle is full of urine?' He met Jess's eyes. 'Good thing your dad didn't try to taste it.'

'That happened on that TV show, do you remember? The one with all the old stuff. Someone brought along a witch bottle not knowing what it was and the so-called expert tasted it thinking it was wine. Ha! Said it tasted odd. Course it did. The real experts later confirmed it was urine and a witch bottle,' said Minerva quickly, before Esther could stop her.

Jess smiled.

'I read about that,' she told them. 'So, once upon a time, someone made a witch bottle and hid it

215

under the floorboards of this house. Except they didn't hide it well. I thought they were usually put under fireplaces and things?'

'They are. Or inside walls. Sometimes they're not found until the whole house is demolished,' said Esther.

'So what was this one doing inside a box with a plate?' asked Jess.

There was a pause from the other end of the line, until Minerva broke the silence.

'I wish we were there to see it,' she mumbled.

'Video call?' Marshall suggested to Jess.

'We can do a video call,' Jess told Esther and Minerva. 'Hang on.' Jess hung up the phone and called them back via video, holding up the phone while Esther worked out how to respond.

'There. We can see you,' said Esther as her image appeared on the screen. She waved at Jess who waved back. Marshall stepped behind her, smiling into the camera. Minerva appeared, sitting beside her daughter, eyes narrowed behind her glasses as she tried to make sense of the screen.

'Oh, clever,' the nearly ninety-year-old remarked. 'And that's the house behind you. The room where you had something thrown at you, Marshall?'

Marshall glanced behind him and nodded.

'Yup. Pretty spooky this,' he murmured into Jess's hair, sending a shiver through her. 'Keep expecting another face to appear beside mine.'

Jess gave a nervous laugh, and then suggested they leave the room and go downstairs. Holding her phone up so they could continue chatting, Jess led Marshall back to the kitchen.

'Don't open that bottle,' Jess warned her father. 'Definitely don't drink from it.' She flipped the camera on her phone and showed Esther and Minerva the box, the bottle and the saucer.

'What's going on?' Ginny asked.

'Oh, these are my parents. This is Esther and Minerva, Erica's mother and grandmother,' Jess introduced. Esther and Minerva waved. Eddie waved back enthusiastically while Ginny blinked, working to catch up before giving a small wave and smile in return.

'I would offer you both a cuppa, but it'd be cold by the time it reached you,' Eddie told them, his voice a little too loud. Esther laughed and held up her cup of tea.

'We think the bottle is a witch bottle,' Jess explained. 'Perhaps made by a witch and hidden in the house to protect it and its occupants. It's likely urine in the bottle, so don't open it,' she warned her father again.

He pulled a face.

'Roger that.'

'Witch bottle? Urine? What are you talking about?' Ginny demanded with a sigh.

'What's urine?' Ruby asked.

'Ruby! Darling! Hello!' Minerva cried, waving

madly at Ruby. Ruby beamed and waved back.

'It's wee,' Marshall told her quietly.

Ruby pulled the same face her grandfather had and then shouted, 'Yuck!'

'Exactly,' said Marshall, turning his attention back to Jess and the phone.

Jess held up the saucer from the box and turned it slowly, giving Esther and Minerva a good look. Minerva leaned forward, squinting a little.

'How big is it?' she asked.

'Erm...' Jess found a teaspoon and put it beside the saucer on the table for comparison. 'Not that big,' she told them.

'And where did you find them?'

'In this box, under the floorboards in a hatch right in the middle of the living room,' said Jess, showing them the box and turning it slowly for the camera. 'Should I show you?'

'Please.'

Jess wandered away from her family and showed Esther and Minerva the hatch. Marshall opened it, using both hands to pull it up, and Jess showed them the dark inside. Then she waited for the verdict.

Esther and Minerva murmured to one another as Jess carried them back into the kitchen.

'Tea?' her father mouthed.

'Not yet, thanks,' Jess murmured, sitting down at the table and stroking Bubbles' head as the dog appeared at her lap.

'Well,' Esther started, 'we don't know. Not for sure. But we do believe that is a witch bottle. Which means it's likely it would have been made for someone in the house by a witch to protect them and the property. You might want to put it back where you found it.'

'And that saucer looks to me like it would have contained offerings,' said Minerva with a sniff.

'Offerings? To who? Or what?' Jess asked, forgetting for a moment that her whole family was there.

'Who knows. An offering to the fairies, perhaps,' said Minerva thoughtfully.

'The...fae?'

'Oh, no, no. The fairies. Think Tinkerbell,' Minerva told her. 'No, can you imagine leaving a saucer of milk out for Eolande? Ha!'

'Oland-who?' Eddie asked in a whisper.

Marshall caught himself before he could answer and looked to Jess for help. She waved the question away.

'Later,' she mouthed to her father.

'They would give offerings often in return for something. Protection or help around the house, or just to show friendship. Of course there are other creatures out there who enjoy an offering. Our folklore is full of them. Fairies, sprites, brownies, hedgehogs,' Minerva continued.

'Hedgehogs?' Marshall interrupted with a short laugh.

'Just because it was with a witch bottle doesn't mean the owner wasn't just helping the local wildlife,' said Minerva with a shrug.

Jess smiled. That's exactly what Erica would have said.

'Could one of those have thrown a book?' Jess asked. 'Ruby said she saw a man, and I know I saw something tall. Not really a fairy. What's a brownie? What does a sprite look like?'

Minerva shook her head.

'None are quite as tall as a man, not even a brownie although they can come close. Any one of them could have thrown a book, though. A fairy would have to be pretty angry, but still. I wonder... Can you give me a tour of the house, Jess? Can you hear me loud and clear? Would I be able to talk to whatever's there and it could hear me?'

'I don't see why not,' Esther murmured, leaning forward with interest.

Jess looked up and met her mother's eyes.

'Is that okay?' she asked. 'If I give Minerva and Esther a tour of the place? See what we can find?'

Ginny looked from Jess to her husband who gave her an amicable shrug, then to Marshall who attempted a comforting smile, then to Ruby who looked up with big, clueless eyes.

'I guess,' she said slowly, returning to Jess. 'Okay.'

Minerva clapped her hands with glee.

'Wonderful! This is the kitchen, I take it?

Probably nothing there. Go back to the living room, Jess, let's start there.'

27

Jess

Jess gave Minerva and Esther a detailed tour of the living room, standing in each corner, moving slowly across the newly exposed floorboards. She even gave them the view from the window, although she suspected that was just Esther being nosey. Trying to keep the camera steady, she explored the hallway with them, the small room to the side that was going to be turned into a downstairs toilet, and the large cupboard under the stairs. The boards creaked under her feet as she took them up the stairs.

There was a chill on the landing and Jess's immediate thought was that her father or Marshall had left a window open. The bathroom's window was closed and the room empty. The front bedroom was also empty but Jess did her due diligence, taking Esther and Minerva around the room, over the threadbare carpet, peering out of the closed window.

'What a lovely house,' said Esther. 'It's got so much potential and character. I can see why your parents bought it.'

Jess made a noise of agreement, but Minerva hushed them both before she could say more.

'Next room, please,' she said.

Jess sighed as quietly as possible and moved back onto the landing.

'Is Marshall going to be helping them?' asked Esther.

'He is. He offered immediately,' Jess told her, almost whispering to avoid being told off by Minerva again. She moved into the back bedroom.

'Wait!'

Jess's heart jolted and she stopped so fast, her momentum forced her to take another step to keep her balance.

'Jess, dear, put the phone down. Prop us up against the back wall, I think. And leave. Close the door behind you until you hear me shout.'

Jess processed this and blinked.

'What?'

Minerva sighed and went to repeat herself. Jess stopped her, holding up a hand.

'Why?' she asked.

'I have a theory,' was all Minerva said.

Jess did as she was told, propping the phone up against the back wall, on the floor, so that it had a view of the room, and then hesitated before closing the door behind her. She waited.

The voices of her parents and the deep rumble of Marshall sounded from downstairs, followed by the light voice of her daughter. Jess continued waiting, straining for anything that sounded like Minerva shouting.

A chill swept over her, the hair on the back of her neck standing on end. Jess froze. All of her instincts told her to look up – no, wait, they were telling her to run. Run down the stairs, grab your family and get out. A vision of the demon from the woods formed in her mind, long arms trailing to the ground, red eyes peering out of the shadows at her. Breathing hard, Jess listened out for Minerva.

Look up.

No, she thought. Nope.

Her mind showed her a memory of the spirit that had haunted Ruby's bedroom. The scratches it had made on her daughter's leg, the hatred it had held for her.

Look up, witch.

'Not a chance,' she whispered.

Something dark moved out of the corner of her eye and, without thinking, Jess spun to face it. There was nothing there. Jess reached out for the bedroom door to steady herself.

'Come on, Minerva,' she murmured under her breath.

That was when she heard it. Not Minerva's shout or Esther's calling voice, but a heavy, laboured, wet breathing. It was coming from right above her head.

In a moment of strange calmness, Jess wondered what to do. Should she look up? Then what? Scream? Run out of the house, grabbing her family and leaving her phone in the bedroom? Or perhaps she could rush into the bedroom, grab her phone and hope that Minerva could help from the other side of the screen.

Before she could decide what to do, and just before her stomach could make the decision to empty its contents, Jess heard Minerva's voice calling her name. The heavy breathing above her stopped and, exhaling in a rush, Jess pushed through the door and headed straight for the phone.

'Are you okay?' Esther asked as Jess's face appeared on the screen. 'What happened?'

Jess shook her head.

'I don't think this house likes me,' she told them.

'Well, I don't think it's personal,' Minerva said. 'There's a couple of things going on here.'

On Minerva's insistence, Jess carried the phone back down the stairs, but only after describing what she'd seen, heard and felt on the landing. She pointed the camera at the ceiling above the door where she'd been standing. There was nothing out of the ordinary. Not a sign that anything had been there at all.

Everyone looked up at she entered the kitchen.

'Can Ruby hear this?' Jess asked before anyone could say anything.

Minerva and Esther looked at one another.

'I don't see why not,' said Minerva at exactly the same time that Esther said, 'I don't think so.'

'What's going on?' asked Jess's mother.

'Hang on.' Marshall dug into the bag he'd brought with him and pulled out a tablet and headphones. 'Put these on, Rubes.' Ruby slid the pink headphones over her ears and took the tablet off Marshall as he set a cartoon playing. 'Sorted,' he told the others.

Jess, her heart squeezing, flashed him a smile and then positioned herself so that Minerva and Esther could talk to everyone.

'Okay,' she said. 'What's happening? Did you see something?'

'I saw lots of things,' said Minerva. 'You certainly have a spirit in the house and given that it showed itself when you start changing things, I would say it's a previous owner or occupant. Keep being polite, tell it what you're doing and why, and I'm sure it'll stop throwing things at you.'

There was a pause before Ginny scoffed.

'We can't get rid...do an exorcism or something?' Eddie asked.

Minerva smiled.

'Unless it hurts you, there really is no need. See how it goes.'

'But that's not all?' said Jess. 'That wasn't the spirit out on the landing with me, was it.'

'No,' said Minerva slowly, her gaze drifting upwards in thought. 'No, that was something else. And I believe it might be cured by you replacing that witch bottle. Put it back under the floorboards and see what happens. Might be that whatever was trying to reach you on the landing will leave or at least calm down, your resident spirit might calm down too.'

'It might be trying to warn you,' Esther agreed.

Jess looked at her father who nodded.

'Bottle goes back under the floor. Check.' He winked at his daughter. Jess didn't dare look at her mother.

'The other thing,' continued Minerva, 'is shadow people.'

A silence descended on the room. Marshall caught Jess's eye and she shrugged.

'What are they?' she asked when it became apparent that Minerva was waiting for a reaction.

'No one really knows.'

Which wasn't the answer Jess had been hoping for.

'Because they're not real,' Ginny muttered.

'Oh, they're definitely real,' said Minerva. 'Lots of incidents, lots of reports, going back hundreds of years, in fact. The most famous being the Hat Man. Although that's not what we saw. Some people see them during sleep paralysis and hope to the goddess that won't happen to you. Awful stuff, that. Others just...see them. And there's no real explanation, although there are plenty of theories. It's generally accepted that they're not spirits, as such, although some argue that they are. They could be demons, aliens, time travellers, versions of us in another dimension, other beings from another dimension.'

Jess needed to sit down. She pulled out a chair and propped the phone up against the box they'd taken from under the floorboards. Wiping a hand down her face, she considered the options.

'Surely if they were from another dimension, Eolande would have told you?' said Jess.

Minerva shrugged her scrawny shoulders.

'Not necessarily. We don't always talk shop.'

Esther pulled a face.

'So, we don't know what they are, but they're in the house. Can they hurt us?' Jess asked, ignoring her mother sighing.

Minerva twisted her lips in a thoughtful grimace.

'Arguable,' she said. 'It depends on what they are, I think. My own theory is that shadow people are not just one thing. Some might be demons, some might be time travellers, but both appear to us as shadows. The time travellers probably can't hurt us, but the demons can. Do you see?'

Jess nodded, mirroring Minerva's grimace.

'So, we've got a spirit and shadow people.' She sighed.

'And something dark,' Minerva added.

There was a pause, until Jess asked, 'There's more?'

Minerva nodded and Esther gave Jess an apologetic look.

'I said there was a lot going on,' said Minerva. 'This other thing is malevolent. You said you've had things thrown at you? When did that start?'

Jess glanced at Marshall who scratched the back of his head.

'After we took up the floor in the living room,' said Jess's father. 'After we took out that box. We went upstairs to take up the carpet there.' Eddie moved to sit beside his daughter, looking into her phone camera. 'Hi there! I'm Eddie, Jess's dad. Do you think this "witch bottle"' – he made air quotes with a big grin on his face – 'had something to do with that? Poor Marshall got a hefty book thrown at him in the back bedroom. As it were. You said something about this bottle being protective?'

Minerva's eyes had been widening with joy as Eddie talked and she gave a quick, excited clap of her hands.

'Oh, Jess. You have your father's inquisitive spirit. Yes, Eddie, that could be exactly it. Now, of course, I can't say if this dark presence was around before that, but if you started to come to harm after the box with the witch bottle and saucer were removed then I would strongly suggest replacing them. As I mentioned earlier.'

Eddie grinned and nodded.

'On it now.'

'This malevolent creature was the thing above you on the landing, Jess, dear,' Minerva continued. 'It certainly didn't look like a shadow person or a spirit.'

A shiver ran through Jess.

'Hang on. How did you see it if it was out on the landing with me while you were in the bedroom with the door closed?' she asked as she moved the phone and handed the closed box, containing the witch bottle and saucer, to her father.

'I saw it in the living room,' said Minerva. Jess nodded once. 'And on the stairs.' Jess hesitated. 'In the bathroom, and then it followed you out of the bedroom when you left us in there.'

Jess stared wide-eyed at Minerva.

'Is it here now?' she breathed.

Minerva looked around and Jess slowly turned so the camera spanned the room, passing across Ginny's disgruntled expression.

'No,' said Minerva. 'But I imagine it's listening. Go replace the box. Let's see what happens.'

Jess didn't like the sound of that.

'Want me to do it, Dad?' she offered.

'Not on your nelly.' Eddie was still grinning. 'Let's see what happens.'

Ginny tutted and made the silent decision to stay behind in the kitchen with Ruby while Marshall and Jess followed Eddie into the living room.

Marshall lifted the hatch and they all jumped back as the hatch somehow ripped out of his grasp and slammed shut.

Jess took a shaky breath. Her exhale came out in a cloud of warm air hitting the sudden chill that filled the room.

'Shit,' she murmured, looking around.

Her father was exhaling over and over, watching his breath cloud, fascinated. Marshall balled his fists, moving to stand over Jess.

'What's happening?' he asked.

'It's in there with you,' said Minerva.

Eddie bent to open the hatch and a loud bang and yell came from the kitchen. They all jumped and Jess practically threw her phone at Marshall as she ran out of the room, towards her mother and daughter.

'Mum? Ruby? Are you okay?' She arrived in the kitchen, breathing hard, to find Ginny with her arms around a bewildered Ruby.

'We're fine,' said her mother. 'The door opened and banged against the wall, scared the life out of me.'

Marshall and Eddie followed behind Jess, her father still carrying the box. They all turned as the living room door slammed shut.

'Oh,' said Jess, realising what was going on. Easing her way past the men, she tried to open the living room door but it wouldn't budge. Marshall followed her and tried, putting all his strength

231

behind it. Jess took her phone from him.

'Erm, if the witch bottle is still in the house, that protects us. Right?'

'Afraid not,' said Minerva. 'It needs to be inside-inside the house. In the foundations or the floor or in a doorway. A lot of people would bury them under the hearth. Why? What's going on?'

Jess looked up at Marshall, their eyes meeting.

'I don't think this thing wants us to put the witch bottle back.'

28

Rick

LONDON, 1864

Rick fretted the whole way to London. DCI Burns, a thin man with a crop of light blond hair and heavy, narrowed eyes, had always been a force to be reckoned with. The man rarely spoke, but when he did it was with such authority that he couldn't be ignored. He'd been Rick's boss for years back...in the future.

Rick closed his eyes, clenching them shut for a moment.

How had Burns found him?

He glanced down at the device on his wrist. It gave off a signature, something for the police staff to follow, to ensure they knew where their officers were and that they were safe. Rick hadn't given it much thought. It would tell his old colleagues that he was alive, somewhere, sometime, but he hadn't considered how easy it would be for them to follow him.

Undoing the clasps that held the device to his wrist, he looked around to make sure no one was watching. Turning the device in his hand, Rick found the enclosed chamber that held the working mechanisms of time travel. He didn't have a clue how it worked inside, although he understood the basic theory and science. He was a detective, not an engineer, and what he needed in that moment was a small, crosshead screwdriver.

Rick blew out his cheeks.

He'd have to wait until he reached London where he could find a shop. How would Burns follow him to London? As far as he knew, the police couldn't trace the exact co-ordinates using the devices; how easy their jobs would have been if they could! He wouldn't have gotten himself into this mess if that had been the case. Instead of going back in time to find the murderer Rachel, who had stolen his own time travel device, and searching the whole of Bristol for the damn woman, bumping into Erica along the way and destroying his whole future, he'd have simply zapped back, apprehended Rachel and zapped them home.

Rick ungritted his teeth.

He'd been about to wish for more technology to aid in his escape, but the more he thought about it, the more he preferred the simple days before technology had gotten out of hand. Looking around the train, he relished in the fact that no one there was staring at a screen.

It would take Burns time to find him in London, and unless he somehow used his own device to travel to London a few minutes before or ahead of Rick – which was incredibly risky, as they'd been told over and over again during safety briefings – he'd have to wait for the next train.

Rick clipped the device back onto his wrist, sat back and tried to relax. Brushing his fingers over the shape of the watch in his breast pocket, he wondered if Alfie had foreseen this. If this was why the fae had been so happy to give him the pocket watch and send him away. If he'd known that Burns would find him, if he knew what would happen to him.

Rick turned his head to stare out of the window at the passing fields through the haze of smoke the train was emitting.

Alfie wouldn't write Rick's future. He was determined of that. Let Burns chase him. He wouldn't catch him.

Despite the brightness of the day, London was dark. The noise was overwhelming. Rick was used to the big city, he'd attended university in London before moving back to Bristol. But this wasn't the London he knew, although he could see the bones of it. The foundation of the city he would come to understand. The noise and smells might be different, but the streets were pretty much the same. Rick found his way to Regent's Park and settled on a bench under a tree, watching people walk past, wondering what to do next.

The minutes passed, until Rick was broken from his thoughts by a man sitting beside him. Rick avoided eye contact; there was plenty of room on the bench for both of them.

'Nice day, today, don't you think?'

Rick froze, eyes wide. He slowly looked up and turned to face the man beside him. Alfie grinned back.

'You,' Rick growled.

Alfie's grin didn't falter. He had the same brown hair that curled around his ears and the same bright blue eyes. His clothing was different, but only just. His trousers were linen instead of denim, but his shirt was similar to his modern one. A flat cap somehow hid his features when he lowered his head.

'We know each other,' Alfie said. 'Although I don't believe we've met yet? Do you know my name?'

'Alfie,' said Rick in a low, gravelly voice.

Alfie chuckled.

'Aelfraed. I go by Alfie where you come from? And where is it, exactly, that you come from?' Alfie looked Rick up and down, studying him. 'You can't answer that. A man who comes from many times.'

Their eyes met and something jolted through Rick. 'We meet in the future,' Alfie murmured.

'We do,' said Rick carefully. 'You gave me a pocket watch.' Slowly, he withdrew the watch from his pocket and showed it to Alfie, the gold glinting in the streams of sunlight that filtered through the branches of the tree above them. 'Do you recognise it?'

Alfie's grin faded.

'It's my father's.'

Rick's breath caught. He hadn't expected that. Alfie lifted his eyes.

'To have given it to you... I must have thought it important.'

Rick sagged into the bench, placing the watch back into his breast pocket and keeping his hand over it.

'Yeah.' He kept his eyes low. Alfie's stare burned into him.

'I've found her, then,' came his voice. 'After all this time, I find her.' Alfie cocked his head a little. 'And she's yours.'

Rick jumped as Alfie barked a laugh, turning away.

'I'm sorry,' Alfie continued, his voice soft. 'For whatever wrong I may cause you.'

'You can't possibly mean the same woman, she's—'

Alfie held up a hand, cutting Rick off.

'Please! I can't know her name. Or what time

you're from, time traveller. Or how we meet. Please, don't give me details. Just know that I know enough, and that I'm sorry.'

Rick's gaze hardened.

'You don't know that you'll win yet.'

Alfie grinned again.

'I don't know that I won't.'

Rick's gut twisted. He looked back to his lap and the ground beneath his feet.

'What can you tell me? About my future? My boss is after me. I'm scared what will happen if he catches me. I could go to prison. I'll definitely be in trouble. And I'll lose...her. If I haven't already. I already have, haven't I? I can't not be with her.' Rick's voice caught as the words tumbled out. 'This is all my fault. All of it. I changed our future and now I've lost my wife and my child. They were everything to me.' He looked up at Alfie as a tear dropped down his cheek. 'Can't you give me any good news?'

Alfie continued to grin, yet Rick didn't have the inclination to smack it off this particular Alfie. The malice wasn't there. This wasn't the man who had stolen Erica's heart, not yet.

'That pocket watch will let you know what to do,' Alfie told him. 'It's why I gave it to you. It might not give you exactly what you want, but it will give you what you need.'

Rick bit his lower lip to try and stop further tears.

'Will I be happy?'

'You will.'

Rick looked up at Alfie.

'Will I be safe?'

Alfie nodded and then leaned back into the bench, shoving his hands deep into his pockets. There, in a flash, was an Alfie more recognisable to Rick.

'I suggest you stop running, time traveller. Good to meet you. Until next time.' Alfie stood and, without looking back, walked away. He followed the path, diverting off, walking behind a tree without appearing on the other side.

Rick sighed and sat back, his fingers tapping against the watch in his pocket, replaying the conversation in his mind.

29

Erica

Alfie made Erica eat something before they left his home on the hunt for Fen and Bethany. She ate small pieces of bread, baked the morning before, as her stomach churned and grumbled. Eventually the small sips of water and bread did the job. Her gut began to settle and colour rushed back to her cheeks.

'Ready,' she said.

Alfie studied her from where he leaned back against his oak kitchen worktop, his arms crossed against his chest. After packing a bag of the bread, some butter and flasks of water, he'd made himself a cup of green tea which he sipped from time to time.

'Give it a little longer,' he said. 'Just to make sure.'

Erica sighed.

'We should have left ages ago. If we'd left when I

said, we wouldn't have to wait for my stomach to settle.' She stood as Alfie flinched. 'We're going now. The longer we wait, the further away they're getting. Sooner we get to them, the sooner I can go home.' Erica stopped and slowly met Alfie's eyes. 'I didn't mean...'

'No, it's okay. Why would you want to stay here? With my neighbours who poison you and a community who use magic to entice your kind into bed. Come on, let's go.' Alfie left his cup of tea in the sink, shouldered the pack he'd prepared and left.

Erica watched him go and then, alone, looked around the room. At the beautifully carved wood, the trunk of the tree that made up one of the walls, the complete absence of flowers.

She followed Alfie out and down the road, staying one step behind him until his shoulders hunched up to his ears and he stopped to take her hand. Erica smiled. Even when angry with her, he still had to protect her.

'I'm sorry,' she murmured so only he could hear. The residents of the fae village were awake now, bustling along the road, at their windows, chatting at their open doors. Some gave them looks as they strode past, some called greetings to Alfie who smiled and responded while pulling Erica on. 'I get why you're not in a rush to go after them.'

As they turned the corner, onto the road with Eolande's house at the end, Alfie slowed.

'And I understand why you *are* in a rush to go

after them,' he relented. 'I just wish I could show you that a life here isn't as bad as you think.'

'Are you kidding? Beautiful colours, living in a tree, no internet, no social media, no humans. Of course living here would be amazing. Just you and me, growing our own food, exploring, having sex. I get it, I do. I don't know why I can't give up my life for it.' Erica looked down at her feet, kicking up the dust as the road became a dirt path.

Alfie smiled and squeezed her hand.

'Because you're human,' he told her. 'And that's why I love you.' He lifted her hand and kissed the back of it, sending a shiver through her.

'Do all fae fall in love with humans?' she asked, unable to take her eyes from him.

Alfie shook his head.

'Not always.' He grinned. 'Before the doors between our worlds opened, we didn't even know what humans were.'

Erica stared.

'Do you remember that?'

Alfie laughed.

'Of course not! That was hundreds of thousands of years ago, how old do you think I am?'

Erica smiled, studying the man who still held her hand as they passed Eolande's house, left his village behind and stepped into the forest.

'I keep asking but you never tell me.'

Alfie gave her a look, a cross between playful secrecy and wondering whether he should give that secret away. The result made Erica want to stop and drag him back to his home and his bed. She found herself considering the trees around them, thinking a little too loud.

Alfie laughed, making her jump.

'That would be a good tree.' He pointed with the hand he clasped hers in. 'The trunk is wide, I could easily lift you up against it.'

A thrill shot through Erica, barely registering Alfie looking her up and down. 'It would be easier if you were wearing a skirt,' he mused.

Erica flushed and laughed. Her step hesitated near the tree and then she shook her head.

'It's too close to the path.'

When she looked up, Alfie was studying her with fascination.

'You're so close to fitting in here perfectly,' he murmured, mostly to himself. 'And no one would mind,' he added, continuing on through the forest. 'The social etiquette is not the same here. You've seen it. We have sex where and when we like.'

Erica glanced back to the tree over her shoulder.

'So, you've used that tree before?'

There was a slight pause.

'Look! A green woodpecker,' said Alfie, pointing up into the canopy.

Erica laughed.

'Well, that's a yes. And in that case, we're definitely having sex against that tree.'

Alfie stopped and turned back to her.

'We are?'

Erica nodded.

'I'm not having some other human woman being better with you than me. If you know what I mean.'

A sly grin spread across Alfie's face.

'I do.' He glanced behind them, back towards the tree. 'There's no one around.'

Erica looked down at herself, wishing she was wearing a skirt. Then she checked in with herself; did she really want this? Yes, her whole body screamed, yes, get on with it!

What about Fen and Bethany?

'We'll have to be quick,' Erica breathed, closing the gap between them, reaching up and pulling Alfie down so she could press her lips against his.

He relaxed into the kiss immediately, scooping her up and carrying her over to the tree. Erica let Alfie take over, trying not to look over his shoulder towards the path or further back into the village. She fought to stay quiet, burying her face in his neck to muffle the noises that escaped as he kissed her, caressed her, lifted her into position and pushed inside her.

Erica's back hurt in the best way as they continued down the path into the forest. It would be covered in scratches, she guessed, from where the bark of the tree had pulled at her. It had been worth it. The throbbing and aching on her back matched the rest of her body, still reeling from Alfie's touch. Sex in this world was somehow better than back home, it always had been. Not only was it better, but it was easier, and somehow more plentiful.

Again, quietly this time, Erica considered whether she could live here and, glancing sideways at Alfie beside her, whether she did in fact want to marry him.

'How long till London?' she asked, breaking through the gentle lull of bird song around them.

'It's quite a way,' Alfie admitted. 'But I don't think Fen is going to London.'

All thoughts of where they'd have sex next left Erica's mind.

'Still? Why?'

'Because Fen hates London.'

'But Bethany wants to go there.'

Alfie nodded.

'And Fen's in love with her. So he'll agree, but I also believe he'll try to dissuade her. He'll go slow, try to find ways of changing her mind.'

Erica pulled a face.

'What ways? Like what we just did?'

Alfie looked up at her, smiling his most charming smile.

'Tell me you didn't enjoy that.'

Erica flushed again.

'You know I did.'

'You want to do it again,' said Alfie.

'Stop reading my mind.'

Alfie chuckled to himself, turning back to the

path.

'No,' he said finally. 'Unless Bethany wants to. Fen will be taking that slowly too. No, he'll try other things. Which is why I think they're going this way, and instead of taking the path on the right at the fork up ahead, to London, I'll bet everything I have that they went left.'

Erica caught herself staring at Alfie and as he turned to her, she looked away. Grinning, Alfie looked up at the trees and continued on in silence.

Erica also looked up and then took a moment to close her eyes and listen.

'Do these trees talk?' she asked.

'Of course.'

Erica's brow creased.

'I can't hear them.'

Alfie stopped to look back at her, his eyes softening.

'These aren't the trees of your home,' he told her.

Something wriggled inside Erica. She jogged to catch up with Alfie and whispered, 'Do they mind that we had sex against one of them?'

'Of course not,' Alfie whispered back. 'Just like they won't mind when we wash in the stream up ahead. And they won't mind when we have sex again in that stream.'

Erica stared up at him and slowly raised an eyebrow.

'We can't have sex every five minutes. We've got a job to do.'

Alfie's gaze lingered down her body, sending a jolt of pleasure through her. She gritted her teeth, trying to stay in control.

'If you say so,' he said.

'I do. Let's find Fen and Bethany, get this sorted and done, make sure she's okay. Then we'll come back to the stream another time.'

Alfie laughed, taking her hand.

'Deal.'

Alfie was right. Up ahead was a fork in the road. They went left instead of right, following his instincts about Fen. After another hour of walking and talking aimlessly, there came the sound of rushing water. Erica's body woke at the noise, remembering Alfie's words.

'No,' she whispered to herself under her breath. 'Stop it.'

'Do you want to clean up?' Alfie asked.

Erica hesitated.

'How far away do you think Fen and Bethany are?'

Alfie looked further up the path, eyes glazing as he thought.

'Four or five hours walk.'

Erica puffed out her cheeks.

'That's not far, considering.'

Alfie met her eyes.

'I told you, Fen will be going the long way. If I was him, I'd have walked her in a circle to begin with. Just in case I could change her mind easily.

But, of course, we don't know if she has changed her mind.' He climbed down a slight bank and gestured to the cleanest stream Erica had ever seen. The water was clear, cold looking, and sparkling under the sunlight that filtered through the trees.

'Wow,' she murmured. 'This is beautiful.'

Alfie smiled and went to undo his trousers.

'Have a quick wash and let's get going.'

Erica watched Alfie undress, her fingers tapping against her thigh. She could have had a quick wash, as he was doing. She barely needed to remove her clothes, but instead she pulled her top over her head and walked to Alfie. Removing his shirt, she pressed her body against him, kissing him deeply as he smiled, his fingers lingering on her bare back.

'Again?' he murmured.

Erica nodded.

'Again. Quickly. One more time.'

Alfie laughed softly and this time, he let Erica take control. He lay back on the bank of the stream and Erica climbed on top, kissing him hard as his hands found her breasts. This time she didn't even consider that someone might be walking past on the path just above the stream. If they did, what did it matter? The sight of two naked people entwined with one another, moaning in pleasure, was common enough in this world. The more Erica visited, the longer she stayed there, the easier it became to just be with Alfie, to not hide away, to not be ashamed of pulling off her clothes so that she could feel his warm skin against hers. Erica let the sound of the running stream and the singing birds fill her mind as Alfie filled her body, and this time she leaned her head back and joined in with the noise, as loud as she wished.

One more time, she told herself, closing her eyes to relish the pleasure. Just one more time.

30

Erica

They walked for a couple of hours after enjoying the stream, stopping in a clearing to eat buttered bread, drink water and make love again in the soft grass.

Erica was beginning to wish that she could always have the excuse of chasing after fae and their teenage loves through the forest with Alfie. As long as Bethany wasn't hurt.

'What is it about this place?' she murmured as they continued along the path. Erica's body tingled and pulsed, and she didn't want it to stop. She was aware of a screaming voice at the back of her mind telling her to get on with it, to find Bethany, that there should be more urgency, but something about the forest kept that voice low and distant.

Erica gave Alfie a sidelong glance.

'Does the forest not want us to find them?'

She smiled as Alfie tripped over an exposed root and looked up at her with wide eyes. He calmed when he saw her expression.

'I told you,' he said. 'This is our way. This is our world.'

'And who am I to come in here and try and change it.' Erica sighed. 'I don't want to change it,' she said a little louder, looking up at the trees. 'I just want to make sure Bethany's okay. That's all. If she's okay and really wants to stay and there's no charm and magic involved in coercing her, then I'll leave well alone.' She turned to Alfie. 'If the forest lets us find her, does that mean no more diversion sex?'

Alfie laughed.

'Don't worry. I'm sure we can make it up later.' He held out his hand and she took it, a warmth shooting through her as their skin touched. She pulled her hand away.

'No. Nope. Not until we've found them.' She gritted her teeth and marched on, Alfie smirking behind her.

They walked for another few hours before Erica complained of needing a rest. Alfie told her to hang on just a little longer. They rounded a bend in the road and there, amongst the trees, was another fae village.

Erica's heart squeezed at the sight.

They entered the village, Alfie once again taking Erica's hand as they followed the main road straight through.

'Aelfraed! My brother.'

Alfie stopped, Erica bumping into the back of him. A man with the same stocky build as Alfie appeared from the side, arms out. His frame was almost identical to Alfie's and for a moment, Erica wondered if they were actually brothers. The fae's blond hair and absence of curls suggested otherwise. When he turned his attention to Erica, his sharp eyes proved he was no relation.

'This one's pretty,' he told Alfie, his hungry gaze raking over her in such a way that she could almost feel the grooves they left behind.

Alfie stepped forward, breaking the hold.

'Minerva Warner's granddaughter,' said Alfie.

At the mention of Minerva's name, the fae quietened, his eyes becoming hooded. He gave Erica a respectful nod.

'Sure can pick them, Aelfraed,' he muttered.

'I'm looking for Fen,' said Alfie. 'Has he been through here?'

The fae nodded.

'He has, with a sweet little thing. They walked straight through at her bidding.' He pointed to the opposite end of the village. 'Only a day ago.'

Erica sighed but held her tongue. Alfie thanked the fae and then pulled Erica on. She glanced back only once to find the man staring after her, winking at her as their eyes met. Rather than turn back, she continued to watch until he seemed to grow anxious and turned away first.

'This one's pretty?' she repeated quietly to Alfie

as they strode down the main street. 'How many girls have you brought here?'

'You've spent most of our relationship openly saying you're going to marry someone else,' Alfie pointed out, dragging her on.

Erica went to argue but couldn't find the words.

They made it out of the village, back into the forest where Alfie paused, cocking his head as if listening to the trees.

'They came through a day ago. We're never going to catch them up,' Erica whined, looking for somewhere to sit as her feet throbbed in her shoes.

'Yes we are. Through here.'

Before Erica could reply, Alfie was pushing through the undergrowth, off the path. Erica blinked, looked up to the vibrant blue sky and then shrugged to herself.

'Fine,' she muttered, following him, frowning as a cobweb snagged her face. 'I'm not doing this all the way to London.'

She didn't have to.

After what felt like an hour, but couldn't possibly have been, they fell out of the undergrowth and into a clearing. Erica began brushing the pieces of leaf and twig and insect from her when she heard a voice.

'What are you doing here?'

Erica looked up to find a handsome young man squaring up to Alfie. Behind him, sitting on a fallen tree, was a teenage girl with long dark hair and tired eyes.

'Bethany?' she asked quietly.

The girl looked up and so did Fen. The young fae pushed Alfie out of the way and stood protectively between Erica and Bethany. The anger came off him in waves, or perhaps that was his charm. His eyes seemed to flame and Erica almost – almost – took a step back.

'Who are you?' Fen growled.

Erica put up her hands in surrender.

'My name's Erica, and Bethany's mother asked us to check that she was okay. That's all.'

'Mum sent you?'

Erica risked looking around Fen. The girl had stood, wringing her hands.

'She did. She knows where you are. She just wants to know you're all right and that you want to be here.'

'Of course she wants to be here,' Fen snapped, but still he glanced back to Bethany.

'Where are you headed?' asked Alfie, hands shoved deep into his pockets.

'London,' said Bethany with a smile.

Alfie cocked his head at Fen.

'London, huh? Didn't think you liked London, Fen?'

Fen's face twitched.

'I do. For her, I do.'

'I'll show him the London that I love,' said Bethany. 'He'll like it then.'

A painful pang squeezed at Erica.

Alfie was still staring at Fen.

'That why you've been walking the girl in circles?'

There was a pause as Fen searched for a response and Bethany turned to him, frowning in confusion.

'We've been walking in circles?'

'He's lying,' Fen said a little too quickly. 'Of course we haven't.'

'When did you leave our village, Bethany?' Alfie asked. 'When did Fen start the journey to London with you? How many days ago?'

Bethany looked from Alfie, back to Fen.

'Two?'

'It's taken us just about a day to reach you,' said Alfie. 'How would that be possible, Fen? If you weren't walking the girl in circles.'

'She might have changed her mind,' said Fen, his voice quieter. Then his angry eyes lifted back to Alfie. 'Like you've never walked a girl in circles around this forest, and for worse reasons. I love Bethany. I am hers.'

The words rankled Erica, making something inside her twitch. Alfie had said that he was hers often enough that she now thought them before he could say them.

'I'm not using her. This isn't a bit of weekend fun,' Fen continued. Erica slowly turned to look at Alfie, but his stare was still on Fen. 'I didn't trick her to come here with me. I just thought...' Fen turned to Bethany. 'I thought that if you could see how beautiful it is here and just how far away London is, you might change your mind.' He sighed, lowering his gaze to the forest floor.

Bethany studied him for a moment. Erica should have been waiting for her reaction but instead, she found herself watching Alfie. Sidling up to him, she lowered her voice so as not to distract Bethany from Fen.

'You tricked girls into this forest to use them?'

Alfie's blue eyes met hers.

'I might have used a little charm,' he admitted. 'I used them as they used me. Everything was consensual. It has to be consensual in our world.'

'Except that you, what? You drugged them? You charmed them. You tricked them.' Erica accidentally raised her voice. When she looked up, both Fen and Bethany were watching her, Fen with something of a smile hinting on his lips.

'I offered them an escape,' said Alfie. 'Which is what my kind do.' His voice had lowered to something of a growl, and anger began to build in Erica's gut in response.

'You stole them away.'

'I offered them something else.'

'You drugged them.'

'I didn't drug them.'

'Then what would you call it?'

Alfie hesitated.

'Charm. Erica.'

'Right. Fae charm. You used your magic. What's the difference between you using magic to trick a girl into this forest with you so you can have your way with her and that stupid neighbour of yours drugging me with flowers?'

'Flowers?' came Bethany's quiet voice.

'I never used it on you,' said Alfie.

'Yes you did and that's not my point,' Erica snapped. 'You used fae charm on me when we first met—'

'And it didn't work,' Alfie interrupted, shouting back.

'No, but it worked on others, didn't it?'

Alfie's chest heaved as he searched her eyes.

'I never hurt anyone,' he told her steadily. 'I never forced myself on anyone. I never would.'

The change in his tone brought Erica back to the forest. She blinked and the tension between them lifted a little.

'No,' she murmured, still unsure.

Fen was smiling, reaching out a hand to Bethany.

'Poor Aelfraed,' he tutted. 'Never could get the girl of your dreams.'

Alfie turned all of his anger and spite on the young fae.

'I never used the tactics you use, Fen,' he said, his voice dangerously low. 'Were there bluebells when you first met, Bethany?'

'I— Yes.'

'And when he took you to his home, were there bluebells?'

Bethany glanced at Fen.

'Yes.'

'Flowers, flowers, everywhere,' Alfie sang. 'I wonder why. Why would you need such potent fae magic around the girl of your dreams?'

'All right, enough!' Erica shouted as Fen went to answer. 'You're both as bad as each other.'

Fen took a moment to study Erica and then snapped round to look at Alfie.

'You brought a *witch* here?' he hissed.

Bethany took a step closer to Fen.

'Yes,' said Erica. 'He did. And this witch is going to have a chat with Bethany right now, away from the two of you and all your magic.' She pointed to the side and gave Fen her best impression of her grandmother when Minerva was angry.

It did the trick.

Fen stepped away from Bethany, albeit somewhat reluctantly. Alfie took him by the arm and pulled him to the side, giving Erica free access to the teenage girl. Eyes wide, Fen stared at Alfie until he let Fen go, pushing him back towards the edge of the clearing.

'You'll let them talk,' said Alfie.

'Why are you allowing this?' Fen hissed, assuming the women couldn't hear.

Erica took a shaky step towards Bethany and the

258

girl looked on with wide eyes, as if she was a deer suddenly caught out in the open, likely to run at any moment. But not without Fen, Erica realised. She wouldn't run without Fen.

Erica held out her hands.

'Can we talk?' she asked gently. 'There on the tree?' She gestured to the fallen tree with a nod of her head.

Bethany blinked, glancing back to the tree trunk.

'Please? My feet are killing me,' Erica added.

Bethany sat down and Erica exhaled, moving to sit beside her. Alfie and Fen were talking in hushed voices off to the side still, so Erica gave Bethany a moment while she waited for the throbbing in her shoes to ease.

'Keep your voice down,' Alfie growled.

Fen snapped his mouth shut and looked past the older fae to where the witch was talking to his love.

'This is our way,' he murmured. 'You'd be doing the same.'

'I know. But this is her way. You would go to London for your love; I would find you and stop you for mine.'

Fen relented and fought back a wave of tears that pricked at his eyes.

'Did you ever hurt the girls before?' he asked, working on keeping his voice steady.

'No. Did you?'

Fen shook his head.

'I never want to hurt them. And I didn't love them the way I love her.' He looked back to Bethany. 'I only wanted them to have fun. To show them a new world.'

Alfie was nodding.

'And to bide our time,' he admitted, glancing over to Erica.

'I guess that too.' Fen sighed. 'I've waited for so long to find her and for her to be of the right age.' He looked up at Alfie. 'What if I lose her?'

A small smile crept onto Alfie's face.

'That is also our way,' he told Fen. 'Even if they choose to stay with us so that we can love them and make them happy, they will still eventually leave us. We must wait for them to come to us, remember.'

'I did,' said Fen. 'I met her in the woods and offered her what she wanted. She could have said no. She did say no.' He frowned at himself. 'She asked me to take her home and I nearly did, but the pull of London is...' He sighed again. 'I don't want to go to London.' A shiver ran over the young fae and Alfie patted his shoulder.

'Love is also about letting go,' he murmured. 'Bethany's fate is in London.'

Fen looked up at him and shook his head.

'You can't mean that.'

'I see it,' Alfie told him. 'And your choice is to go with her or wait for her.'

Fen looked back to Bethany, talking quietly to Erica.

'And if I wait for her? Will she come back to me?' Alfie smiled.

'Do you really want to know?'

'Of course!'

Alfie leaned closer to Fen and whispered, 'She comes back to you.'

Fen's world stopped. His heart skipped a beat, his stomach threatening to push up into his throat. Struggling for a breath, he blinked away the tears.

'She is yours,' said Alfie. 'You are hers. She comes back to you.'

Fen sniffed, wiping the tears away as they fell.

'Does your witch stay with you?' he asked, glancing up at the older fae. Alfie's smile was gone, his eyes sad.

'My future is unknown.'

Fen shook his head.

'That's the problem,' he murmured. 'Things change. Humans change.'

Alfie looked back down to him.

'Which is why you have a choice, Fen. You can go with her to London or you can stay behind and hope.'

Jess

Jess left her parents in the kitchen, having a hushed heated debate. Marshall fretted over Ruby, brushing back her hair and asking her if she saw anything, if she was feeling okay, did she need anything. Holding up the phone, Minerva and Esther still on the screen, Jess stepped into the garden and shielded her eyes from the sun.

'What is it?' she asked. 'This thing that's in my parents' house. You saw it. Is it a demon?'

The women on the screen shifted uncomfortably.

'Could be.' Minerva sniffed.

Jess's eyebrows shot up.

'Could be?'

'Chances are,' Minerva said.

Jess waited for more, but the woman shut her mouth and pressed her lips together. Jess growled softly, looking around the garden.

'How has this happened? Has this thing been

here all this time?'

'Probably,' said Esther. 'It must have been waiting and when the witch bottle was removed...'

Jess groaned.

'Seriously? This thing has been waiting here all this time? How old is that witch bottle? It must be a hundred years, maybe. This thing has been waiting a hundred years?'

'A blink of an eye for whatever this thing is, I imagine,' Minerva agreed. 'And it's entirely possible that it's longer. You don't find many witch bottles these days.'

'What do I do? How do I get rid of it? It's in my parents' *house*,' Jess hissed. 'I need it gone. Where can I put the witch bottle if not back under the floor?' She turned to look up at the house. 'In the fireplace? Under the hearth, you said?'

Minerva and Esther nodded.

'But that'll mean pulling up the hearth,' Esther pointed out. 'And if all it had to do was slam a door and hold it shut to keep you from putting it back under the floor, imagine what it might do if you start pulling up the hearth. It'll take too much time.'

'Agreed. You might have to get sneaky,' said Minerva.

Jess stared at them, her teeth gritted.

'Or I can just get Alfie and Eolande here, right?'

Minerva and Esther exchanged a look.

'Alfie's busy with Erica,' Esther began.

'Eolande won't go,' finished Minerva.

Jess held her breath to stop herself from screaming up at the sky.

'Then what do I do?' she shouted. 'Can you come here? Maybe Minerva just walking in the house will scare the damn thing off.'

Minerva barked a laugh, grinning as Esther rolled her eyes.

'That as may be, but you're forgetting something, Jess, dear,' said Minerva, leaning closer to the camera. 'You're a witch too. You can do this.'

Jess shook her head.

'Not on my own.'

'Yes, on your own.'

'With my whole family here.'

'Because your family is there.'

Jess stared at Minerva and the hesitation turned into a pause which grew into a pregnant silence.

'Fine,' she said eventually, her insides twisting, her shoulders lifting up to her ears. 'Where else can I put this witch bottle?'

Esther appeared thoughtful.

'You know, I'm not sure there is another place as easy as under those floorboards. You might just have to try there again.'

'But be sneaky about it,' Jess murmured.

Esther nodded.

'Of course, there is someone else there who might help you,' came Minerva's voice, quieter than usual. Jess watched the screen as Esther turned to her mother, her eyes brightening with realisation.

'Oh yes, that would be worth a shot.'

'What?' Jess asked.

'There's a spirit in the house with you,' Minerva told her. 'The one that's likely a past resident. Might be worth asking them. And of course, you know how to contact spirits.' She sat back, proud of herself.

Jess's mind whirred. She'd never contacted a spirit directly by herself, but she'd watched Erica do it over and over. Deep down, she knew how to do it. Deep down, she realised, she could do it.

'There's probably a cavity up in the loft.'

Jess squealed at the sudden low voice, and span, raising her hand to throw her phone at her attacker. Marshall widened his eyes and blinked, slowly lifting his hands.

'It's me,' he said.

Jess lowered her hand and phone, breathing hard, heart thumping so hard her ribs hurt. She tapped him on the arm.

'Don't. Do. That.'

Marshall gave her his most charming lopsided smile and wrapped an arm around her waist, kissing her cheek.

'Sorry.'

Jess held the phone back up to discover both Esther and Minerva smirking.

'You saw him coming, didn't you.'

Minerva laughed and Esther nodded, apologising quietly.

'Great,' Jess mumbled as her mind sorted through the facts. There was a wobble and tears sprung into her eyes. She forced them back, blinking hard, sniffing. Marshall watched with concern.

'Err, we'll call you back,' he said, his eyes on Jess as he took the phone from her and hung up. 'I'm sorry. I honestly didn't mean to creep up and scare you.' He held her tightly as she pushed her cheek against his broad chest. She breathed him in, closing her eyes.

'It's okay,' she murmured into him. 'It's not you. It's just...' She looked up at him. 'This is never going to stop, is it?'

Marshall searched her eyes.

'You could quit,' he told her gently. 'Today. Call Erica, tell her to come fix whatever mess this is and then quit. We'll figure it out.'

A smile pulled at Jess's lips as her insides pointed out the obvious to her. She looked up at him, running her hand down his chest.

'Thank you. But I don't want to quit. I love this job. More than I've ever loved any job.'

Marshall studied her.

'And they're right,' he added quietly. 'You're more than capable of dealing with this. You defeated a demon in the woods,' he whispered.

'Erica, Minerva and the fae did that,' said Jess.

'You got rid of that horrible thing in Ruby's bedroom.'

Jess's chest tightened.

'It threatened my baby.'

'And this thing is threatening your parents.'

Jess focused on her fiancé.

'The damn thing threw a book at you,' she declared, her voice raising.

Marshall smiled and kissed the top of her head.

'So what are you going to do about it?'

'Put that witch bottle back and get rid of it,' said Jess, the uncertainty returning with every word. 'Because everyone keeps telling me that I'm a witch.' Even the angry spirit in Ruby's room had called them witches. Her and her daughter. Jess frowned, glancing back to the kitchen door where she could hear her mother fussing over Ruby. 'I need a moment,' she said, staring past Marshall. 'Can you go check on them all? Keep them safe? And bring me my bag? Please.'

'Anything I can do, I'm here to do it.' Marshall kissed her lips so gently that Jess could almost forget all this nastiness, then he vanished back into the kitchen.

He reappeared for a moment, carrying her handbag and asking if she wanted a cup of tea. Once he'd been sent back into the kitchen, Jess moved to the furthest corner of the garden, tucked herself away between overgrown weeds, out of sight of the kitchen, and sat on the ground. To hell with the dirt that would cling to her clothing.

Pulling a box from her bag, she crossed her legs,

closed her eyes, took a deep breath and centred herself. Eyes still closed, Jess opencd the box and lifted out the pack of cards. They were familiar beneath her touch so she concentrated on her breathing as she shuffled them. Her mind settled, reaching out to the boundaries of the garden, and she allowed it, just as Alfie had taught her. The bird song that filled her ears began to fade, along with the noise of traffic from the nearby high street. There was a shout from a nearby neighbour, but Jess pushed it away.

There. On the edge of her hearing, thumping in the darkness, was *something*.

Jess flinched. She didn't want to talk to the creature and she certainly didn't want to invite it closer. Gently, she eased away from the thing and went back to herself. Lifting her face to the sky, she asked in a whisper, 'What is this thing?'

Jess pulled a card and opened her eyes.

Blowing out her cheeks, she shifted her position – her hips were beginning to scream, she was far too old to be sitting cross-legged on the ground like this – and reached for the book that explained each tarot card. She'd studied the book over and over, between practising pulling the cards, listening to Alfie's advice on channelling her gift of foresight. It meant that she didn't really need to look at the book to know what this card symbolised, but given the situation and the pounding of her heart, it wouldn't hurt to double check.

She flicked through the pages until she found the card and ripped her gaze from the title.

The Devil.

It didn't mean anything. It was like pulling the Death card. It wasn't literal, no one was going to die. This would be the same. Just because she'd pulled the Devil card didn't mean that there was evil, even though she knew there was, and it didn't mean it was a demon, even though she had a suspicion that the two were related.

Calmly, breathing through her nose, Jess read the section about the card with the Devil drawn on it.

Just as she thought, it didn't necessarily mean evil. The Devil was about your darker side, about the negative forces within. All those bad habits, the nasty relationships, negative thinking. The Devil represented choosing short-term pleasure, whatever the consequences.

'In effect, you're selling your soul to the Devil.'

Jess's eyes fixed on that sentence. There were more words below – she already knew what they said – but her gaze kept reading that one sentence over and over.

Shaking herself out of it, she sat back, lowering the card, and glanced back to the house. What did this have to do with her issue? She'd asked what this thing was and had been given the Devil card.

This creature wasn't the Devil, her gut could tell her that. It was, however, negative. That was an under-statement.

Perhaps it was the negative forces of addiction and pain and bad relationships from the house's past made into something a little more solid?

Jess sighed and chewed on the inside of her cheek. She glanced back to the words written beneath that sentence, now engraved in her thoughts.

This card would be pulled when the person in question should face up to the negative forces in their life. A light needed to be shone on the darkness.

In a small paragraph at the bottom, the book mentioned that sometimes the Devil can represent sexuality and exploring wild fantasies and fetishes. Jess hoped to every being listening that those words didn't apply in this situation.

'Right,' she murmured, placing the card back into the deck. 'A new question.' She closed her eyes, shuffling the cards. 'How do I get it out of my parents' house?'

Jess pulled a card, opened her eyes and sighed deeply.

The Devil stared back up at her.

'Well,' she mumbled. 'That's not great.'

Packing her cards away, Jess stared at the house from her corner of the garden. It wasn't much to go on, and she was sure that if Alfie had been there, he would have given her a new lesson in foresight. She had to be missing something.

But Alfie wasn't there. She was on her own.

Which was fine. She was a witch. Apparently. She could do this. Apparently.

Jess shook her head and repeated those thoughts.

I am a witch. I can do this.

'Hell yeah, I can,' she whispered, instantly regretting her choice of words. Pulling a face, Jess scrambled to her feet and made her way back to the house.

A light needed to be shone on the situation and negativity had to be faced. The thing in the house was old, but then perhaps so was the spirit. Esther and Minerva had been right – of course they were, Jess never doubted them. It was time to make contact with the ghost in the house.

33
Jess

'Absolutely not!'

Jess stared at her mother.

'I don't know what else to do, Mum. We can't open the living room door to put the witch bottle back. You are not going up into the loft,' she added quickly as Marshall opened his mouth. 'That thing has already thrown a book at you. Imagine what it'll do if you go up there. Nope. Not happening. No arguments.'

Marshall closed his mouth. Ruby shook her head as she coloured in a unicorn she'd drawn.

'That means you can't say anything more about it,' she quietly told Marshall.

Jess's heart jolted and Marshall gave her a soft smile before moving to sit beside Ruby, reaching for a crayon to help her colour.

'But...what if the thing that's throwing the books and slamming doors and stuff *is* the ghost? If you contact it…' Ginny's eyes reddened as she held back tears.

'Minerva and Esther say there are two separate things here,' Jess soothed. 'And we can trust Minerva and Esther. I trust them both with my life, with Ruby's life. Please, Mum. I'll get them on the phone again, yeah? They can help out?'

Ginny fretted, wringing her hands, looking to her husband who gave a small shrug.

'I'm up for contacting a ghost,' he told the room.

'What about Ruby?' Ginny asked.

As a family, they all turned to look at the little girl who sat with her head down, the tip of her tongue sticking out of her mouth as she concentrated on giving her unicorn a rainbow mane. Feeling their eyes on her, Ruby slowly looked up.

'I'll stay with her. We'll go back to your old house,' Marshall offered.

Jess went to agree but her stomach twisted.

'No, no,' said Ginny. 'If you're going to do this thing, I'll take her back. And the dog. I don't want to be involved.'

Still, Jess hesitated.

'No,' she said eventually. 'I think I need you here, Mum.'

'What? Why?'

Jess sighed and searched her mother's eyes. Jess had inherited their colour. The older she'd got, the more it felt like looking into her future when she locked eyes with her mother. That thought sealed her decision.

'Mum, it turns out that I'm able to do...stuff. Foresight. That's what it's called. Like, I know things. I see things. I can, I don't know, *sense* things. Minerva and Alfie have been helping me hone it, and—'

'Who's Alfie?'

'Erica's...boyfriend.'

Ginny sighed.

'What does he know about it?'

'He's a...' Jess drifted off, blowing out her cheeks. 'He knows about these things. It doesn't matter right now. What matters is that it's real. I have it. And you remember that angry spirit that was in our house last year?'

'That what?' Eddie jumped up from his seat. 'Like a...poltergeist?'

Jess and Ginny turned to him.

'What do you know about ghosts?' Ginny asked.

Eddie shut his mouth and slowly sat back in his chair.

'Nothing,' he muttered under his breath.

Jess gave her father a strange look before Marshall caught her eye, raising his eyebrow.

'Anyway, Mum.' Jess turned back to her mother. 'Remember? I told you. It referred to Ruby as a witch. And—'

'Should you be saying this in front of Ruby?' Ginny asked.

'I know I'm a witch,' said Ruby, not looking up as

she moved on to the unicorn's tail.

'—That means it maybe runs in the family, like it does with Erica,' Jess continued. 'And if Ruby inherited it from me, then that means that I inherited it from...' She drifted off, hoping her mother would get the point.

Eddie turned wide-eyed to his wife and gasped.

'You're a witch, Gin!'

Ginny's mouth had straightened, her eyes narrowing. She shook her head.

'No.'

'Mum—'

'No!'

'I just think it might be helpful if you stayed. I'm not saying you need to learn...anything. Or even do anything.'

Ginny blinked back tears, folding her arms about herself.

'I don't mind staying,' came Ruby's voice.

'That's very sweet, thank you,' Jess told her.

'I don't think whatever's in this house is quite ready for you, though, Rubes,' Marshall told the girl gently.

'Is it like the ghost in my room?'

Marshall nodded.

'A bit, yeah.'

Ruby shivered and looked up at Jess.

'I don't mind helping.'

Jess moved over to her daughter, wrapping her arms tightly around Ruby and kissing her hard.

'Thank you, baby. You can help by staying safe in Granny's old house with...' Jess glanced up at her mother, relenting at the sight of her red eyes. 'Granny. Yeah? You can help to keep her and Bubbles safe.'

Ruby nodded and began packing away her colouring pencils and crayons.

'How will you do it?' Eddie asked, clapping his hands a little too gleefully as he rose from his seat. 'Ouija board?'

'No!' cried Jess and Marshall in unison.

Ruby looked up at them both with wide eyes before shaking her head and continuing to pack away her things.

'Ouija boards are really dangerous,' Jess explained. 'You need to be experienced to use them, otherwise you risk opening something, letting something through. You know, contacting something you didn't mean to contact. No, we're going to reach out to the supposed one and only spirit in this house. The last thing we need is that horrible dark presence pretending to be the spirit and chatting away to us.'

'But you always said that talking about your differences is good,' said Ruby.

Jess hesitated.

'Well, yes. I have said that. And it's true. But... not in this situation.'

'Why not?'

Jess fell into a chair and rubbed her hands over

her face.

'Because we don't know what this thing is,' Marshall offered, helping Ruby put her drawings into her little backpack.

'Then why don't you ask it?'

Marshall looked up at Jess, who glanced at her parents.

'Because I want to talk to the spirit first,' Jess told her daughter gently. 'And you really don't have to worry about this, okay? You just go with Grandma and keep her safe.'

Ruby nodded, growing slightly taller with the responsibility being placed on her tiny shoulders.

'Good. Right. Let's try making contact in here,' said Jess as her father jumped up and bounced on his toes, waiting for instructions. Jess began clearing the table, considering what equipment she might need and whether the apps on her phone would be enough. Her stomach churned, but there wasn't time to dwell on that. Marshall helped Ruby from her chair and led her over to Ginny along with Bubbles who jumped up when Ruby moved. Marshall held out Ruby's bag and Ginny stared through them all.

'Mrs Tidswell?' Marshall murmured when Ginny didn't move. 'Ginny?' He looked to Eddie and Jess helplessly.

'Gin? Take Ruby home,' said Eddie.

'Mum? Are you okay?'

Ginny shook her head, focusing back on the

room.

'I want to stay,' she declared.

Her family exchanged glances.

'Are you sure?' asked Jess.

Ginny nodded.

'Yes. What you said... It makes sense. I want to stay. This is going to be my home. So, I'm staying.' She nodded, although her lower lip quivered.

'Okay.' Jess glanced at Marshall, going through her options as quickly as possible.

'I can take Ruby to the other house,' said Marshall.

Jess shook her head.

'Well, I'm staying here,' said Eddie. 'There's no way I'm missing this. Sorry, love,' he added to Jess, but Jess didn't mind. She was staring down at her daughter as Ruby looked up to her. A silent conversation passed between them, an understanding. Jess smiled to herself.

They had done this a lot when Ruby was a baby. She would stare up into Jess's eyes and Jess would just *feel* it. The connection. The understanding. The communication. She'd considered herself mad, perhaps eccentric, and not told a soul. Perhaps every parent had this connection with their child. What did Jess know? She was a new mother and Ruby was her world.

'Rubes, sweetheart, do you want to stay or go?' Jess asked quietly.

'She can't stay!' Ginny gasped.

Jess and Ruby ignored her.

'I want to stay,' said Ruby. 'I'll be quiet.'

Jess glanced around the kitchen.

'Sit in the corner, over there.' She pointed to the far corner of the kitchen table. 'Do your colouring. Marshall will sit with you and he'll be with you all the time. Okay?'

Ruby nodded and took her bag from Marshall.

'Jess, I really don't think this is the place for her.' Marshall closed the small gap between him and Jess, keeping his voice low. 'I can take her away. Keep her safe.'

Jess smiled at him, taking his big hand in hers and squeezing.

'I know. But it'll be okay. I think we might need her.'

Marshall frowned.

'For what?'

'Power,' said Jess. 'Three generations. When we fought back the demon, I didn't do much but I was present. Just being there helped. When we fought the spirit in our house, we needed all those witches. This is all we have here.' Jess looked over at her family. 'Three generations of witches. I think we need her here. And I need you to keep her safe. Please?'

Marshall's expression made something inside Jess twist.

'Please?' she whispered.

With a sigh, he turned his bulk towards Ruby

and settled beside her.

'We'll all keep an eye on her,' said Eddie. 'What can I do?'

'I don't know,' Jess murmured, staring down at the table. She pulled her phone from her pocket. 'Just...get comfortable.'

Eddie sat back at the table while Ginny stood apart, resting against the kitchen worktop, her arms still crossed.

Jess pulled up the recording app on her phone, the one she used when doing this sort of thing with Erica, and placed the phone in the middle of the table.

'Do you have a torch?'

Ginny passed her the torch from the kitchen worktop. Jess placed it next to the phone.

'What else,' she murmured. There was another app she could use, but it was on Erica's phone. She'd need to download it onto someone else's mobile. Jess sat at the table; she'd do that if none of this worked.

Taking a deep breath, Jess centred herself.

'Should we hold hands?' Eddie whispered.

Jess shook her head.

'It's not a séance. Let's just see what happens.' She took another deep breath. From under the table, Bubbles let out a whine.

'Do you want to call Minerva? You said you might need more witches.' Marshall offered Jess his phone.

Jess contemplated this and then agreed, taking the phone and calling Esther's number.

Once the video call had been established, everything had been explained and the phone was propped up so that Esther and Minerva could see what was happening, Jess began. She tapped the red button on her phone to start the recording.

A wave of self-consciousness swept over her. She'd never done this in front of so many people. Or in front of anyone, for that matter. How did Erica start this?

'Just say what comes naturally,' came Minerva's voice.

Jess nodded and glanced around the kitchen, to the spaces between people.

'Hello,' she started. 'I would like to speak to the spirit here. My name is Jess. Erm...we spoke earlier, remember? My parents here have bought your house, they want to make it into a home again. We're sorry that we removed the witch bottle, we didn't know what it was. But we do now and we'd like to make things right again. And we need your help. Can you please do something so we know that you're here and you can hear us? Say something. My phone is recording this, it'll pick up your voice. Or turn the torch on. Or any appliance. Turn on the oven or the kettle. Or the light. Whatever you can.'

They all waited. Eddie looked around the kitchen, his hands splayed on the table in front of him.

Nothing happened.

After a couple of seconds, Ruby whispered, 'Nothing's happening.'

Jess glanced at Marshall.

'We don't know that yet.' She stopped her phone recording and played the file, holding the phone to her ear with the volume turned up. They all listened to her voice and the complete absence of any background noise.

Jess sighed, and was about to ask Minerva what to try next when her phone battery drained from ninety-six percent to two percent, the bar flashing red. She watched it, blinking, and then reached into her bag for the charger.

'Okay,' she said, plugging it in. 'Hang on.' She went to the app store on her phone. 'I know just the thing. This won't take a moment.'

34

Rick

LONDON, 1864

Two weeks had passed since Alfie had joined Rick on that bench in Regent's Park. Rick had stayed in London, wondering if that was what Alfie had meant by not running, but also secure in the knowledge that London was a dense city. It was easy to hide. Still, that didn't mean the streets weren't dangerous. Rick tried to keep to the busy areas, so that afternoon he found himself on Oxford Street, walking past the shops, avoiding the horse drawn cabs and carriages, and the people in the street. He kept his head down, avoiding eye contact with most people, unless he found himself in the path of someone when he would lift his eyes and apologise.

He jolted as someone stepped into his path.

Swerving, Rick looked up.

'Sorry,' he said, eager to move on.

DCI Burns smiled at him.

'That's all right, Cavanagh.'

Burns put out an arm to block Rick's way and the men stared at one another. Rick's chest heaved as his mind whirred. He could run. He would have to dodge and weave, but he could do it. He only needed a second and he'd be lost again in this crowd.

'Don't run, Cavanagh. I just want to talk.'

Stop running, time traveller.

Alfie's voice sounded in Rick's head and he relented, giving in to Burns.

His old boss led him to a place where they could buy a drink and Burns treated them both to a pie each. They found somewhere to sit, in the corner of the establishment, and Burns took a moment to enjoy his food. Rick left his untouched, watching the other man.

'Are you going to arrest me?' he asked eventually.

Burns shook his head.

'Not yet.'

Rick frowned.

'Why not?'

Burns looked up at Rick, wiping the crumbs from the corners of his mouth.

'Because I have a proposal for you.'

Rick frowned, and in the pause that followed,

Burns sipped his drink and pulled a face.

'They haven't perfected coffee yet.'

Rick made a noise of agreement.

'What's the proposal?' he asked eventually.

Burns sighed through his nose, tapping his long fingers on the table between them.

'A job,' he started, his eyes flicking up to Rick. 'You understand that you can't continue as a detective, not in the same capacity, at least.'

Rick's frown deepened.

'I was under the impression that I would be fired, arrested and possibly sent to prison for what I've done.'

Burns laughed, catching the attention of the table nearby.

'You won't be sent to prison, or arrested for that matter.'

'What? Why? It says in the handbook—'

'We have to say that. For legal reasons.'

'But... We are the law. We're the police.'

Burns shrugged.

'Would you prefer to go to prison or do you want to hear this job proposal?'

'Job proposal,' Rick murmured, his stomach turning.

Burns pulled out a piece of paper and a pen from his pocket, pushing them over to Rick.

'NDA,' he explained. 'Sign it and we'll continue. You can't talk about what I'm about to tell you with anyone. Although, I guess right now that isn't a problem, is it.'

Rick swallowed against his dry throat, pulling the paper and pen closer. He scanned the fine print as Burns watched him. Then, with trembling fingers but sure that he wasn't signing his life away, he scratched his signature onto the form.

Burns took the paper and pen, slipping them back into his pocket, and returned to pulling the pastry from the remains of his pie.

'You'll know about the different levels of detective positions,' he started. 'Constable, sergeant, inspector, chief inspector.'

Rick watched him, a tiredness seeping into his bones.

'Yeah.'

'We also have a branch of undercover detectives. In a way.'

'The undercover branch was discontinued four years ago,' said Rick. He remembered the fall out of the decision, and the horrific circumstances that had made the decision such an easy one to make.

Burns shook his head.

'The public wanted it gone, so we made it disappear. But it still exists.' He lifted his eyes to Rick, waiting for his reaction.

Rick gritted his teeth.

'You lied to everyone,' he murmured.

'Not me personally. Except, in a way, yes.'

Rick took a steadying breath as his stomach churned.

'Dealing with crime requires undercover work,' Burns continued. 'We lost the funding, so the higher ups made a deal with MI5.'

Rick almost laughed.

'MI5? So, what, they all became spies?'

Burns smiled.

'Not exactly. They're still detectives, not agents. But they work to the strict rules of MI5, they follow their code of conduct, and in return, we get use of their funding and resources.'

'Their code of conduct? Sir, last year an MI5 agent went rogue and murdered his family.'

'Yes, that was regrettable.'

'And since then, agents have been caught committing abuse, torture even.'

'Hmm.'

'They're no better than we were four years ago. So, nothing's changed. Has it? The public revolted and our bosses said they would do what was right, but they didn't. Did they.' It wasn't a question, but Rick let it linger there, curious as to Burns's response.

'You'd have a purpose, a higher salary – yes, it would be a promotion – more freedom than before, you've proven yourself more than capable of thinking outside the box, more responsibility, more authority, and your pension. What do you say?'

Rick shook his head.

'I haven't proven myself capable, sir. I broke the rules, didn't think it through and I've lost my wife and child. I've lost everything I loved.'

Burns's smile was cruel.

'Which means you have nothing left to lose, except for your freedom.'

Rick leaned back.

'Are you blackmailing me?'

'Of course not, Cavanagh. I'm just pointing out that if you don't take this position, I'll probably have to arrest you. I can't just let you swan off into whatever time you want and get away with it.'

Rick swallowed on a lump of bile.

'Sounds like I don't have much of a choice.'

Burns searched his eyes.

'I don't see the problem, Cavanagh. I'm offering you a promotion, your pension and new opportunities. You'll travel through time, meet new people. You might meet a new woman. Fall in love. Start a family. Your wife might still fall in love with you and you'll get your old future back. Who knows. Bouncing around time aimlessly like this certainly won't help or change anything.'

The golden watch burned against Rick from its secret place in his pocket.

'Think about it,' Burns continued. 'I'll give you a week.' He pulled a card from his pocket and passed it to Rick. 'Go to this time, these co-ordinates, when you've made your decision. If you miss the deadline, then we'll hunt you down.'

Burns stood and brushed the crumbs from his long coat. He gave Rick a swift nod, turned on his heel and left. Rick watched him go and then scrambled outside, vomiting violently into the street.

35

Erica

'I really don't want to mess anything up,' Erica started, her eyes still on Alfie and Fen off to the side. 'If you're here because you truly want to be, then that's fine. Your mum just wants to know you're okay.' She turned to Bethany and found the girl staring forward, eyes glazed, looking at nothing.

'It's a lot to take in,' she murmured.

'It is?'

'Magic and...fae.' Bethany blinked, glancing sideways at Erica. 'I've known Fen...' She drifted off.

'All your life?'

Bethany bit her bottom lip.

'No. I don't know. He knows my parents, though. I can trust him.'

'Fae are older than they look,' Erica explained, looking back to Alfie. 'They're not like us. Well, except that sometimes they are. Maybe over the centuries we've rubbed off on them a little, I don't know.'

Bethany was frowning, deep in thought.

'I feel like I've known him for so long,' she murmured.

'You have,' said Erica. 'You know that circle of mushrooms in your front garden? Shows up every spring and autumn, I'm guessing?'

'Yeah?'

'It's a fairy circle. My best guess, it's Fen's way of claiming that property, a way of marking you out as his. Don't worry, it's more of a protection thing. No other fae will go close to your family because of Fen. The way your mum talked, Fen's been known to your family since you were a baby.'

Panic flashed across Bethany's face.

'It's okay,' Erica told her with a small smile. 'Alfie found me before I was born. When my mum was pregnant with me.' She gave a small laugh. 'Apparently he got over-excited when he realised what I would be for him and told my mum. She became protective, as she should have, and forbade me from meeting him. I only met him about a year ago.' She looked back to Alfie. 'Sometimes I wish I'd met him earlier. Sometimes I wonder what would have happened if I'd met him when I was your age.'

'Fen's been around since I was a baby?' Bethany murmured. 'That's...that's so creepy.'

Erica chuckled and Bethany flinched.

'Yeah, I guess it is. But it's their way.'

'And then he was just waiting in the woods and I happened to stroll by so he invited me into his world?'

Erica nodded.

'Extremely creepy,' she agreed. 'Lots of countries have their own folklore about being tempted into other worlds by supernatural creatures. Especially the Celtic folklore. Scottish stories of fairies and fae are full of the dangers of being tempted into their world. The reality isn't always like that, though.'

Bethany was hugging herself, slouching, making herself as small as possible on the tree trunk.

'What am I doing here?'

Erica turned her body to face Bethany and studied the girl. Her stomach turned.

'What are you worried about?' she asked gently.

Bethany shook her head.

'Who can I trust? Mum and Dad didn't tell me about Fen, Fen's tricked me here, or so you say, and who the hell are you? Fen said you're a witch. Maybe you're the liar in all this.'

Erica sighed and sat back, wiggling her toes in her shoes as the throbbing eased.

'That's fair enough. And right that you should think like that. You can't be sure who you can trust right now. But your gut knows. Your gut knows if you should trust me and your gut knows if you should trust Fen. And yes, I'm a witch, but that doesn't mean anything other than that my family know about the fae and other things that most people don't know about. It's nothing scary. I promise you.'

Bethany searched Erica's eyes for a moment and then glanced over to Fen, nibbling on her lip. She was going to make it bleed.

Erica took a steadying breath.

'The fae have the use of magic. I don't fully understand it myself, but my mother and grandmother do, to a degree.'

'Are they witches too?'

'Alfie's been using my grandmother's name to put the fear of whoever these guys worship into them whenever they try to...I don't know, intimidate me or whatever it is they think they're doing.' Erica nodded. 'She's also in a relationship with a fae and you can bet your arse there was no coercion used there. No tricks, no magic. My grandmother wouldn't have allowed it.' Erica glanced away. 'It is possible to have a healthy, good relationship with a fae without magic.' She looked over at the men. 'I don't know why they feel they have to resort to magic. I guess they get a little desperate, knowing what they know.'

'What do they know?' Bethany asked quietly. She was still hugging herself but her grip was loosening.

Erica smiled at her.

'I think we'd call it soulmates,' she tried. 'Some of them have gifts, if you want to call them that, but all fae know when they find the person they will fall in love with. They know the moment they lay eyes on them. And they live for so long, although Alfie won't tell me how long. So, Fen knew he would fall in love with you when he first met you, maybe when you were a baby – it's not as creepy as it sounds. It's sort of like they can see into our souls. And then he's had to wait all these years for you to grow up and to find out if you'll reject him or not.'

Bethany looked past Erica to Fen still talking to Alfie.

'Soulmates,' she murmured.

Erica studied her.

'But that doesn't mean you have to say yes,' she told the girl. 'You don't have to fall in love with him, you don't have to be with him, you don't have to do anything he says. Just because there's something in your souls that are connected, or whatever, doesn't mean you're not your own person, Bethany. You make your own life choices. And you can always change your mind.'

Bethany sighed.

'This is a lot.'

Erica laughed, dragging Alfie and Fen's attention.

'Yeah. Tell me about it.'

There was a pause as both women went into their own worlds.

'I don't know how I feel,' said Bethany after a moment.

Taking another deep breath, Erica pulled up her

bag and found the bottle her mother had given her. She showed it to Bethany.

'My mum's a herbalist witch. A garden witch, if you like. She doesn't like the fae much and she doesn't really deal with spirits or the spiritual world. What she likes are plants, flowers and herbs. And trees. She loves trees. And while me and my grandmother will talk to spirits and, apparently, gallivant with fae, my mum will make potions. Like this one. She knows the charm magic that the fae use and this is something of an antidote. If Fen has used magic to coerce you into being here and cloud your mind, this will clear it. If he hasn't, then, well, it won't do anything. I assume it'll taste nice.' Erica pulled the stopper from the bottle and sniffed it. 'It smells nice.' She offered it to Bethany who leaned away a little.

'It won't do you any harm and just a sip should do,' Erica told her, putting the stopper back and making it tight. 'You don't even have to drink it now. Here. Just take it. Do what you want with it.' She offered it again and this time Bethany tentatively took it. Studying the bottle, she placed it beside her without a suggestion that she might taste or even sniff at the contents.

'What was that?' cried Fen, rushing over. 'What are you giving her, witch?'

Erica gave Fen a look.

'Something that will clear her head if you've been using the bluebells to cloud her judgement, that's all. She doesn't have to take it, it's just an option. And if you haven't been coercing her, then it won't matter, will it?' She gave Fen a sweet smile, but he only had eyes for Bethany. His breath came hard, his chest heaving, and he reached out a trembling hand to her.

Bethany looked at it and then up at him.

'Let's go to London,' he told her. 'Now. Right now.'

'You've been walking me in circles, haven't you,' Bethany murmured.

Fen shook his head as Alfie appeared behind him, exchanging a look with Erica.

'Be honest with me, Fen. If I mean anything to you, you need to be honest with me,' said Bethany.

Erica didn't dare move so she kept her eyes on Alfie, not wanting to intrude on the young couple.

Fen's exhale came out in a rumble of emotion.

'I may have...we may have...yes. But only a little. And only because I wondered if you might change your mind.'

'You hoped I would change my mind,' Bethany corrected him. 'You really hate London that much?'

Fen looked down at his feet.

'In Fen's defence, it takes a special kind of fae to go to London,' said Alfie, crossing his arms over his chest. 'It's a big city overflowing with magic. Sometimes it's hard to breathe there.'

'And the city fae are terrifying,' said Fen.

Over Fen's shoulder, Alfie gave the younger fae

an amused look.

'The city is terrifying,' Erica muttered before she could stop herself.

They all turned to her and Alfie's amusement turned into a grin.

'I don't find it scary,' Bethany murmured.

'The fearlessness of youth,' said Erica. Fen nodded but stopped when Bethany looked up at him.

Falling to his knees in front of her, he took her hand and looked up with large green eyes.

'But I will go there for you. I will do anything for you.'

Erica's heart squeezed and she instinctively looked up to Alfie to find him staring back at her. His grin gone. He gave her a small twitch of a smile and Erica's whole body reacted. The desire to leap into his arms, to kiss his lips, was overwhelming, but she remained seated, transfixed by his blue eyes.

She jumped as Bethany burst into tears.

36

Erica

Fen scrambled to his feet, bending over Bethany and taking her in his arms in an awkward embrace.

'My love! What is it? What's wrong?'

'I just want this to be over,' she told them quietly, between sobs.

Alfie and Erica exchanged a pained look.

'Want what to be over?' Erica soothed, reaching out to lay her hand on Bethany's back. The girl pulled away from Fen and wiped her wet cheeks with the back of her hand. Erica scrambled through her bag and pulled out some clean tissues.

'This?' Fen asked quietly, leaning back, his eyes wide.

Bethany shook her head as she dried her face.

'No,' she said, shuddering as another sob threatened to take over. 'My exams.' She sniffed, her bottom lip quivering as she fought back another wave of tears.

Erica smiled.

'Exams feel like they'll go on forever and that they mean the world, but they don't,' she told Bethany gently. 'Is that why you want to go to London now?'

'I'm supposed to get my A Levels and go to London and become a famous fashion designer. But I need the grades to get into university to get the graduate jobs.'

Erica made a *pish* noise, catching Bethany's attention.

'Or you could just make the best designs you can and get through on talent. Your exam grades aren't going to make or break you, they'll just give you more options. I got good grades and look at me! I ended up in the career I thought I wanted and hated it, and myself. I dragged myself to work every day, got passed over for promotion again and again, worked myself to the point of exhaustion and for what? Now I'm in business with my best friend and I'm in love with...' Erica glanced up at Alfie. 'A wonderful man,' she told him as much as she was telling Bethany. 'And I'm happy.' She turned back to the girl. 'I'm earning less, sure, and there's no career path as such, but I'm incredibly happy. And that's what's important. To have fun, to do things that make you happy and to have adventures.' She glanced at Fen whose face twitched.

'My parents argue all the time. It's my fault,' Bethany murmured. She was staring at the ground now, rocking back and forth ever so slightly as her body tried to soothe itself. Erica scooched closer to her.

'It's not your fault.'

'They argue when I don't study. They argue when I get upset. They even argue when I talk about wanting to go to London.'

Erica smiled.

'They're worried about you, Bethany. They want the best for you and they're scared. My parents did something similar. My mum wanted me to have the career and big job, but my dad was worried about what it might do to me. My mum didn't want me to meet Alfie, ever. She was scared that... Actually I don't know what she was scared of. Her little girl running away with a fae who must be really old because he won't tell me his age.' She gave Alfie a look. He smirked and winked at her. 'But here I am, my own boss, no job security and in love with Alfie. My parents are fine. Everything's fine. It didn't feel like it would be, especially when I was your age, but things work themselves out. This is just life. Exams suck, and then they're over and you just get on with life.' Erica leaned closer, trying to make Bethany concentrate on her. 'The important thing is that you make your own decisions. And running away with a fae isn't necessarily the answer to how you're feeling right now.'

Fen scrambled back to Bethany, taking her hands again.

'I'm here for you,' he told her quietly. 'Tell me what you need. I'll take you to London right now. We can go right now.'

Bethany focused on him, blinking, a final tear rolling down her cheek. Fen reached up and stroked it away with his thumb.

'Did you drug me?' she asked quietly.

Fen froze, staring up at her. Finally, he shook his head.

'A little,' he admitted. 'I waited among the bluebells because I thought they might... But I didn't *drug* you.'

'Are the bluebells, or whatever, strong enough to make me come here when I really didn't want to?' she asked. When Fen didn't answer, she glanced down at the bottle Erica had given her, now resting by her side. 'Can I trust them?'

Fen gawped.

'What?'

'Can I trust them? These two?' Bethany gestured to Erica and Alfie. 'Can I trust you?' she added quietly.

Fen seemed to collapse in on himself. He rocked back on his heels and nodded.

'You can trust them. You can trust me. None of us mean you harm.'

Bethany didn't respond, she only stared at Fen, as if trying to read his mind. He watched her, panic growing in his eyes.

'Bethany.' Erica's quiet voice drew the girl's

attention and Fen inhaled sharply, broken from the spell, shuddering a little. Alfie moved behind him, his presence steadying the younger fae. 'To withstand the fae, you must know yourself,' said Erica.

Both Fen and Alfie looked at her.

'You must know yourself enough to understand what you want.'

Alfie scoffed at that and Erica glanced up at him.

'Okay, I might not know exactly what I want,' she told him.

'Yes, you do. You just won't admit it,' he mumbled.

'But I know myself enough to know that I am here out of my own choice.' Erica turned back to Bethany. 'Fae live for a really long time, Bethany. Fen will have waited so long for you, but he can wait longer. We only have short lives. If you want to be with Fen, then that's fine, but don't forget to live your own life. Fen wants to spend your life with you, but you need to live your life too. However you want. You know? Go to London, meet other people, discover who you are and who you want to be, and what you want to become. You're allowed to go out into the world and fall in love, get your heart broken and fall in love again.'

Bethany slowly looked back to Fen whose eyes had grown wide, shimmering with building tears. He shook his head at her.

'And how did that work out for you?' Alfie asked

quietly, his voice low.

Erica's heart jolted painfully and she met his eyes.

'Well...'

Bethany turned to her expectantly.

'We're all different,' Erica continued. 'Okay, fine, I didn't know Alfie existed when I was your age. We were kept apart so I just went out and lived my life like anyone else.'

'And,' Alfie prompted.

Erica sighed.

'And nothing. I'm in my thirties and never had the big love. Not until...' Erica looked back to Alfie and sighed. 'We're all different,' she repeated to Bethany. 'We all have different experiences. Some people are happy to fall in love at your age and spend the rest of their life with that person, some people aren't. I'm just trying to tell you that you have choices. And deciding to be with Fen doesn't mean that's the end. You can leave whenever you want to.' Erica gave Fen a look but the fae was rigid, eyes brimming with unspent tears, fixated on Bethany. 'And you'll have those choices throughout your life. Whether you do well in your exams or not. You always have a choice over what you do next. I don't want you to ever feel trapped or resentful. Don't have regrets.'

Alfie softened, cocking his head slightly to the side in thought as he watched Erica. She tried to ignore him.

There was a silence as they waited for Bethany and the girl stared down at her hands in her lap. Fen inhaled sharply as Bethany reached for the bottle Erica had given her. She removed the lid and sniffed the contents.

'This is safe?' she checked.

Erica and Alfie nodded and, eventually, so did Fen, the motion finally spilling his tears down his cheeks. Bethany hesitated at the sight. Her free arm lifted towards him but then stopped and she took a deep breath. Raising the bottle to her lips, she took the smallest of sips and then looked at Erica.

'Do I have to drink all of it?'

Erica shook her head.

'As much as you want to,'

Bethany studied the bottle.

'It tastes nice.'

Erica smiled.

'That's because my mum made it,' she murmured.

Bethany looked down at her lap.

'I miss my mum.'

Fen made to move but Erica got there first, sliding close and putting an arm around Bethany's shoulders.

'You can go home whenever you like, can't she, Fen.'

Fen nodded, moving closer and crouching back down so he could peer up at Bethany.

'Whenever you like,' he whispered.

Bethany reached out and brushed the tears from his cheek. Fen closed his eyes and leaned into her touch.

'I'm sorry,' he murmured, eyes closed. 'I'll always be here for you. Always. I am yours. And I promise to always do my best to make you happy. I'll make sure you have everything you need and want.'

Bethany pulled her hand away and, after a beat, lifted the bottle and drank the contents.

37

Bethany

The liquid tasted sweet and fresh, and Bethany's body welcomed it. She drank as much as she dared and then, licking her lips, replaced the bottle's top and passed it back to Erica. The woman took it, placing it back in her bag. For a moment, Bethany was catapulted into her childhood, eager to ask the strange woman with the reassuring tone and aura of safety whether the drink would make her grow or shrink.

A laugh bubbled up inside and she slapped a hand over her mouth as it escaped.

Fen – soft, sweet Fen – watched with wide eyes. She wished he wouldn't look so scared. She wished he would be strong for her. She was so tired of having to be strong.

'I feel like Alice in Wonderland,' she murmured, and Erica gave a soft snort beside her. Bethany looked up, beyond Fen, to the fae standing behind him. Alfie. He was handsome, more rugged than Fen, older, more mature. Would Fen grow old with her?

Her gaze dropped back down to him.

Stomach roiling as it filled with the potion, Bethany swallowed on a wave of nausea that quickly passed. Her vision seemed to clear momentarily, making everything brighter and then dull. She kept her eyes on Fen, wondering if he'd slowly morph before her, from the attractive young man to a hideous creature.

He didn't.

Fen stayed as he was, as he'd always been. A hand on her stomach, Bethany felt it in her gut. All of it. The knowledge that he'd been there when she was too young to remember, the fact that he'd waited all these years for her.

Gritting her teeth, Bethany fought against the emotions.

That wasn't her fault. She never asked him to wait. She didn't owe him anything.

As if hearing her thoughts, Fen's face fell.

Still, she was drawn to him. Inexplicably drawn to him. There might as well be magnets under their skin, pulling them towards one another.

Bethany glanced at Erica.

'You love your fae?' she murmured.

The woman looked up at Alfie and smiled.

'I do.'

'You're happy?'

Erica turned and met her eyes.

'I am.'

Bethany waited for more. A warning. That such happiness had come at a cost, that she should stay away from such magic. But Erica only sighed.

'I just don't want you to miss out,' she repeated. 'But ultimately, you need to follow your gut. Your gut knows best. How are you feeling?'

Bethany swallowed and waited to see what her stomach would do. It had settled. In fact, she felt great.

'I'm okay,' she said warily.

'Do you want to go to London?' Fen asked quietly.

She met his eyes and studied him, waiting for her gut to tell her what to do.

'Yes,' she said finally. 'But not now. I think I want to go home.'

'But—'

Fen was cut off by Alfie placing his hand on the younger fae's shoulder.

'She'll still be,' came Alfie's quiet voice.

Fen closed his mouth and nodded.

'I like it here,' said Bethany, looking around the forest. 'I like you,' she told Fen. 'But I'm not sure about... I think I want to go home. I want my mum.'

Jess

Ruby watched her mother playing with her phone. Beyond her stood the ghost. Even the witches on the phone screen, resting on the table, didn't seem to notice him. Beside her, Bubbles lifted her head. Ruby watched the dog staring at the man. The dog didn't growl, so Ruby didn't say anything. Even when the man approached her, walking around her mother and leaning down, his gaze on Ruby.

'Hello, Ruby.'

Ruby shivered.

'I'm James.'

She kept her eyes down on her drawing.

'It's ever so kind of your parents to help me.'

She lifted her gaze to him and found kind eyes staring back.

'You remind me of someone I used to know. She was a pretty girl, just like you. But she was not as good at drawing.' He looked at the papers in front of her. 'These are very good. You have a talent for art.'

Ruby smiled and glanced back to her work, her chest swelling.

'I do hope we can be friends, Ruby,' said the man. 'Especially if your family will be living here. I am sure we will see a lot of each other, hmm?'

Ruby went to open her mouth, but snapped it shut as Bubbles jumped up and growled.

The man disappeared as she blinked. Her stomach in knots, she looked up at her mother. Bubbles shoved her head into Ruby's lap, licked her hand and then settled beside her. Ruby took a deep breath as Marshall, on her other side, leaned into her.

The ghost reappeared in the corner of the room. He gave her a small smile before turning his attention to her mother, still fiddling with her phone.

Ruby found herself staring at him, his words repeating in her head as she drew comfort from Bubbles' proximity, leaning into Marshall to steady her swirling stomach.

∞⊗

Satisfied, Jess sat back from the kitchen table and cleared her throat.

'All right. This machine' – she gestured to the app on her phone in the middle of the table – 'will give us words. If you can, use your energy to choose which words you would like the machine to say. Okay, let's give this a go.'

On her phone's screen, words popped up at random. Jess kept her eye on it as the room about her stilled. 'I understand that you might not be strong enough to use this machine. But can you please try,' said Jess, keeping her tone gentle. 'Is this your house?'

They waited.

Esther and Minerva sipped their tea, listening quietly.

On the screen, words flickered as they changed.
Home.

Eddie made an *oomph* noise as he startled. They all stared at the phone in the middle of the table where the four letter word remained. The app fell silent, and after a moment, the words began to flicker again, ready for the next question.

'What was that? Did the spirit say "home"?' came Minerva's voice.

As one, everyone turned to Jess.

She smiled to herself.

'Yes,' she said for Minerva's benefit. 'This was your home,' she clarified, ignoring her family for the time being. Ruby blinked and then returned to her drawing as Marshall placed a hand protectively on her back. 'Thank you,' Jess continued. 'Do you know what's in this house with us?'

'Clever girl,' Minerva murmured softly.

Time.

Everyone turned to Jess again.

'Time? Well, there's time everywhere,' said Eddie. He leaned forward across the table. 'This is amazing,' he whispered to his daughter.

Jess swallowed a bubble of laughter.

Evil.

Her laughter died of its own accord. She stared at the word on her phone screen.

'Time is evil?' asked Eddie.

'Oh, this is ridiculous,' Ginny muttered from behind them.

'The shadow people,' Esther suggested.

'Are the shadows the time?' Jess murmured, leaning across the table towards the phone.

There was a long pause, long enough that Jess wondered if they'd lost contact, and then—

Yes.

'But the shadows aren't evil.'

Devil.

Jess's blood ran cold. Leaning back, she hugged herself, gritting her teeth, her tarot pack burning a hole in her bag by her feet.

'Jessica,' came her mother's warning.

'It isn't the Devil,' said Jess, knowing it as a truth in her gut. 'Is it a demon?' She glanced sideways at her daughter just in time to see Ruby hesitate.

Evil.

Jess glanced to Minerva and Esther, but Minerva only gestured for her to continue.

'We need to put the witch bottle back,' Jess explained. 'But I think we'll need help doing that. Can you help us?'

Witch.

Jess bristled.

'Witches aren't evil,' she murmured gently, her stomach turning.

Help.

Off to the side, Marshall sighed.

'Is there no other way of doing this?' he asked, a thick arm now around Ruby.

'Can you see the spirit?' Jess asked Minerva.

She shook her head, sipping her tea.

'Sorry, my love. I can't. My guess is that it doesn't wish to be seen.' Placing her cup down, she shuffled closer to the screen, and shouted, 'We don't wish you any harm! We want to help! Show yourself to me so we can talk!'

Esther pulled a face.

'You don't need to shout, Mum.'

'Not to them, no. But who knows what this spirit can and can't hear.' Minerva sat back and returned to her tea while she waited.

'You can see spirits?' Eddie asked.

'Usually,' Minerva told him. 'As I say, when they wish to be seen. Make yourself known!' she shouted.

'Mum!' Esther chided.

'Try using more words,' said Jess. 'Can you do that? Try using more words to say what you mean.'

There was a pause, and then Jess asked, 'Do you need help?'

They all watched her phone screen on the table.

Devil.

Jess held up a hand to silence her father who opened his mouth to speak.

Sent.

Jess's gaze flicked up to Minerva who slowly lowered her cup of tea.

'The Devil sent it,' Jess murmured. She turned back to her phone. 'Is it a demon?'

The words on the screen flickered, jumbling, as if the spirit was searching for the right letters.

I.

Jess swallowed, glancing again at Minerva.

M.

Minerva's eyes widened.

P.

The phone screen went blank and then the usual flickering words appeared.

'Imp,' said Eddie. 'It spelled out imp.'

'The Devil sent an imp,' said Jess.

Minerva and Esther leaned forward.

'Have you heard of imps before?' Jess asked them.

Minerva nodded.

'We have.'

Jess waited for more but Minerva didn't seem inclined to elaborate.

'Okay.' She turned back to her phone. 'How do

we stop it?'

Her phone struggled, the low battery warning flashing again despite it being plugged into the wall.

Witch.

Bottle.

Witch.

Cottage.

Witch.

Help.

The words came in a strange garbled rush, and then Jess's phone died.

'Well,' said Minerva. 'That was exciting.'

'Any idea what all of that meant?' Eddie asked.

Jess was reaching for her phone. They needed to give it some time to recharge before she could turn it back on.

'Something about a witch,' Marshall mumbled. 'You think we can trust this thing?'

Jess nodded.

'Witch bottle,' she said. 'We know what that is. Witch cottage. Presumably they go together. Which might mean that "witch" and "help" go together too.'

'We are witches who want to help!' Minerva shouted into the camera. Esther glared at her.

'Witch cottage,' Jess mumbled, attempting to turn her phone on. It refused, giving her a low battery symbol instead. She shook her head, leaving it charging, and reached for the phone currently video calling Minerva and Esther. 'I'm going to take you both outside and you're going to explain imps to me,' she told them. When she realised her tone, she bit her tongue, hesitating.

Smiles crept over Esther and Minerva's faces.

'Of course,' said Esther.

'Absolutely,' said Minerva.

'Witch cottage,' Ginny murmured.

Jess glanced at her mother. Ginny shrugged and looked away. Jess exchanged a look with Marshall. His eyes were dark – he was anything but happy with the situation – but he tightened his grip on Ruby and gave Jess a nod.

'I'm coming too!' Eddie declared, standing and following Jess out into the garden. Bubbles trotted out after them. Eddie took the patio chairs to the bottom of the garden and sat beside his daughter, staring into the phone screen.

'You're really enjoying this, aren't you,' Jess murmured.

Eddie nodded.

'I can't believe this is your job.' He gently elbowed his daughter and she swallowed a laugh.

'Yeah. Well. Don't get too excited. It's more scary than exciting at this point.' She turned back to Esther and Minerva. 'So. There's an imp in the house.'

Minerva was nodding.

'Fascinating creatures,' she began. 'Originating in hell, supposedly. They're a form of demon, so it makes sense that the spirit would say that the Devil sent it.'

'So we are dealing with a demon.'

'In a way,' said Minerva. 'But not like you're thinking. This isn't the demon in the woods, Jess. This is something else.'

'Imp. A creature of chaos who seeks to destroy,' Esther read from a book she'd produced seemingly from nowhere.

'Marvellous,' said Jess, looking back to the house. 'That thing's in there now with my mum, fiancé and little girl.' She turned to the phone. 'What else do you know? Should we go get them out now?'

'I wouldn't worry,' said Minerva.

'Imps became a popular notion in the sixteenth century for working with the Devil,' Esther continued, her eyes scanning the pages of her book. She closed it, putting it down beyond the camera. 'But, of course, in the seventeenth century some pious man decided they must work with witches instead, given that any woman with the power of healing or who lived on her own must be evil.' Esther bit down on her words and sighed heavily.

'So...when the spirit says "witch", it might be more of an accusation?' Jess attempted.

Minerva screwed up her face.

'Some witch bottles were put in place to catch witches.' She glanced at Esther who sighed again.

'Brilliant.' Jess rubbed her hands over her face. 'Great. Another spirit who doesn't like witches.

Maybe that's why it's acting up. Because of me and Ruby?'

'And your mother,' Minerva agreed.

Eddie clapped his hands.

'This is wonderful.'

The women stared at him.

'How is it wonderful?' Jess asked her father.

'It's interesting. Fascinating. Oh, come on, we'll get it sorted. Your mother and I wanted an adventure and we're getting one.'

Jess's stress gave way to mild horror.

'Not like this, Dad.'

Eddie met her eyes and hesitated.

'Right. Okay. So, what do we do?' he asked Minerva and Esther.

'Put the witch bottle back,' said Esther.

'Talk to the spirit some more,' said Minerva.

'And maybe sell the house,' Esther suggested.

It was Minerva's turn to give her daughter a dirty look.

'And why would they want to do that? No, no. There's no need for that. We'll figure this thing out.'

'First things first, then,' said Jess, standing. 'Let's get my daughter out of there. Come on, Dad.'

They wandered back into the kitchen, and as Jess opened her mouth to declare that Ginny would take Ruby back to their old house, her mother spoke.

'The witch cottage is the one down by the woods.'

Jess stared at her and then flinched as Eddie

slapped his thigh.

'Of course! What's it called? Rose Cottage? Something pretty like that. By the woods. The one in all the stories.'

'What stories?' Jess asked, placing the phone holding Minerva and Esther back on the table and checking the battery level on her own phone. It turned on without a problem. She glanced over at Ruby who was still drawing, Marshall's hand on her back. Bubbles plonked herself down at Ruby's feet.

'Some old stories people tell about this town,' Eddie explained. 'The folklore. This is a medieval market town, you know.' He lifted his chin, proud.

Jess waited and then prompted further, 'And what are the stories?'

'A witch lives in the cottage at the edge of the woods,' Ginny murmured, her voice low and her eyes glazed. Jess studied her. 'A witch has always lived in that cottage, for as long as anyone can remember. It gets passed down, from witch to witch.'

'From mother to daughter?' Jess asked.

Ginny shook her head.

'No child has ever lived there.'

'Or so the stories go,' Eddie clarified. 'It's a nice little cottage. But it's small. Tough to raise a family in there these days, I reckon. Low ceilings and small windows.'

'I wonder if the witch there made witch bottles,' came Minerva's voice.

Jess had been pondering the same thing. She opened the app on her phone and glanced around the room.

'Hello? Are you still there? Is this what you meant by "witch" and "cottage"?'

They waited. Ruby continued colouring, Marshall continued leaning protectively over her. Ginny shook herself and filled the kettle while Eddie watched over Jess's shoulder.

Yes.

Eddie whooped.

'It meant the cottage!' he declared.

'Did the witch there make this witch bottle?' Jess asked.

There was a long pause, but finally her phone spoke.

Yes.

'Why?' Eddie asked.

Jess shook her head.

'You need to be more specific. Did they make this bottle because of the imp?'

Yes.

'The imp that the Devil sent?' asked Eddie.

Yes.

'How do you know your phone isn't just broken and repeating itself?' Ginny muttered.

Jess twisted her lips in thought.

'What's your name?' she asked after a moment.

Minerva clapped her hands.

'Good girl,' came her soft voice from the phone

beside Jess's.

J.

'Jay? Good name,' said Eddie. He closed his mouth when Jess hushed him.

A.

M.

The letters stopped, the words flicking.

'Jam?' Eddie rubbed the stubble on his chin. 'Not such a good name. Maybe a nickname, I suppose.'

'James,' Jess whispered. 'Is your name James?'

The kitchen light blinked on and Ginny squealed.

'Mummy.'

Jess snapped round to Ruby. The little girl had stopped colouring and was leaning into the warmth and comfort of Marshall.

'The man says you need to put the bottle back, Mummy.'

A shiver ran over Jess.

'What man, sweetheart?'

Ruby pointed to the empty corner of the kitchen, by the closed door.

'That man.'

'Oh good god,' said Ginny, stepping away from the corner. Eddie studied the empty space, placing himself between the invisible man and his granddaughter.

'Is the man's name James?' Jess asked Ruby.

Ruby nodded.

'He says you need to be quick. It's coming.

What's coming?'

'Don't answer that!' Jess yelled towards the empty corner of the room. 'Okay. Mum, get Ruby out of here. Now. Dad, where's the box and the witch bottle? Marshall, I need your help. We're getting back in the living room.'

'I want to stay,' said Ginny.

Eddie passed the box to Jess and then stared at his wife.

'What? But you hate all this stuff.'

Ginny hugged herself and shrugged.

'This is my home. My daughter. My grand-daughter. And I want this thing gone. I'm staying.' Despite the way Ginny lifted her head high, there was still a tremor in her voice.

'Good for you,' said Minerva. 'Let her, Jess. You're going to need all the witches you can muster. And we're here. Of course. Now all we need is a plan.'

Jess stared down at her daughter.

'I'll take her,' said Marshall.

Jess shook her head.

'I need you,' she murmured, and in that moment she couldn't voice exactly why she needed Marshall there. She had a feeling there were just too many reasons. She needed his strength and his protection, his warmth, his logic, his encourage-ment. She needed *him*.

He appeared torn, looking between Ruby and Jess.

'I can't explain why. It goes against everything I would normally say, but Ruby is going to stay,' said Jess quietly. As the words were spoken, her gut stopped churning. Yes, this was right. She met Marshall's eyes. 'And I need you to stay with her. In here. Shut the door behind us, keep her safe.'

Marshall nodded, taking Ruby in his large arms.

Jess turned to Minerva.

'How do we do this?'

39

Jess

'Quickly,' said Minerva. 'And don't forget to take us with you.'

Eddie picked up the phone, holding it up so that Esther and Minerva could see.

'Erm, excuse me, Eddie?' came Esther's voice.

'Round the other way, Eddie!' Minerva shouted.

'Oh, sorry.' Eddie turned the phone around.

Jess looked to her father and then her mother. Both gave her a tenative nod. Gripping the box containing the witch bottle, Jess threw open the kitchen door and stormed into the hallway. Eddie followed at pace and Ginny stepped through after him, closing the door behind them. Jess was already at the living room door, pulling on the handle, but the door wouldn't budge.

Jess hissed through her teeth.

'Anything you can do, James?' she called.

Despite there being no windows open, a chill ran

over them, and then the lightbulb above them exploded. Ginny screamed as they covered their heads.

Jess glanced around the hallway, her gaze resting on the shadows of the stairs, just that little bit too dark to be natural.

'Try upstairs, Jess.'

Jess shook her head involuntarily. Minerva repeated herself.

'Upstairs. There's a fireplace in the bedroom. That's as good a spot as any.'

Jess told her legs to move, to run up the stairs and rush towards the fireplace, but every instinct held her in place.

Eddie moved the camera from Jess to the stairs, and Minerva gave a soft, 'Oh. Right.'

'What?' Ginny was near screeching. 'What are we doing?'

'It's on the stairs,' Minerva explained. 'The imp is on the stairs.'

The shadows shifted and Jess's mind's eye gave her the memory of the spirit of the witchfinder, drifting and swirling down her staircase towards the coven of witches. Jess's stomach turned. If only this was another spirit. If only this could be banished by getting Minerva's friends round.

Instead, she had only her family around her. All she had to do was place a witch bottle into the fibre of the house, but she had to keep her parents safe, and her daughter. Jess swallowed against her dry throat. This had all been a mistake. She should have sent Ruby away, she should have demanded that her parents leave. They should be in the other house, the good house, the one without spirits and shadow people and an imp. They should be safe, and Jess could wait for Minerva and Esther to arrive. They could deal with this while Jess sat at home, protecting her family and doing... paperwork.

Jess blinked, her chest tightening.

'Up the stairs,' she murmured.

'Jess, wait!'

Jess hesitated, her legs wobbling. She glanced to the phone screen her father was holding up.

'Pull a card,' said Minerva.

Jess studied her for a moment and then looked back to the stairs.

'I shouldn't go up and try and end this?'

'How?' said Esther. 'You're going to have to take the fire surround off, and that'll take time. The imp is right in front of you, Jess. It'll get there before you can. It'll stop you again. Mum's right, pull a card.'

'What does that mean?' asked Eddie, his eyes wide.

Jess looked back to the stairs. The shadow began to take on the shape of something that made her bowels loosen. She gave the living room door another go, shaking the handle. The shadow on the stairs shifted and then dissipated.

'Where did it go?' Jess whispered.

'Up,' said Minerva. 'It's gone up. Go pull a card, Jess.'

Exhaling in a puff, Jess herded her parents back into the kitchen and brushed off the curious look Marshall gave her.

'What's going on?'

'Living room door's still jammed shut and the imp-thing is on the stairs,' said Eddie, grinning. Marshall gave him a horrified look.

'Why are you enjoying this?' Ginny elbowed her husband.

'Oh, come on. You wanted an adventure! What happens if we just go upstairs?' he asked Jess.

'I imagine it'll throw something worse than a book at you,' she mumbled, her trembling fingers placing down the box and pulling her tarot cards from her bag.

'Are you okay?' Marshall murmured, leaning forward across the table while keeping one arm around Ruby. 'You don't have to do this.'

Jess stopped and watched her shaking hands as she balled them into fists and stretched them out.

'I think I do.' She barely recognised her own voice.

'No, Jess. You don't. We can leave. Together. All of us.'

Jess looked up and met Marshall's kind eyes.

'Every time something like this happens, I think I'm not cut out for it,' she told him quietly, edging closer. 'And every time, I think maybe it won't happen again. But here we are. And it's in my family's home. Again.' Her eyes filled with tears and her throat constricted with the effort of holding them back. 'Everyone tells me I can do this, but I don't know if I can.'

'Oh, you can,' Marshall told her. 'I know you, Jess. You can do anything you want. You're the most incredible, strong, defiant woman I've ever met. But just because you can, doesn't mean you have to. You don't *have* to do this.'

Jess's vision blurred as she resisted the urge to sink into Marshall's warmth.

'I can help, Mummy.'

Jess grinned, tears breaking through her defences and dropping down her cheeks. She wiped them away with the ball of her hand and turned to her daughter.

'You are helping, sweetheart. You're keeping Marshall safe.' Jess leaned over and kissed Ruby's head.

When Jess turned back to the room, she found her parents, Minerva and Esther watching her. Pulling herself together, sniffing loudly, she moved to the middle of the table and unboxed her tarot cards.

'What are we doing now?' asked Ginny, watching the cards warily.

'Jess is going to pull a card,' said Minerva matter-of-factly. 'We need a display of power. Show this imp who and what it's messing with.'

Jess faltered.

'You don't have to,' came Esther's gentle voice. 'There are other ways.'

'Oh? What ways?' asked Minerva, turning on her daughter.

'They could all just leave and we can make the journey. You can get rid of the damn thing. With my help.'

'But Jess is more than capable—'

'That as may be, but...' Esther hesitated, beckoning to the camera with her head, trying to silently finish the sentence in a way Minerva would understand.

Minerva sighed and studied Jess.

'I know it's hard,' she started. 'I know it's scary. And it *is* scary. And dangerous. And you're there with the people you love most in the world. Because this thing is invading your home. Once again. Once again, the people you love the most are being threatened. But the thing is, if this happened to anyone else, they wouldn't know what had hit them. Someone with sensitivity might see the shadows and feel the spirit, but they wouldn't know about the imp until it had sunk into their nightmares, slowly breaking them down until they were shells of their former selves. Someone without that sensitivity wouldn't stand a chance. But this isn't happening to them, Jess. It's happening to you and your family. And that imp doesn't know who it's messing with. It's no coincidence that your mother has bought this house. This is a special house of significance, all the activity proves that. And it needs a witch to protect it. Pull a card, Jess. Ask any question you like. Show your power. Believe in your power. You'll gain the upper hand and you'll be stronger for it. I promise.'

'You keep saying that,' Jess murmured. 'Every time this happens. You tell me I'm a witch and I was made for this, but that it'll get easier. It hasn't gotten easier, Minerva. It just keeps getting harder. That damn thing doesn't need to infiltrate my nightmares. There are already demons and spirits galore in there.'

A silence descended over the kitchen.

'I think we're done,' said Ginny, although she didn't move. 'Let's go. Come on, Marshall. Come on, Ruby.'

Bubbles, sensing the tone, jumped up from under the table and wagged her tail. Ruby and Marshall looked at Jess.

'I'm sorry, Jess,' said Minerva. 'Perhaps it won't get easier. Perhaps it just is what it is. Demons and spirits and imps. It's scary, I know. But I know that you're more than capable.'

'Capable doesn't have to mean willing,' proclaimed Ginny, holding out an arm to her daughter. 'Come on. Let's go home.'

'But, but, what about...' Eddie floundered, looking back to the kitchen door.

'Our daughter's mind is more important than any of this...stupidity,' Ginny spat. 'Jess. Now. Come on.'

Jess blinked, glancing back to the box on the table containing the witch bottle. Finally, she gave a subtle nod.

Marshall was immediately on his feet, gently pulling Ruby with him and grabbing her bag. Ginny took Bubbles' lead and, despite Eddie's groaning, they headed out the back door.

Jess was the last to go. As she moved past the kettle, it clicked on. She studied it and then looked around the room as the water boiled for no one.

Silently, she pulled out her phone and opened the app.

Please.

Something inside Jess's chest caught.

Please.

Witch.

Please.

Help.

Jess glanced back to her family waiting for her on the patio.

Bubbles growled and then started barking, pulling Ginny back towards the kitchen. Ginny gave a squeal as the large dog pulled the lead from her hands. Bubbles bounded back into the kitchen to stand beside Jess, staring at the kitchen door, her hackles raised, her teeth bared.

Without thinking, eyes on the door, Jess lowered

herself to sit cross-legged on the kitchen floor, the comforting bulk of her dog beside her. She pulled her tarot cards from her bag, lifted her chin to the room and began to shuffle them.

There were no yes or no questions for the tarot. That's not how they worked. Not that it mattered. Jess could reframe the question.

Quietly, aloud, she asked the room, 'Should I stay and fight or should I leave? Am I a witch or should I be doing the paperwork?'

Something banged beyond the kitchen door. Bubbles whined but stood her ground, returning to growling and giving the door two deep barks for good measure.

'Jess. What are you doing? Get up! We have to go.'

Jess jumped as the back door behind them slammed shut, followed by the raised voices of her family and Marshall's bulk as he tried to force it open.

'Was that you, James?' she murmured.

Please.

Jess took a deep breath, continually shuffling her cards.

'What do I do?' she asked them.

She pulled a card, and before she could look at it, the kitchen door swung open, smashing against the wall, and Bubbles fell silent.

40

Erica

Erica slapped her thighs and stood up.

'Let's get you home, then.'

'Wait!' shouted Fen, finding his feet. 'You said you're not sure. Not sure about what?' he asked Bethany, still sitting on the tree trunk.

She gave a small shrug, looking down at her feet.

'About this,' she offered. 'About...anything.' She looked up into his eyes. 'I'm eighteen, Fen. I want to go out and explore the world. Meet people. Meet...' She drifted off and Fen's expression shifted. Gone were the sad eyes and downturned lips. His mouth straightened, his eyes hardening.

Erica stood, catching Alfie's eye.

'Meet other men,' Fen growled softly.

Erica moved to stand between them, facing Fen.

'Stop,' she told him. 'Calm down.'

Fen reached out to grab Erica, to push her out of the way, shouting, 'I'll curse them all!'

He didn't get close to touching Erica. As his arm swung out, fingers stretching towards her, Alfie clapped and each of them jumped.

When Erica gathered her wits about her and looked around, they were no longer in the forest. Chest tightening, she called out for Alfie and the fae appeared beside her, taking her hand.

'Where are we?' she whispered, wishing she hadn't called his name so loud when she didn't know where they were or who might be listening. Fen and Bethany were no longer with them. 'Where's Bethany?'

'She's safe,' said Alfie calmly. 'We haven't moved. We're all still in the forest.'

Erica looked around.

'We are definitely not in the forest,' she said.

There were no trees, no grass beneath their feet, no bird song. There was just grey, as if everything had been deleted from the world except for the two of them.

'It takes a moment,' Alfie told her, as if that explained everything.

She stared up at him.

'What does?'

He turned and gave her something of a playful smile.

'Do you wish we'd met earlier?' he asked.

Erica opened her mouth, but before she could summon an answer, the world of grey started spinning around them – although she wasn't sure how she could tell the difference. Her stomach knew, though, as it slid and turned. She clung to Alfie's arm until he wrapped himself about her and she pressed her cheek to his warm chest, clamping her eyes shut.

As her stomach settled, she carefully opened one eye and gasped.

They were back in the forest, but in Alfie's village rather than the clearing. Erica spun round, still clinging to Alfie.

'What's going on?' she demanded. 'How did we get back here?'

'We're not back here,' said Alfie, his voice level. He kept hold of her, holding her hands until she stopped and looked up at him. 'We're still in the clearing.'

Erica leaned towards the fae.

'What. Is. Going. On,' she whispered.

Alfie smiled. He raised an eyebrow and gestured with a gentle nod for her to turn around. There, on the road behind her, was Fen and a woman who looked strangely like Bethany.

'This is their future,' Alfie murmured in her ear. 'About five years from now.'

Erica watched the couple approach.

'Can they see us?' she hissed.

'No.'

Fen and Bethany walked hand in hand, Fen whispering to her and Bethany nodding along. She wasn't smiling. If anything, she looked tired.

'Is she okay?' Erica whispered.

Alfie didn't reply.

Erica jumped as a couple appeared beside them.

'What's happening?' asked eighteen-year-old Bethany. 'Is that me?'

'Aelfraed,' came Fen's hushed voice. 'What are you doing?'

'Bethany is unsure of what her future holds. I wanted to show her one option,' Alfie told them. 'Here you are, together, living in our world. This is what will happen if you don't go home and finish your exams, if you don't go to London, if you stay here with Fen instead.'

Fen spluttered, glaring up at Alfie.

'Why are you doing this?'

'She has a right to know,' Alfie told him. 'This is but one possible future,' he continued to Bethany. 'If you go to London and Fen joins you, your future will be different. If you take yours exams and then return here, your future may be different.' He shrugged. 'One simple choice can change everything.'

Erica stared at him, blinking away hurriedly as he glanced down at her.

'I look awful,' said Bethany.

The older couple – the future couple – walked past them and the group turned to watch.

'You look beautiful,' said Fen, although his tone betrayed him.

Alfie smiled.

'Love isn't about trapping a person,' he said gently. 'Love is about care, and when you care about someone, you want them to be safe and happy. Does she look happy to you there, Fen?'

Fen shuffled his feet.

'I will give you anything you want,' he murmured to the Bethany standing beside him.

'Well, I don't want to look like that,' she mumbled.

'Love is about letting go if that's the right thing,' Alfie continued. 'To love someone is to want them to be themselves.'

Erica flinched as Alfie clapped his hands and a bright light fell over them. When the light fell away and Erica's stomach came back from her throat, they were on a street, bustling with people.

Fen gripped onto Bethany while a grin split her face.

'London!' she declared.

Erica was still reeling from the bright light, forcing away the memories of travelling through time with Rick when she'd first met him. Of the blinding light, the rising nausea, vomiting onto the floor while he tenderly stroked her back.

Reading her mind, Alfie's hand landed softly on the small of her back, a reassuring presence that instantly calmed her nerves. She leaned into him, taking a shuddering breath.

'There.' Alfie pointed with his free hand to an older, much happier Bethany. She wore a long dress and her dark hair floated around her as she strode towards them, a smile lingering on her lips, a bag over the crook of her arm.

'Wow,' Bethany murmured. 'Look at that dress.'

'Where am I?' asked Fen. 'Am I here?'

'I don't believe you could ever let Bethany out of your sight for long,' Alfie told him.

Erica scanned the crowds and across the road, towards a park, searching for any sign of the fae. She couldn't see him.

The older Bethany passed them, a skip in her step.

'I'm going to London,' said eighteen-year-old Bethany. 'Definitely.'

Fen glared up at Alfie.

'And what of me?' he growled.

The group turned to watch the older Bethany and Alfie held up a hand to quieten Fen.

'Whether you come to London with Bethany or not, I believe she will be happy.' He looked down at the younger fae.

Fen shuddered.

'London,' he spat.

'I'm afraid so,' said Alfie, his arm now around Erica's waist. She watched the proceedings thoughtfully.

They all jumped as Alfie clapped his hands. This time, Erica was ready. She clenched her eyes shut against the bright light and waited for her stomach to tell her it was safe to open them.

They were back in the forest, back in the clearing, bird song filtering through the white noise in Erica's ears. As she steadied herself, Bethany bounced on the spot.

'I'm going to London!'

Fen groaned, slowly looking up at Alfie before squaring off to him.

'It is not our way to interfere like that,' he growled.

Alfie levelled his gaze at Fen.

'She deserves to have a choice.'

'Just because your chance of love was ruined doesn't give you the right to ruin mine,' Fen continued, his eyes darkening.

Alfie flinched and turned to face Fen.

'Alfie,' Erica murmured.

'This is not personal,' said Alfie.

'Of course it is,' Fen spat. 'You just can't bear to see someone else happy.'

'Happy?' Bethany almost screeched. Fen snapped round to her, his expression changing instantly. 'Do you think I looked happy? Living here with you? I'm not going to give up on my dream, Fen. Not for you. Not for anyone.'

Hidden behind Alfie's back, Erica smiled to herself.

'But—'

'No,' Bethany interrupted Fen. 'I don't know what that was or how it happened, but I'm not turning into...that.' She waved her arms around and looked to Alfie. 'I want the second version of me. In London. Wearing that dress. I want to see what that life will be like.' She crossed her arms defiantly and for a moment, Erica wondered if she was expecting Alfie to clap his hands again and make it so.

Fen shuddered, his eyes full of rage but his shoulders drooping.

'This is our way,' Alfie told him quietly. 'We watch and we wait and we hope.' He glanced at Erica.

'Not strictly true,' she muttered, unable to take her eyes from him, and her heart jolted as Alfie gave her a private smile.

Fen sighed and went to argue, but Bethany gave him a look.

'Please,' she started. 'If you love me, you'll let me find out what life could be like in London.'

Fen, jaw jutting out as he ground his teeth, sighed again through his nose. When he didn't answer immediately, she looked to Erica.

'Can I go home now?'

Erica nodded.

'Absolutely. Let's go. It's quite a walk.'

'No need,' said Alfie, holding up a hand. 'This way.'

41

Erica

Alfie led them to a path which they followed back to
the small village. Fen took Bethany's hand and Alfie
took Erica's, both on instinct. Alfie's friend was still
there, and while he narrowed his eyes at Erica, his
gaze turned hungry when he spotted Bethany. Erica
glared at him, channelling everything her grandmother had ever taught her, and watched in
fascination as the fae flinched and turned away
from them.

'Here,' said Alfie, leading them across the village
and towards a line of trees marked by a bed of
bluebells.

Bethany stopped.

'No.' She pulled Fen to a stop. 'This is a trick,' she
murmured. 'More bluebells? More flowers?' She
looked at Alfie and Erica. 'What are you going to do
to us?'

Erica looked up at Alfie and then stepped closer

to Bethany.

'This is a door. Right?' Erica checked with Alfie who nodded. 'Back to our world. Just like the one Fen led you through before. I guess the bluebells are – what? A doormat?'

Alfie chuckled.

'Something like that. They tell us when the bluebells on the other side are in bloom.' He stopped himself as if realising what he'd just said.

Erica raised an eyebrow.

'Oh yeah? So you know when you can come and tempt poor unsuspecting humans through?'

Alfie grimaced.

'Do you want to go home or not?'

Erica rolled her eyes and looked back to Bethany.

'Come on. Let's get out of here and get you back to your family.' She stepped through where Alfie pointed and hoped that Bethany would follow.

The world immediately dulled, although they were still surrounded by trees and birdsong. Looking around, she tried to get her bearings.

These weren't the local woods.

'Where are we?' she murmured, turning on the spot.

Alfie appeared behind her, followed closely by Fen and Bethany.

'We're close,' Alfie told them. 'About half an hour's drive away.'

'Great, and where did you leave your magic car?'

Erica asked with a huff, wondering which direction to take that would lead them to civilisation.

Fen seemed to know the way. Without a word, he led Bethany down the path. Alfie followed and, not wanting to be left behind, Erica jogged to catch up.

'How are we going to get home?' Erica hissed to Alfie.

The fae glanced back to her and then shrugged, his hands deep in his pockets as he walked.

'Call Jess to pick us up?' he offered. 'Or Bethany can call her family to collect her and we can go back to my world and walk back, just the two of us?' He smirked.

As tempting as more sex in the forest was, Erica's limbs were heavy. What she wanted more than anything in that moment was a hot shower and to fall into bed, alone, so that she could sleep. She pulled out her phone and checked for a signal, then she messaged Jess.

'Where are we?' she asked. 'I can't ask for a ride if I don't know where we are.'

'Chipping Briar,' said Alfie.

Erica stopped and Alfie turned back to her.

'That's where Jess's parents live.' Erica smiled and then laughed. 'She's here! She's visiting her parents, isn't she. Introducing them to Marshall and Bubbles.' Reaching out, Erica wrapped her arms around Alfie in a hug and then rushed past him to catch up with Bethany and Fen. 'Do you want a lift too, Fen?' she asked.

Fen's shoulders lifted in defence and he glanced at Bethany who looked back silently.

'Okay, well, you two figure that out and let me know,' said Erica. 'Do you want a lift?' she asked Alfie.

He took her hand and squeezed.

'Let's wait and see. I can go back with Fen if need be.'

Erica nodded and typed out a message to Jess, wondering if they'd be able to fit everyone in one car and doubting it.

The woodland path led them out into the sunshine, and on the edge of the treeline stood an old cottage with an array of glorious spring flowers around the front. While the roses were developing buds and foxgloves were growing taller, there were bluebells and cowslips already in bloom. The cottage was just as pretty, painted white with black framed windows and a slate tile roof. Erica cocked her head at it, wondering if it had ever been thatched. Net curtains hung at each of the windows and a light grey smoke plumed from the chimney. It was like something a child might draw, something from a fairy tale, and that was when Erica saw one of the net curtains twitch.

Trying not to stare, she watched out of the corner of her eye until something pulled at her attention. A pair of eyes, dark and gleaming, watching them from inside the cottage. They were fairly low down, suggesting either a short person or a child.

Adrenaline surged through Erica in a painful jolt as their eyes met, and then the person was gone, the net curtains swishing back into place.

Acutely aware of Fen and Bethany continuing down the path, Erica looked up at Alfie and was surprised to find him also staring at the window.

'Did you see that?' she murmured.

He gave a singular nod.

'Probably annoyed that people are walking past,' Erica ventured, studying the fae.

Alfie didn't respond and, annoyingly, gave nothing away in his expression. Then he turned away from the cottage, making to follow Fen and Bethany, before murmuring, 'Careful where you stand.'

Hands in his pockets, he strode off, leaving Erica looking down at her feet. She was standing on the path, marked out in rock and stone with grass and weeds attempting to grow between and, in places, through them. Her brow creased in curiosity, Erica crouched and ran her fingers over the rock. It wasn't just a path.

'It's a road,' she murmured.

Sitting back on her heels, she followed the road with her eyes. With the suddenness of looking at a patch of grass and realising you were standing on an active ant nest, Erica saw the rest of the road. She straightened and walked over it, where another rocky road crossed over the one they were walking on.

It was barely visible, overgrown as it was, and the road was broken enough in places that it hardly existed. But there it was.

'A crossroads,' she murmured.

Movement caught her attention and she snapped up to see those eyes watching her again from a different window in the cottage. Carefully, Erica stepped off the forgotten crossroads. A wind lifted her hair, sending a shiver over her. Alfie and the others were a good distance away now and she called after them, running to catch up, grateful to leave the cottage and the woods behind her.

Alfie waited for her, wrapping an arm around her waist when she reached him.

'What was that?' she asked, working to catch her breath.

'What?'

Erica hesitated.

'Any of it,' she decided. 'What was any of that? What the hell just happened?'

Alfie considered her and then shrugged.

'We found the girl, we're taking her home,' he said.

'What's with that cottage?'

Alfie smiled.

'It has a history. A long one. I thought Jess grew up here, has she never told you the stories about it?'

'She didn't grow up here, her parents moved here later. What stories?'

Alfie pulled Erica close and pressed his lips to

her head, breathing in her hair.

'About the witch.' His voice was muffled but still, the words loosened something in Erica. She turned to look up at him.

'A witch lives there?'

Alfie shrugged again.

'Used to,' he said. Erica waited for more but apparently that was all she was getting.

'Okay, fine. And what was that back there in your world? You never said you could show us our futures,' said Erica quietly, mindful of the young couple in front of them.

'You never asked.'

Erica pursed her lips and offered Alfie a glare. He laughed, tightening his grip on her.

'It takes a lot,' he explained. 'I don't do it often.'

'Could you...' Erica drifted off, unsure of whether she wanted to ask that question after all.

'I could,' Alfie said in a low voice only just audible. 'But I won't.'

Erica swallowed and bit her lip. He was right. Even if he did show her what the future held for them, she wasn't sure she wanted to know. Not like that.

'Can you forgive me?' Alfie asked as they reached the point where the path became tarmac, leading into the town.

'For what?'

'For my past transgressions. For the things I have done before you came into my life. While I was waiting but didn't know what I was waiting for. And then, while I was waiting and impatient for you.'

Erica looked up at the man beside her. His brown hair curled about his ears, his skin was softly tanned and brought up memories of being pressed against his warmth. When he turned to her, his blue eyes sparkled with something inhuman, but also a touch of sadness and an age that, apparently, couldn't be defined.

'Promise me you never hurt anyone,' she whispered, terrified of the answer. 'Promise me.'

Alfie stopped walking and she turned to face him. He met her eyes and lifted a hand to run the back of his fingers across her cheek.

'I promise,' he told her. 'I swear on my love for you, on my life and on everything that I hold dear in this world, my world and the next. I promise I never hurt anyone.'

Erica slowly wrapped her arms around Alfie's neck and pulled him close, pressing her lips against his. He kissed her back, gently at first, and then harder, clenching her clothing into balled fists.

When the kiss broke, she bumped her nose against his.

'You ever try and use charm on me, I'll know about it and there'll be hell to pay,' she murmured.

Alfie laughed, those sad eyes disappearing into a sparkling grin.

'Don't I know it.' He kissed her again and then let her go. Taking her hand, they rushed to catch up with Fen and Bethany.

Erica checked her phone as they wandered towards the high street. Jess hadn't responded. Sighing, she rang her mother, holding the phone to her ear.

'Right, who's coming with me and Bethany?' she asked as the phone rang and went immediately to voicemail.

Fen glanced at Bethany and then, carefully, untangled his hand from hers.

'You go,' he told her. 'And I'll see you soon.'

Bethany went to argue, but Fen shook his head, stepping away from her and towards Alfie. Without a word, Bethany leapt to him, wrapped her arms about him and kissed his lips. Shocked, Fen froze for a moment before sinking into the kiss.

Alfie pulled a face when they didn't break away from each other.

'All right, kids,' he said eventually. 'Come on, Fen. I'll go home with you.'

The kiss broke and Bethany eased herself out of Fen's grip. She gave him one last longing look before turning away and joining Erica.

Erica and Alfie's eyes met and she smiled at him.

'See you on the other side.'

Alfie, hands back in his pockets, grinned and turned away, wandering back to the woods with Fen in tow.

42

Jess

The hallway beyond the now open kitchen door was empty. When nothing moved for a good half a minute, Jess reached an arm around Bubbles, digging her fingers into the dog's fur, and looked down at the tarot card she'd pulled.

She bit her lip at the sight of two cards stuck together. She hadn't felt two cards when she'd pulled them, but there they were. Looking up at her from the kitchen floor was the Devil. Jess's bowels loosened.

Over the top of the Devil, however, was the Magician.

Jess studied the card, wracking her brain for its meaning. Unsure of herself, she reached for her little book and found the card inside.

'Potential,' she read, glancing back to the card. A smile slowly grew on her face. 'As above, so below. The Magician is the conduit between the physical and spiritual. Convert spiritual energy into real-world action.' Jess glanced up and froze as a dark shape moved from the hallway and up the stairs.

Above her head, the kettle clicked off. Bubbles licked her lips, yawned and pushed her head into Jess's lap.

'Well,' she told the dog. 'I don't think we're going anywhere.' She untangled herself and stood, brandishing the cards she'd pulled. 'You hear that?' she shouted into the house.

There came a creak and then a loud bang. Another creak, and a loud bang. The living room door opening and slamming shut, over and over.

It was toying with her.

Come and play.

Jess smiled. She reached for the box on the table and then unwittingly squealed as the kitchen door slammed shut. Heart pounding, she shook her head.

'Was that you, James?'

Her phone remained silent. No, that wasn't him. That was something trying to keep her from the rest of the house.

Cradling the box and the witch bottle, Jess went to open the back door where her family stood in a huddle with wide eyes.

'What the hell, Jess?' Marshall hissed, one arm keeping Ruby behind him.

Jess leaned against the door in case something decided to slam it, although the imp had seemingly not made it into the kitchen yet. Jess didn't have time to wonder on that.

'I pulled a card,' she told them. 'I'm staying. I need to finish this. Where are Minerva and Esther?' She glanced at their hands for the phone.

'We hung up,' her father told her. 'But we can call them back, right? I'm staying with you. Your mother and Marshall can take Ruby and the dog home.'

'No!'

They all turned to little Ruby hiding behind Marshall. She stepped out and stared up at her mother silently. Jess searched her daughter's eyes.

'No,' she murmured slowly. 'Ruby stays.'

'Jess!' Marshall would have thrown up his arms – Jess saw his shoulders twitch – but that would have meant letting go of Ruby. 'This is insane.'

Jess levelled her gaze at her fiancé.

'You encouraged me to get into all this,' she said matter-of-factly.

'Because I didn't think you'd be putting yourself and Ruby in danger. I'm not—' Marshall caught himself, taking a moment to breathe and lower his voice. 'I'm not losing either of you. Your nightmares are bad enough as they are. Ruby is still having bad dreams. Let's just go. Erica's family can sort this out.'

Ruby looked between Marshall and her mother, awaiting the outcome.

'He's right, Jess,' Ginny murmured.

Eddie sighed heavily through his nose.

Jess looked at each of them in turn and smiled.

'Okay, so I had a wobble. I'm sorry. This stuff is scary. But I know I can do this.'

'A *wobble*?' Marshall muttered.

'How?' Ginny crossed her arms.

'Because of this.' Jess held up the tarot cards she'd pulled. Beside her, Bubbles sat down almost defiantly. 'Because I have potential. Because I have a spirit on my side. Because it's time to convert that spiritual energy into real-world action.'

Her family blinked at her.

'You what?' her mother demanded.

'Yes!' Eddie punched the air and went to take a step forward, but his wife's glare held him back.

'It's a card. It doesn't mean anything. What are you talking about?' Ginny demanded.

Jess sighed and glanced at Marshall for help, but he'd set his jaw, staring back at her, his eyes flickering as he considered his options.

'Marshall. Please. You know me. You know we can do this.'

He shook his head and gave a trembling sigh. 'This is some scary sh–stuff, Jess, and our daughter is here.'

Jess's heart caught and she smiled before she could think. Marshall realised what he'd said and smiled back. They both glanced down at Ruby.

'I want to stay,' she told them.

'You don't understand what that means,'

Marshall told her.

'Yes I do,' said Ruby. 'There's something bad in the house. Worse than the thing that was in my bedroom. But the man in the corner said a witch can get rid of it and that Mummy is a witch.' Ruby shrugged. 'I want to stay.'

Jess looked back to Marshall with a glimmer of hope.

'You'll protect her,' she murmured to him. 'I know you will.'

'I'd die for her,' Marshall said in a low voice. He searched Jess's eyes and then softened, reaching out for her. 'And for you. And I don't want to die. I'd prefer to just go somewhere safe for everyone. You know?'

'I know.' Jess moved into his reach and he scooped both her and Ruby into a large hug. Bubbles barked and bounced into them, trying to get involved. Marshall opened the hug to let the dog in. 'We can do this,' Jess murmured in his ear. 'I can do this.'

Marshall kissed her cheek.

'I know. It's just—'

'I know,' whispered Jess. 'Therapy sessions. All right? Let me do this and I'll go to therapy.'

Marshall chuckled, soft and warm against her cheek.

'If you can find a therapist who will listen to you talk about ghosts and demons, then absolutely.'

Jess kissed his lips as they broke the family hug.

'So...are we doing this?' Eddie asked.

'We are.' Jess turned to her mother. 'What do you want to do?'

Ginny looked from Jess and down to Ruby who gave her grandmother a thumbs up.

'I'm staying,' said Ginny. 'I'll help.'

'Great. Marshall, get Minerva and Esther on the phone. I'm confident now, but I'm not stupid.' Jess took a deep breath and then led her family back into the kitchen.

They made Marshall, Ruby and Bubbles fairly comfortable in the corner at the table, within easy reach of the back door which was left open. Marshall was given strict instructions: keep them safe, get them out if need be.

Minerva and Esther concocted a plan and Jess took the lead, cradling the box with the witch bottle. Ginny followed, holding up the phone so that Minerva and Esther could see what was happening. Eddie took up the rear, in one hand was a piece of scrap metal from the garden that he was eighty per cent certain was iron, in the other was Jess's phone, held up so that James the spirit could talk to them using the flashing words from the app.

The living room door wouldn't budge, so Jess led the way up the stairs.

'Are we sure about this?' Ginny whispered.

Minerva bobbed her head, as if her moving in her kitchen miles away would help her to see around Jess in front.

Jess hesitated on the landing, waiting for something to jump out. Instead, the door in front of her slowly opened as if pushed by an absent breeze.

Fire, said her phone from behind.

Jess nodded and entered the bedroom, heading straight for the cracked fireplace.

'How are you going to get the fireplace off?' came Esther's voice.

'Need that big man of yours, Jess,' said Minerva.

Jess hesitated, looking at the small, dusty Victorian fire surround. Eddie and Ginny squealed as the door was slammed shut behind them, and then they held their breath as a new noise filled the room.

'What's that?' Ginny hissed.

Eddie was looking up at the ceiling, eyes wide, chest rising and falling too fast for Jess's liking. Jess stood her ground, squared her shoulders and glanced around the room, waiting.

Come on, she willed silently. Come on.

The noise grew louder. Wet, heavy breathing from directly above their heads. Ginny and Eddie stared up, but something told Jess to turn around.

She had vivid memories of the demon in the woods, of the long limbs and red eyes. She'd expected the imp to look similar.

It was smaller than the demon, which sense. Although its dark outline was eerily familiar. There were no red eyes, no eyes at all that Jess could discern, and yet she knew deep in her gut that the imp was looking at her. Its claws were long, as long as its fingers, and there was something...odd about the way it moved. It flickered, as if the reception wasn't quite what it should have been.

The imp moved as it breathed, shuddering up and down with each breath. The creature opened its maw with a wet sound and Jess's knees weakened. She wanted to run. To turn around, grab her parents and run. She'd grab Marshall, Ruby and Bubbles on the way, and they wouldn't stop running until they were safe. Back at her parents' old house. Back at Jess's house, even.

Instead of running, however, Jess spoke. She wasn't sure where the courage to find the words came from, this was one of those moments where she didn't feel particularly in control. Despite that, she had the imp's full attention.

'How long have you been waiting?' she asked.

The imp's breath faltered, if only for a second.

'You have been waiting, haven't you?' Jess continued. 'Waiting for the witch bottle to be removed. You shouldn't have waited. You should have left. There is nothing for you here.'

The imp shuddered, flickering until Jess's eyes began to hurt, and she realised belatedly that the thing was laughing.

'Why are you here?' she asked. Around its feet, pools of what Jess assumed was drool formed on the original floor boards. She pulled a face. 'Did the Devil send you?'

The laughter stopped.

The imp hissed and approached Jess.

'Jess!' came Minerva's voice.

'Back away!' shouted Esther.

'Jess.' Her mother's voice was quiet, full of fear, but louder than Jess had anticipated. She glanced across to find Ginny at her shoulder. The two women stared the imp down as it stepped closer. It raised a claw and Jess threw out an arm to push her mother back. Before the imp could slash at them, it stopped, raising its head and listening.

No.

Jess thought quick.

'You can't leave, can you?' she shouted.

The imp glanced at her and she could have sworn its eyes – wherever they were – narrowed.

'You can't leave until the job is done. What's the job, huh? Why are you here?'

The imp hissed again and then vanished, leaving Jess with tears in her eyes, a pounding heart and the name *James* whispered in her head.

'Where did it go?' asked Eddie. He'd followed his wife and stood with an arm around both Ginny and his daughter. 'What do we do?'

Jess's world fell apart as a high-pitched scream filled the house. She was out of the door and thundering down the stairs before her parents could fathom that the scream belonged to Ruby.

43

Jess

'Ruby!'

'Keep going, Jess! We're okay.'

Jess skidded to a stop at the bottom of the stairs. The imp was in the living room, flickering and shuddering, pulsating with rage at the sight of Marshall lifting the hatch in the floor.

'You're not okay,' Jess murmured. 'Hey! You didn't answer me.' She rushed into the room before anyone could stop her. Ginny followed and Eddie was close behind when the door slammed closed. He cried out, stepping back from the force, dropping Jess's phone on the floor. The door swung back open.

Ginny went back for him, propping up the phone holding Minerva and Esther against the wall while she checked her husband for injuries. The moment they were both out in the hallway, the imp slammed the door and held it shut.

Jess could barely hear for the sound of her heart pounding in her ears.

'Are you all right?' she yelled, keeping her eyes on the imp.

'We're fine. But we can't open the door. Jess? Are you okay? Is Ruby okay?'

'We're fine,' Jess lied. How could they possibly be fine?

'We're still here, Jess. You still have us,' came Esther's voice.

'You can do this, Jess, love,' said Minerva.

Keeping her eyes on the imp in the corner, Jess began to work her way around the room to place herself between the imp and Marshall and Ruby.

'Where's Bubbles?' she murmured between gritted teeth.

'Kitchen,' said Marshall, keeping Ruby behind him and his gaze on the creature in the corner. 'I should have left Ruby in there but she was adamant.'

'It wants James, Mummy.'

Jess stopped and glanced back to her daughter. 'What?'

Ruby looked up at her with big eyes.

'The monster wants James.'

Jess turned back to the imp.

'It's talking to you?'

Ruby nodded.

'James is scared.'

'Minerva! Esther?' Jess called, still creeping

around to defend her family.

There came no response. Jess risked a glance over her shoulder and saw that the screen of the phone propped against the wall was blank. Her own phone lay nearby, the screen blank. She cried out when both phones gave a *pop!* and the one against the wall slid down to the ground.

She turned back to the imp, eyes wide, mouth dry.

'You killed the *phones*?'

The imp hissed, giving a suggestion of teeth.

'Mummy. It can't have him, can it?'

Jess blinked.

'Rubes, sweetheart, I can't hear the imp talking. Can you tell me exactly what it's saying, please?' She took another step towards the shadowy, flickering creature.

'It says it wants James,' said Ruby, hiding behind Marshall.

Marshall and Jess exchanged a look. Behind Marshall's back, near Ruby, was the box containing the witch bottle. Jess kept her own decoy empty box in sight of the imp, clutched to her chest.

'Why does it want James?'

There was a pause while Ruby listened, and Jess considered throwing her box at the imp to give Marshall the opportunity to place the witch bottle back under the floorboards. Would the box hit the imp? Or would it pass straight through?

'Because he owes his soul. What does that

mean?'

Jess faltered, staring up at the imp.

'The Devil did send you.'

Ruby huffed and went to move around Marshall, but he caught her with his free hand, pulling her back, forcing him to step away from the open hatch in the floor.

'Well, you can't have him!' she yelled at the shadow in the corner. The imp flickered and writhed, but it didn't advance. 'He lives here. He belongs here. And you don't. So you can go away and never come back. Go away and never come back!' Ruby shouted at the top of her voice.

'Jess? Ruby?' Ginny and Eddie pounded on the closed door and Bubbles began to bark and whine longingly.

Jess studied the imp.

'James sold his soul to the Devil. Is that right? You're here to collect but James put the witch bottle under the floorboards before he died, right? Before it was time to collect? You've been waiting ever since.' Jess blinked. 'If we let you take James, you'll go away forever?'

Jess didn't need Ruby to translate. The imp nodded its odd-shaped head, its invisible eyes boring into Jess.

'No, Mummy. You can't!'

A twinge of pain hit Jess between the eyes.

'Ruby, sweetheart. Is James still here?'

'Yes.' Ruby looked behind her to an empty corner

of the room. Marshall went to move but Jess warned him against it with a subtle gesture of her hand.

'Ruby, sweetheart, please ask James what deal he made with the Devil.'

'What deal did you—' Ruby stopped and listened. Then she turned back to her mother. Jess waited, her palms sweating as she held the empty box close, her mind whirring.

There were tears in Ruby's eyes.

Jess's chest tightened.

'What is it, sweetheart? Ruby? What did he say?'

Marshall crouched down to the five-year-old's level and Ruby's large eyes glanced up to meet his.

'He says we should put the bottle back,' said Ruby, then she lowered her voice. Jess struggled to make out the words. 'He killed someone. He says she deserved it, that it had to happen. He killed her.'

Marshall's shoulders tensed as Jess made sense of what Ruby was saying.

'The deal was to keep him safe?' Marshall murmured.

Ruby nodded, tears spilling down her cheeks. Her gaze dropped to the box in Marshall's hand.

A cold breeze swept over the side of Jess and she froze, her breath coming in short, jagged rasps.

Justice should be served.

The voice was new and sent a violent shiver through Jess. Slowly, she looked up to find the imp standing beside her. Its eyes, while sunk deep into the shadows that made up its form, stared at her. Willing her to make her next move.

'Who did he kill?' Jess whispered.

The imp shifted, as if studying her, and then painfully slowly, it turned to face Ruby.

Jess couldn't breathe.

In front of them, Ruby shook her head, the tears now falling freely. Marshall wiped her cheek, leaving it damp.

'It's okay, Ruby,' he murmured. 'Everything's going to be okay.'

Ruby lifted her gaze to his and something passed between them, something that Jess only caught a glimpse of. Before she could speak, Marshall opened the box he was holding, his fingers wrapping around the witch bottle.

A wind picked up around the room and Jess jolted. This wasn't the imp. It was the same wind the spirit of the witchfinder in Ruby's room had swirled around her home, pushing at the coven of witches attempting to banish it.

'James. Settle down,' Jess called, her voice trembling as the imp flickered beside her. 'Come on, now. We still need to talk about this.'

'It's over, Mummy,' said Ruby, reaching out to the box in Marshall's hand. He was ahead of her, raising the bottle over her head and out of her reach. He looked down at her as she went to protest.

'You're not doing this,' he told her. 'This isn't your decision. I told you I would always protect you, and that's what I'm going to do.'

Marshall threw the bottle into the open hatch with all his strength. The imp screeched with surprise and the light bulb above their heads smashed, sending glass over Marshall as he shielded Ruby with his body.

There was a moment of quiet as they looked around, wondering what had just happened.

Slowly, gently, a laughter filled the room. Ruby snuggled into Marshall's grip, pressing her face into his chest. The imp surged forward and dissipated, the shadowy mass creeping up the walls and along the floor. It avoided Marshall and Ruby, regrouping on the other side of the room, and Jess fell to the floor as an ear piercing scream cracked the window behind her.

Then a true silence fell over them.

Mouth dry, Jess lifted her head. There was no sign of the imp. She reached out for Marshall but couldn't quite touch him. Scuttling towards her family, she glanced down into the open hatch. The witch bottle lay in pieces, the glass smashed, the wood beneath soaked with the urine, the nail and thread lying out in the open air for the first time in a century.

Jess's breath caught and she found her feet, rushing to Marshall and Ruby, throwing her arms around them. Marshall opened the embrace to let her in.

They held each other tightly, until the door burst open and Ginny and Eddie fell inside. Bubbles bounded past them, jumping on Marshall and licking Ruby's cheeks.

'What happened? Are you all right? Are you okay? Ruby? Talk to us? What did you see? Why are you crying? What did it do to you?' Eddie's words came in a rush as he fell upon his granddaughter.

Marshall was wiping Ruby's face dry when Eddie reached them. Ruby looked up into her grandfather's eyes and gave him a small smile.

'Are you all right?'

She nodded.

'What happened?' Ginny demanded, peering into the hatch at the smashed witch bottle.

'The imp wanted the spirit.' Marshall shrugged. 'If we'd put the witch bottle back, the imp would have always been here, waiting.'

'Oh, but...' Ginny looked at Jess, sitting on the floor, watching her family with large, unseeing eyes. 'I thought James was on our side?'

'No, Mum,' Jess murmured. 'We were on James's side, until we found out why the imp was here.' She blinked and looked up at Ginny. 'It's gone now and it won't be coming back.'

'I smashed the witch bottle so the imp could take the spirit. Two stones with one bottle,' said Marshall.

Ruby shuddered and wrapped her tiny arms

around his waist as far as she could. Marshall hugged her back.

'And they're gone? They're really gone?' Ginny asked, looking around the room.

'And all that's left is the smell of hundred-year-old urine,' said Eddie, wrinkling his nose as he looked down into the hatch.

'I've got some cleaning stuff that'll clear that up,' Marshall told him.

'They're really gone,' Jess confirmed, finally finding her feet. She scooped Ruby up in one movement, holding her daughter tight, breathing in her hair.

'He was a bad man, Mummy,' Ruby whispered.

'I know, sweetheart. Did he tell you what he did?'

'He said he killed her and she deserved it.'

'Did he tell you anything else?' Jess asked, her heart in her throat.

'That he would do it again if he could.'

'Anything else?' Jess managed.

Ruby considered this and shook her head. 'Why did she deserve it?'

'I don't know, baby. But it's over now. No need to think any more on it,' Jess told her, kissing the side of her daughter's head. She placed more kisses on Ruby's face and then released her. Marshall picked Ruby up easily, holding her tight, and she grabbed hold of his top in her small fists.

'I think we might all need therapy after that,' Ginny told Jess quietly.

Jess smiled and went to follow her family out of the room. Bubbles pushed her head into Jess's hand, licking her fingers. As Jess paused to give the dog a cuddle, something at the window caught her eye. In a flash, it was gone, but as Jess left the room, her mind put the pieces of what she'd seen together: a small, strange looking man with large eyes, peering through the window, looking from her to the hatch in the middle of the room.

44

Rick

LONDON, 1864

The sun was just rising over the horizon, sending tendrils of pink light among the clouds and giving the park a hazy glow. Rick stood on top of the hill looking out over the city. The park was relatively empty but cities rarely slept. The odd jogger had rushed past him, along with a couple of ambling dog walkers. For now, he was alone.

Three days had passed since Burns have given him the ultimatum. Three days of enjoying the city with the freedom of not having to look over his shoulder. A freedom which he couldn't enjoy; his thoughts weighed heavy, churning and turning over and over as he wandered from street to museum to street to pub to hotel. His money was running out, and so were his choices.

By his side, his fingers gripped Alfie's pocket watch. Rick urged it to do something, to throb, to chime, to rattle. Anything that would call him to Erica. But the watch only continued ticking, calm and quiet.

Erica didn't need him.

Erica didn't want him.

Unless Alfie was wrong, unless he'd set Rick up.

There were too many what ifs and not enough certainties other than the options Burns had given him.

Rick Cavanagh was at a loss.

He sat on the bench behind him and studied the pocket watch and all its finer detail. What would Erica tell him to do?

She would tell him to listen to his gut. He smiled. That had always been her answer. Should he take this promotion? Listen to your gut. Should they have a baby? Listen to your gut. Where should they go on honeymoon? Listen to your gut.

Rick laughed to himself at the memories. She said it so often that he would often say it with her after asking a question, wrapping his arms around her waist to kiss her.

The empty space she'd left in his soul ached with a pain that was almost unbearable. The empty space their baby son had left was a pain like no other.

Rick turned the pocket watch over in his hand.

What was his gut telling him to do?

Wiping his eyes, Rick stood and looked over the city once more. Glancing around, he checked no one was there to see, then he slid the watch back into his pocket. Pushing up his sleeve, he revealed the device on his wrist and turned the dials.

That dawn, the people in the city who were awake and happened to be looking in the right direction at the right time claimed to see a bright, sudden light on the horizon. It even made the newspapers. No one had been close enough to witness what had caused the light at the time, and when those in the park ventured up the hill to investigate, there was nothing to be found.

45
Jess

The change in the Victorian house was immediate. Sure, there were still shadows where there shouldn't be, but they weren't malicious, they didn't make the skin crawl, they didn't even seem to notice Jess and her family were there.

'The difference is amazing,' Ginny murmured as they watched Marshall loading up the car. 'I hadn't even noticed how dark the house was. I just thought some new curtains and a lick of paint would brighten it all up.'

'When actually, all you needed was to get rid of the imp on the periphery,' said Jess.

Mother and daughter looked at one another and broke into grins.

'What you do is terrifying, do you know that?' said Ginny.

Jess nodded.

'I'm more than aware.'

They watched Eddie leading Ruby and Bubbles over to the car.

'What about Ruby? The things she saw and heard in there…'

Jess shifted her weight.

'We'll keep an eye on her, don't worry. Maybe get her someone to talk to.'

'Yes. You've always been good about talking with her,' Ginny agreed. 'She was very brave.' She looked at Jess. 'Like her mother.'

'Like her grandmother,' said Jess, smiling and taking her mother's hand. 'Maybe Minerva is right. We're a family of witches.'

Ginny laughed.

'As long as we never have to go through that again, you can call me whatever you like.'

Jess squeezed her mother's hand and Ginny smiled at her. 'And now we can concentrate on planning the wedding!'

Jess's expression fell.

'Yeah, but something small, yeah? Let's not go overboard. Something small and intimate would be nice. You know? Good food, good music, not too many people.'

Ginny had returned to watching the men fastening Ruby in to her car seat and letting Bubbles into the back of the car.

'It'll be nice to see all your cousins again. And I haven't seen Uncle Mark in a very long time.'

'Yeah. Small, though, Mum. Yeah?'

'And we'll have to invite Sharon and Bert.'

'What? I haven't seen them since I was...I don't know, sixteen? Why are we inviting them?'

'They watched you grow up, Jess, it's only polite.'

'But, small and intimate, Mum. Remember?'

Ginny wasn't listening.

Jess sighed and squeezed her mother's hand again.

'What about the house? Need to renovate it before the wedding, I guess,' she tried softly.

Ginny's expression shifted.

'Hmm. We do have a lot of work to do. You'll come and help sometimes?'

'Of course,' said Marshall, approaching with Eddie. 'Anytime. I can come up next weekend, if you like.'

'Splendid! We'll put the kettle on,' said Eddie, clapping his hands. 'And bring Jess and Ruby and Bubbles, of course.'

'All hands, huh, Dad?'

Eddie grinned and gave his daughter a tight hug.

'After all that, I want to see a lot of you girls. And I want to hear all your stories,' he added in a whisper.

Jess laughed, hugging him back.

Eddie shook hands with Marshall and Ginny gave him a tentative hug, then Jess and Marshall fell into the car. Jess and Ruby waved manically as Marshall drove the car off the driveway and onto the road. They waved until Jess's parents were out of sight.

'Well,' said Marshall. 'That went well, I thought.'

Jess laughed and pulled out her phone. The screen was cracked but it seemed otherwise unharmed. Unlike Marshall's poor phone.

'What are you doing?'

'When we get home, I'm looking up this James character. See what he did,' Jess murmured. 'I'm sorry about your phone.'

Marshall grinned.

'It's all right, I'm due an upgrade anyway.'

Jess watched her fiancé drive, her gaze travelling from his eyes, down his neck to his thick, strong arms. The arms that had held Ruby so close, the arm that had smashed the witch bottle.

'Thank you for looking after us,' she whispered.

Marshall smiled.

'It's what I do.' He reached for her hand and, without taking his eyes from the road, pressed it to his lips.

'And I love you for that. And so many other things,' Jess told him. 'You still want to marry me?'

Marshall laughed.

'Wild, demonic imps couldn't keep me away,' he told her.

Jess's phone, lying in her lap, gave a beep. A message from Erica flashed up in her notifications.

Hey! Is your phone not working? It goes to voicemail when I call. Are you okay?

*We're in Chipping Briar. Don't suppose you could
give me and Bethany a lift home?*

It beeped again before Jess could even consider
a response.

*Just saw your message. Looks like a witch bottle
to me. Not sure about that plate though. What's
that? Is everything okay? You won't believe where
I've been.
Call me.*

Jess chuckled to herself.

'Hang on,' she told Marshall. 'Pull over.
Apparently Erica's here and she needs a lift home.'

Marshall did as he was told while Jess called
Erica.

On their way to pick up Erica and Bethany, Jess
sat back, closing her eyes, listening to Marshall
humming beside her, her daughter and dog safe
behind her. No demons or angry spirits jumped out
at her against the darkness of the insides of her
eyelids, there was no heavy, wet breathing or red
eyes.

Eddie had told them he would keep the saucer
they'd found, just in case. It was safe in a cupboard
for now. Jess's memory handed her the image it
had pieced together of the strange little figure
watching them from the living room window, but
the memory soon faded as she opened her eyes and

spotted Erica standing by the side of the road with a teenage girl.

46

Fen

One week. Seven days. It had seemed as long as a year, if not more, to Fen. It was as long as he could manage before he found himself standing outside Bethany's house, looking up to the bedroom windows. On the front lawn, the fairy circle of mushrooms pushed through the grass, feeding off his presence. He stood with his hands in his pockets, not really knowing what he would do if he saw her. His heart pounded at the thought.

Mouth dry, he waited.

There came no twitch at the curtains, no angry parents rushing out to send him away. Eventually, he managed to turn and walk back to the woods, staring at his feet the entire way. The trees were whispering but he didn't want to listen. Fen wasn't in the mood for the gossip of trees.

Still staring at the dirt path beneath his feet, hands deep in his pockets, he wandered through the woods until he reached the clearing.

'Hi.'

Fen stopped, his heart leaping into his throat, and looked up to find Bethany watching him. A year had gone by, surely, but she looked the same. Of course, because only seven days had passed.

'I missed you.'

Her voice was quiet, a whisper, and if the trees hadn't repeated her all around him, Fen would have wondered if he'd heard correctly.

'I went to your house,' he managed, unsticking his tongue from the roof of his mouth. 'You weren't there.'

Bethany smiled and opened her arms.

'Because I'm here.' She looked down at the bluebells around her feet. 'Waiting for you.'

Fen had to stop a laugh from bubbling up.

Bethany stepped closer to him.

'I'm going to London after my exams,' she told him.

London, the trees repeated in their hushed tones, the word carried on the wind.

'While I'm at university. I don't know after that.' She paused, biting her lower lip, and it took everything Fen had to not close the gap between them. 'But that's not until September. We have the whole summer to spend together.' Fen swallowed. 'And you can visit me in London? And then, afterwards...' Bethany trailed off and stood watching Fen. 'What do you think?'

Fen smiled and slowly approached her, stepping through the bluebells.

'Are you sure?' he murmured.

Bethany nodded, and then his hand was in her hair and his lips were on hers. As they kissed, his hands slipped down to her waist and her fingers brushed over his arms.

'I would like nothing more,' Fen whispered as the kiss broke. He held her close as she smiled, reaching up to kiss him again.

'And you'll take me into your world whenever I want?' she asked.

Fen nodded.

'Like, now?' she said.

Fen searched her eyes and, again, nodded. He took her hand. Bethany turned to face the doorway to Fen's world, surrounded by a welcome mat of bluebells, before he led her through, into colour and sensation and a wonderful summer.

47

Erica

Surrounded by boxes, Erica sat on her bed in her parents' house and surveyed her packing so far. She hadn't always lived with her parents and just because she was once again moving out, didn't mean she wouldn't return. Erica didn't know whether to laugh or cry.

The majority of her friends from school were married with mortgages and children, yet here she was without any of that.

Sighing, she opened a small, delicately painted box she'd been about to pack and removed a bag. Tipping it out onto her bed, she picked up Rick's warrant card and rubbed her thumb over it. She'd had a future with him, a marriage, a mortgage, a baby.

All these years, she'd thought that was what she wanted. It was certainly what she'd wanted the day she met Rick from the future, the man who claimed to be her husband, the man who made her insides tingle, who she always wanted to be close to.

She placed the warrant card back in its bag and lifted the promise ring Rick had given her when he'd left to travel through time, to wait for her to be ready. Rick had never led her astray, there'd never been any hint that he could trick her. Although, she supposed, it was always possible for anyone to use flowers to get what they wanted.

Erica smiled, sliding the ring onto her wedding finger and admiring it.

There was no sudden rush of emotion, no longing. There was no love.

Frowning, Erica slid the ring off and turned it around in her fingers thoughtfully.

What would she feel if Rick were to appear right then in her room? Would she want to run to him?

Did she want him to appear?

She sighed but it came out with a shudder. There was a voice at the back of her head screaming at her but she ignored it, unwilling to process the words just yet.

A knock on her door made her jump and she turned to find her father surveying the boxes.

'Nearly ready?' he asked.

'Probably not. I don't know how I managed to get so much stuff,' said Erica.

'Well, you don't need to take it all with you,' he told her. 'This will still be your room.' He moved to sit on the bed beside her and subtly glanced at the ring in her hand. 'Alfie give you that?'

'No. Rick.' Erica looked up at her father. 'All these years wondering if I'd ever find a man I really wanted to be with, and then two come along!'

Her father smiled.

'Really? Or do you just want to be with one of them but you don't want to hurt the other?'

Erica looked back down to the ring and her father sighed. Leaning close, he murmured, 'Don't be with the normal man just because your mother approves. Heaven knows I want you to be with someone who's going to keep you safe, but you're not your mother. If anything, you're more like your grandmother.' He did a good job of not pulling a face. 'And while this Rick guy is probably a lovely bloke, you have to follow your heart. I know your grandmother loved your grandfather with all her heart, I saw it. But I also get the feeling she's annoyed she waited so long to be with Eelando.'

'Eolande,' Erica corrected with a smile.

'Yeah. Her. Alfie is the scary choice.' Her father sniffed. 'And if it was up to me, I'd choose the normal one, but...I don't think you'd be happy. And the only thing I've ever wanted for you in this life, since the day you were born and I first laid eyes on you, is for you to be happy.'

Erica held back the tears that threatened to build and met her father's eyes.

'Alfie looks after me,' she whispered. 'He protects me.' Her father nodded and Erica looked back down to the ring. 'Rick went off travelling to wait for me.'

'Which means he's not here,' came her father's voice, and something inside Erica gave way. He put a rough arm around her, hugged her tight and kissed the top of her head. 'Want a hand with packing?'

Erica shook her head.

'No. No, I think I'm nearly there. Thanks.' She offered him a smile and he left her bedroom, leaving the door open behind him. Erica put the ring back in the bag with Rick's warrant card and the note he'd left her. The bag went into the box which was shut and placed into a bigger cardboard box. Erica stood back, hands on her hips, and sighed.

Part of her wished Rick would appear right in that moment, if only so that she could make a decision.

Her family's two Labradors started barking as there was a knock on the front door and Erica jumped, hand on her heart as she turned to face the hallway.

'Erica! Alfie's here,' came her mother's voice.

A smile pulled at Erica's lips and she bounced down the stairs just as her mother was pulling the dogs into the kitchen and closing the door. Alfie was waiting for her just inside the house. She hugged him, throwing her arms around him and gripping him tight.

'Are you okay?' he asked, his lips in her hair, his breath warm.

Erica nodded.

'I've been thinking,' she told him, her voice muffled against his shirt.

'What about?'

'You. Us.' Erica let go and led the way up the stairs to her bedroom and all the boxes she'd need help taking down. Instead of making a start, she sat back on her bed and Alfie sat beside her.

'And? Should I be worried?' he asked.

Erica looked up into his blue eyes and shook her head. Slowly, she leaned forward and just before she pressed her lips against his, she murmured, 'I'm yours.'

Erica and Jess return in

Bedevilling

In autumn 2023

If you enjoyed this book...

Authors love getting reviews.
It's one of the best ways to support
authors you enjoy.
I would really appreciate it if you could leave a
review of this book on Amazon.

Printed in Great Britain
by Amazon